Chase ran the back of his hand along her cheek

Sylvie could hardly breathe. Everything in her waited to hear what he would say, what he would do.

He gave in and pressed his mouth to hers, holding motionless, as if waiting for the spark to flare. And oh, did it flare. Just like all those years before, pure desire poured through her.

They were reliving a memory, fixing it. For once in her life, she was going for it. Arousal sparked along her nerves, like strings of twinkle lights. She felt light-headed and pulled back just long enough to take in a gulp of air. With their hands on each other's faces, their upper bodies close, the embrace was tender and hungry and wild all at once and she never wanted to stop.

Dear Reader,

I have to confess: I'm not a good shopper. I walk into a mall and get overwhelmed. That dates back to childhood when my mother would take me shopping for a special dress and I'd find something in the first store, but she would say, "Shall we keep looking for something better?" Better? There might be something better? So off we'd go, to store after store after store. All that choice wore me out.

So why would a non-shopper write a story about a woman who practically grew up in a mall and loved it like home, its employees like family? Because malls fascinate me. A mall is a world unto itself under an air-conditioned sky. I used to have a fantasy of spending the night in the mall and exploring all the stores. You'll see that happen in the book. Boy, did I have fun with those pages!

This story is also about family—about how family is what you make of it. With her mother largely absent from her life, Sylvie created a family out of the mall and Chase's relatives. The book takes place around Christmas, and even I love the crazy, festive fun of a mall at Christmas. Starlight Desert Mall does Christmas right, I think.

So we've got malls, family, Christmas and falling in love. Can you see why this story was a delight to write? This is my first book for Harlequin Superromance, so I hope you'll find it a worthy fit.

Let me know what you think at dawn@dawnatkins.com or visit www.dawnatkins.com.

Best,

Dawn Atkins

A Lot Like Christmas
Dawn Atkins

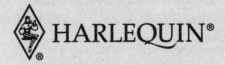

TORONTO • NEW YORK • LONDON
AMSTERDAM • PARIS • SYDNEY • HAMBURG
STOCKHOLM • ATHENS • TOKYO • MILAN • MADRID
PRAGUE • WARSAW • BUDAPEST • AUCKLAND

Recycling programs
for this product may
not exist in your area.

ISBN-13: 978-0-373-71671-5

A LOT LIKE CHRISTMAS

www.eHarlequin.com

Printed in U.S.A.

ABOUT THE AUTHOR

Award-winning author Dawn Atkins has written more than twenty novels for Harlequin Books. Known for her funny, poignant romance stories, she's won a Golden Quill Award and has been a several-times *RT Book Reviews* Reviewers' Choice Award finalist. Dawn lives in Arizona with her husband and son.

Books by Dawn Atkins

HARLEQUIN BLAZE

Don't miss any of our special offers. Write to us at the following address for information on our newest releases.

Harlequin Reader Service
U.S.: 3010 Walden Ave., P.O. Box 1325, Buffalo, NY 14269
Canadian: P.O. Box 609, Fort Erie, Ont. L2A 5X3

In memory of my mother, the Starr of our family

Acknowledgments

Thanks to Thomas Randall, manager of Paradise Valley Mall, who graciously squeezed my questions into his jam-packed schedule. Any errors are my own.

I'm also indebted to Paco Underhill, whose books *Why We Buy: the Science of Shopping* and *Call of the Mall* gave me enough intriguing shopping facts to last a lifetime.

Sylvie had a complicated relationship with the McCanns. Her mother, Desiree, had been best friends with Starr and when Sylvie moved in with her grandparents due to Desiree's travel schedule when she was seven, Starr had treated her like family.

Now Sylvie feared Marshall still thought of her as the teenage assistant who served muffins at mall meetings or the little girl sitting quietly at the noisy McCann holiday dinners.

That was why she'd included her work history and accomplishments in the update she'd prepared—to assure Marshall that the mall was in capable hands.

Now this vandalism threatened her moment. It felt as though she were about to host a foreign dignitary with a pile of dirty laundry on the porch. Worse, it might make Marshall believe the slight down-tick in profits meant more than it did.

Just as Sylvie grabbed her cell phone to call the head of security, Randolph emerged from the mall, shoulder to shoulder with Betty, the maintenance manager, loaded with paint gear.

"We're on it," Randolph told Sylvie when they got close.

"Graffiti-buster primer," Betty said grimly, hefting one of the three paint cans. The other two were gold and turquoise, the two colors the ugly scrawl had been sprayed over.

Most malls were blah beige boxes. Starlight Desert was a feast for the eyes—a colorful take on an ancient Hohokam village, with rounded corners, wooden posts and decorative ladders, its walls painted gold, turquoise, salmon and purple, all cozily tucked into the parklike setting of shade trees and desert landscaping also owned by McCann Development.

CHAPTER ONE

THIS MALL SUCKS!

The spray-painted scrawl across the whimsical pu
style exterior of Starlight Desert Mall hit Sylvie Stark
a poison dart. Starlight Desert was her second home,
store owners and employees practically family.

Now the area looked like the aftermath of a frat part
Trash bags from the Dumpster had been torn open, th
contents strewn about, and festoons of toilet paper dang
from the thorny mesquite trees and soiled the silver
hedges.

The timing couldn't have been worse. In an hou
mall's owner, Marshall McCann, would arrive to
Sylvie the new general manager—her dream almos
she started working here at age fourteen.

Currently second-in-command, Sylvie was t
ous choice to replace Mary Beth Curlew, the for
who'd left abruptly two weeks ago to care for
mother in Michigan.

Mary Beth did tend to take credit for Syl
but she'd surely recommended Sylvie to Fle
shall's younger son, the McCann Developm
the mall.

Still, Sylvie felt uneasy. Marshall was
maker and he hadn't been to the mall si
wife, Starr, passed away from cancer thre
mall had been Starr's baby.

"Marshall is due soon, so just a quick coat for now," Sylvie said.

Betty nodded and set to work. Two of her crew had spread out to gather the trash, determined as soldiers. Sylvie's heart lifted at the sight. Everyone who worked here was as devoted to the mall's well-being as she was.

"Who would do such a thing? Is this a post-Halloween prank?" she asked Randolph.

"It was either those Goth kids I gave hell for banging into your mom's kiosk or those delinquents from that art group."

"The art kids love it here." Sylvie had convinced Mary Beth to lease a hard-to-rent space to Free Arts, which taught art to kids from drug rehab programs or foster homes. They had to earn the privilege of coming. "At least it's not gang tags."

"Just you wait," Randolph said. "That's coming."

"Hold on. You're sounding like Councilman Collins." A modest increase in home foreclosures and petty crime in the area had Reggie Collins politicking in the press about the need for urban renewal funds and more police patrols.

Everyone loved Starlight Desert, the homey heart of Phoenix's oldest suburb. If there were problems, Sylvie was determined Starlight Desert would be part of the solution.

"This wouldn't have happened if I had more guards," Randolph said. "Leo's nephew needs a job, you know. We could hire him at least."

"Let's just be more watchful for now." Randolph took his job very seriously, which Sylvie appreciated, though she had to rein him in from time to time. If he had his way, he'd ground every teenager who walked in the place.

With ten-year-old twin daughters, the man was terrified of puberty.

"You'll mention it to Marshall? About the new locks and about replacing the golf carts?" Randolph pushed.

"Let's get our revenues up first." She had a plan for that to show Marshall, too. "If you've got this handled, I'll go set up for my meeting." She patted her laptop, which held the presentation she'd run through at home until she'd nearly memorized it.

"You'll do great," Randolph said. "You're sure dressed like a boss." He nodded at her outfit with a wistful smile. Recently divorced, Randolph had a bit of a crush on Sylvie they both wisely ignored. "Is that from Margo's?"

"Yes." She'd spent too much on the white silk shirt and navy suit, but Sylvie supported mall shops whenever she could. She felt sweat trickle down her rib cage. It was nerves, not heat. Summer had released its death grip on Phoenix and the early November air was pleasant, the sun gentle.

Randolph held the mall door for her and Sylvie stepped inside. *Home.* The feeling never failed to cheer her.

She paused to breathe in the aroma of flowers and fruit from Heaven Scents, the lotion shop, and pick up light jazz on the loudspeaker. In a couple of weeks the smells would be cinnamon, clove, peppermint and pine and the music would be Christmas songs.

The prospect made Sylvie's heart swell with joy. The holidays here were so festive, so full of promise and surprise, of people wanting to show their love in tangible ways. To her, Starlight Desert was a lot like Christmas.

Maybe it was weird to love a mall, but Sylvie and Starlight Desert had *history.* Her happiest memories with Desiree and her grandparents were here. She even had the same birthday as the mall—a sign if she'd ever heard it.

"Want a ride to the stairs?" Randolph asked.

"Just to the bakery to pick up my order, please." She climbed into Randolph's security cart, happy not to scurry the length of the mall in her new pumps and the itchy lace-topped stockings Margo had talked her into instead of her usual sensible panty hose.

They rolled past the pet store and Sylvie craned her neck for a good-luck look at the puppies in the window. They were Cavalier King Charles spaniels and cute as buttons. She'd given them all reindeer names in honor of her favorite season.

Randolph hit the brakes, and Sylvie was rocked forward and back. "Want to pick one out? Jed would give you a good price. He needs the room for the rescued dogs."

"I can't have a pet," she said, watching her favorite, Dasher, tumble over the one she'd named Rudolph for his very pink nose. "I'm here twelve hours a day. He'd be alone too much."

"That's the point, Sylvie. You deserve more of a life. A dog, a husband, kids." His kind eyes looked her over.

"I've got plenty of time for all that." She was only twenty-nine. She waved her hand at the distant prospect of a family. Frankly, since Steve left for Seattle three months ago, she'd been glad to reclaim her free time. Their breakup had been amicable and she'd visited him in Seattle. The sex had been nice, but relationships needed too much nurturing. That was tough enough when you lived in the same city but nearly impossible long-distance. The truth was she didn't have space in her life for anything serious just yet.

"Don't wait too long. That's all I'm saying. Marriage is a wonderful thing. I wish I'd appreciated the good times when I had them."

"Did the girls' visit go better this time?"

"Yeah, thanks to you. We played that board game all weekend."

The twins had been bored during their previous visit to Randolph's new bachelor apartment, so Sylvie had given them the game as something they could all do together. "It was Toy Town's top seller, so I thought it might work."

"You always take care of us."

"Just doing my job, Randolph," she said. "We're all in the Starlight Desert family. You can let me off here." She bounded away before he could get mushier. Or, worse, romantic.

Breathing in the sweet and yeasty smells of Sunni's Bakery, she bopped into the kitchen for her order of the award-winning cranberry-nut scones she knew Marshall liked, then dashed up the stairs to the mall offices.

Once she had her PowerPoint presentation set up, Sylvie left the refreshments for Cyndi, the GM's assistant and receptionist, to arrange, and dashed out to check on the cleanup effort.

When she got there, she could barely see where the new paint had been added and the crew was prying off the last of the toilet paper from the sage bushes.

Spotting a few streamers at the top of a mesquite tree, Sylvie braced a ladder against the trunk and climbed up to retrieve them.

The damned paper was just out of reach. She stretched higher, but fell partly into the scratchy branches. Yikes. Her heart racing, she lifted a leg to balance herself.

Thank God there was no one below her to get flashed.

"Can I help?"

The voice came from beneath her. Sylvie cringed, then twisted to see who might have glimpsed her panties.

Chase McCann, Marshall's older son and Sylvie's first

crush, grinned up at her from the bottom of the ladder. What the hell? The man did investment deals all over the U.S. and Europe and was rarely in town.

"Chase? What are you doing here?"

"Helping you, looks like." Humor danced in his dark eyes, so he'd definitely seen. Damn.

He braced the ladder, forcing her to climb down into his arms, while he looked her over, not the least apologetic that he'd perused her underwear.

"You hurt yourself?" he asked, checking her out in that amused older brother way he'd always had with her.

Except that one night.

That one fizzled-out fire of a night.

Her twenty-first birthday and she'd intended to lose her virginity to him until he figured out what she was doing and backed away as if she were contagious or radioactive or both.

"Not at all. I'm perfectly fine." The backs of her hands stung from scrapes and she'd snagged her jacket, but no way would she admit that.

"You've got…leaves." Chase reached over and tugged mesquite twigs from her curls.

"Thanks." She stepped back, needing distance from the man and to retrieve the tatters of her dignity.

"You're all dressed up." He shaped his hands in a body curve, not sexual at all, but his golden-mocha eyes held her tight. He had a way of really looking, as if he knew her well and was damned glad about it. Chase was a charmer, for sure.

He looked good in trendy jeans and a black microfiber shirt that molded itself to his chest. He clearly squeezed gym time into his jet-setting party schedule. Mary Beth kept Sylvie updated on his exploits through Fletcher.

"I've got a meeting." She looked at her watch. Uh-oh. She had to get upstairs.

"I'll get that." He nodded up at the fluttering toilet paper she'd been unable to grab. "You can head in. Dad's already there."

"He is? Damn. Thanks." She spun on her heels and ran. She was halfway down the mall before she realized Chase had never answered her question: Why *was* he here?

FROM THE TOP OF THE LADDER, Chase watched Sylvie take off, blond curls bouncing, backside firm in that tight skirt. Hardly any jiggle to it. Mmm, mmm, mmm.

Distracted, he nearly took a tumble himself. *Focus, bro.*

He grabbed the fluttering toilet paper and lowered himself to the ground.

The stockings had been a surprise. He'd have pegged Sylvie as a bare-legs girl—practical, simple and easy.

She did need help, Fletcher was right about that. Why the hell was she out here doing yard work in a suit?

She seemed worried and looked exhausted, probably from juggling two demanding jobs.

According to Fletcher, she was eager to join her boyfriend in Seattle, so Chase taking over the GM job would be a relief to her. Funny, but Sylvie didn't strike him as someone who would arrange her life around a guy, but people changed, he guessed.

She was still a wound-up coil of energy, for sure, with a spark in her green eyes and a plan cooking every second. She still had that steady serenity about her that he'd loved. She made him want to slow down and just pay attention.

Even flustered, falling into a tree, flashing the world her underthings, she'd remained her solid self. *Ah, Sylvie.* He had to smile. She always made him smile.

He needed it, too. Chase's focus in Phoenix was getting his new project off the ground, but his father and brother were in a tug-of-war over the fate of the mall, and Fletcher had asked Chase to bring his dealmaker eye to the situation.

If his family needed him, Chase was there, regardless of the personal land mines he'd have to dodge.

Bailing Sylvie out was a nice bonus.

Chase handed the ladder off to a worker and tossed the paper in the trash on his way into the mall.

He stepped inside and was hit with sick dread, reminded instantly of the months he'd run the mall once his mother became too weak to make the drive. He'd been barely there, a ghost, going through the motions, his attention on his failing mother. The mall was her joy.

It was named after her because she was the light of their father's life—all their lives, really. Starr had smoothed Marshall's rough edges and oiled the friction between the two brothers, building a decent family out of the four of them. After she died, they'd fallen apart, bumped heads, scraped words, grieving in their separate ways.

If emotions ruled, they couldn't sell this place fast enough to suit Chase. But he did business based on facts, not feelings. So Chase would gather the data, drill down to the bottom line, then lay out the case for either keeping the mall or selling it based on what he found.

Which likely wouldn't resolve the issue. Fletcher was as stubborn as their father, whom they called the General. Marshall would never sell away his wife's dream while Fletcher was convinced that selling was the only way to go.

Chase took the stairs to the mall offices, where his father stood in the doorway to the meeting, munching on a pastry, a china cup puny in his big hand.

"You're holding up the show, son," he boomed, his voice as big as his presence. Marshall McCann took up a lot of space. He motioned Chase inside.

Sylvie looked startled to see him. "You're sitting in? Oh. Okay." She bit her lower lip, a move Chase felt below the belt. Sylvie had the most kissable mouth he'd ever tasted, before or since that ill-advised night.

"Grab him a chair, would you, hon?" his father said to Sylvie. "And some of this good coffee, too."

"That's not her job," Chase said, shooting Sylvie an apologetic look. "I can get my own coffee." He helped himself to a scone while he was at it and pulled up a chair.

Sylvie stood there looking stunned. What the hell?

"You all right?" he asked her, munching on the pastry. God, it was delicious. Tangy and moist. Sunni Ganesh knew how to roll dough, for sure.

"The team's on the field, let's put the play in motion," his father said, rolling his hands like a referee.

Good grief. The man had gone from gruff to sexist to clownish in a few short words.

"The team?" Sylvie's smile went stiff as plaster.

"That's right," his father said. "Team Starlight Desert Mall. Sylvie, meet your new head coach. And, Chase, Sylvie's your able assistant coach. Let's kick off."

"Head coach?" Sylvie repeated. "Does that mean...?" She turned to Chase. "*You're* the new general manager?"

"That's the plan," his father answered for him, beaming.

"Oh." Sylvie looked like she'd been punched in the gut. "I didn't realize..." So much for easing her burden the way he'd expected. Judging from her stricken face and the storm clouds in her green eyes, Chase had just gone from hero to villain in ten seconds flat.

CHAPTER TWO

MARSHALL HAD GIVEN CHASE her job. Rocked by the news, Sylvie bumped the table, jarring the computer mouse so the first slide of her presentation flashed on the screen.

It was a photograph of all the store owners grouped in front of the mall wearing sunglasses. Underneath, the caption read, The Future's So Bright, We Have To Wear Shades.

Meanwhile, Sylvie's future had just gone black.

Her loyalty, devotion, hard work and brilliance meant nothing. Marshall trusted family over her and that hurt. Bad.

"Sylvie? Are you okay?" Chase asked.

"Sorry. Yes. Let's, um, get started, shall we?" She would go through her presentation and figure out a solution as she went along. She managed a smile at her audience, Chase and Marshall, who would determine her fate, her heart just aching.

"In tough economic times, shoppers must be selective about where they shop and how much they spend." She somehow kept her voice steady, her tone upbeat. As she spoke, she clicked through slides of the stores, one at a time, each with its owner in smiles and sunglasses. She'd been so proud of this presentation.

Now she just felt sick.

"Weary of huge malls, with their generic stores and indifferent salespeople, today's shoppers want a place where cheerful, caring employees guide them to the goods they want at the prices they need. Just like the famous *Cheers* pub, they want to go where everybody knows their name." She paused.

"And where is that?" She tried for the grin she'd planned, but her face muscles lagged. "Starlight Desert Mall, of course, where our forty shops are one-of-a-kind, where every salesperson is eager to assist, where prices are fair and customers are treated like royalty."

Her tongue stuck to the roof of her mouth, so she took a sip of water. "And how do we know this? We asked our customers!" She clicked through several charts from a recent survey and summarized the positive findings.

Next came the tough part—the revenue dip.

She flashed to the graph with its visible down-tick. "Though the general economic downturn has resulted in a slight drop for us, we've replaced four of the six lost tenants and in a blip of time we'll hit our financial stride again."

She paused. "However, to be certain we were on firm ground, last week I met with a top mall renovation consultant and she declared us solidly positioned to survive the downturn. Here are some excerpts of her report."

Sylvie flashed quotes about the mall's stability, its unique niche, its staying power.

She glanced at Marshall, who was nodding along, clearly impressed. Chase's face was neutral. Should that worry her? Maybe he just didn't care. This was hardly his area of interest. He'd been a piss-poor manager those months he'd been in charge after Starr got sick, hardly there and unresponsive when he was. The rest of the team had soldiered on, leading themselves.

And now he would be her *boss*. She made a fist of her nonmouse hand to contain her frustration.

"Starlight Desert is what's known in the industry as a 'destination mall,' she continued. "People don't just go to the mall. They go to Starlight Desert. They know they'll get a special shopping experience within these colorful walls. That's why, in these difficult times, while generic malls lose revenue or close their doors, Starlight Desert will not only survive, we will thrive." She paused for a breath.

"Excellent presentation," Marshall said, pushing himself heavily to his feet. "Thank you, Sylvie."

"Oh, I'm not finished yet." She smiled at him.

"That's fine. I'll let you and Chase carry on from here."

"You're leaving?" She was stunned.

"I think that's best." He looked briefly around the room. "Starr surely did love this place." He cleared his throat, his smile wistful.

But he couldn't leave. Not when she'd worked so hard. "Please stay, Marshall. I'm nearly finished." She held her breath, her heart banging her ribs, waiting for his answer.

"Five minutes," he said sternly, lowering himself again, his bushy eyebrows dipping into a frown. Marshall did not like to be disagreed with. Eccentric, obstinate and cranky, he gave Fletcher, his second-in-command, hell, according to Mary Beth.

"Thank you." Sylvie's pulse raced. *Make it good. Make it count.* "The Black Friday promotion I've planned, 'A Starlight Desert Christmas,' will dramatically boost our revenues, but I'll save that portion for another time—" she clicked quickly through those slides "—and move straight to what's most crucial now—mall leadership."

She stopped at the slide that showed her career path, from gift wrapper, to mall maintenance crew, to cashier at the card shop, then hobby shop manager, GM secretary, marketing assistant, and finally operations manager for the past two years, where she handled the budget, maintenance, capital outlay and more.

Marshall seemed restless, and Sylvie heard her voice tighten with tension as she explained how she'd cut expenses, negotiated discounts with vendors, met tenant needs in a timely fashion, been active with the Retail Association and coordinated community events—a heart-healthy foods cook-off, a karate kick-a-thon for cancer, a community theater production and a skateboard competition.

These tasks were Mary Beth's responsibility, but Sylvie had taken the lead, assisted by Olive, their part-time marketing assistant. Sylvie, like Starr before her, believed Starlight Desert should be as good a neighbor to the community as it was a family to the employees and shop owners.

She clicked to the final slide of her and Sunni outside the bakery, Sunni with a basket of scones on one hip, sunglasses on the tops of both their heads, holding up red umbrellas on which Sylvie had stenciled *The Starlight Desert Family: Together we weather any storm.*

Her cuticles still sported black spray paint from stenciling an umbrella for each tenant. She'd planned to hand them out on her walk-around announcing her new job.

Then she delivered her bottom line: "I hope you can see that with my skills, experience and commitment, I'm uniquely suited to lead the Starlight Desert family through the economic storm into its bright and sunny future."

She stopped, her pulse throbbing in her ears, waiting for Marshall's reaction. He looked bewildered and so did Chase.

Eventually Marshall spoke. "We're kind of caught off guard here, Sylvie. We hoped you'd stay on as operations manager as long as you remained in Phoenix."

"As long as I remained? What does that mean?"

"Mary Beth let Fletcher know you were headed for Seattle. There's someone special there?" He smiled faintly.

Mary Beth told Fletcher about Steve? "Not anymore, no. I mean, we dated, but... Never mind." No way was she discussing her love life with the McCanns. "The point is I'm not leaving."

"Well, then, that's good news for us. You'd be tough to replace, in point of fact." Marshall seemed to hesitate. He glanced at Chase, then cleared his throat again. "Which is why we'd like to, uh, offer you a bit of a salary increase."

"That's nice and all, Marshall, and I know we'd have to hire someone for my old job, but I'd happily train that person." She smiled, forcing more confidence into her voice than she felt. "With the holiday season approaching, we need strong, knowledgeable leadership. And that would be...me."

"No can do, Sylvie. I'm sorry. We feel this is best."

"I have to respectfully disagree. I—"

"Let me tell you a personal story that might help you," Marshall said. "When I was a young man, I worked as a clerk in a drugstore. I loved the job and before long they offered me a position as shift manager. I jumped at it—it was more money, more responsibility, more prestige. The only problem was—" he paused for effect "—I hated it. I was a terrific cashier, but a miserable manager. I should have stayed with what I loved, with what I was good at. Do you see my point?"

"I'd be great as GM," she said woodenly, feeling the ground slide beneath her. She was lost. "With all respect to Mary Beth, I've already taken on many of her tasks."

"And we appreciate that. You're tremendous at what

you do, so we want you to keep doing it. And at a higher salary, now, I insist." He wagged a finger at her. "I'll let you and Chase decide on the proper amount."

"It's not about the money, Marshall," she said, her mind a riot of arguments and despair. Marshall didn't believe she was up to the job and that broke her heart. She hoped her face wasn't as red as it felt.

"I'm sure you'll come to see this arrangement is best for all concerned." He stood, signaling the end of the discussion.

Not for her. For her it was the worst. Her throat burned and she'd dug half-moons into her palms with her nails.

"Can we count on you to stay with us? I'm sure Mega-Malls would snap you up in a Mall-of-America minute."

"I'm happy here, Marshall. And I'll do what's best for the mall." Her insides seemed to sag like her spirits.

"We wouldn't expect anything less. Hell, you've been practically part of our family." Marshall leaned forward for another scone. "These things are sinful. Great coffee, too."

God, he *did* think of her as the snack girl.

"I'll leave you two to work out the playbook." He lumbered out the door without looking back.

If only Starr were alive. Starr would have known what was going on, how hard Sylvie worked, how qualified she was. Starr would have fixed this.

Water wobbled in Sylvie's eyes, but she would not let one tear drop in front of Chase, who stood and joined her, his expression uneasy and full of pity.

"Look, I'll be counting on you a lot, Sylvie," he said, as if that made it better. "If you want we can comanage the place. How's that? The title's not a big deal to me."

Anger flared. "Well, it is to me. It's a huge deal to me.

And as far as comanaging goes, operations is a full-time job. So is the general manager's if it's done properly."

"Calm down, Sylvie. I'm on your side here." He was trying to mollify her as if she were an angry child who'd lost her Popsicle.

"Really? Then post my job and give me yours."

"That's not possible at the moment."

"Then you're not on my side." She turned to go, before she said what she was really thinking. This reeked. She'd worked for every scrap of success and Chase had swooped in and stolen the dream job he thought was *no big deal*.

If he ran it the same way he had last time, well, she wouldn't stand for it. No, she wouldn't.

"Hold on," he said, moving to block her from leaving. "Whatever you're thinking about this, just stop. We can work this out. I promise you."

"What do you want with this job anyway? Don't you have deals to broker somewhere else?" The words came out snottier than she'd intended.

"Not at the moment, no," he said, not seeming offended. "As a matter of fact, we're starting a new project here. It's different from what I usually do."

"Yeah?" she said. "What is it?" She had to be polite.

"We'll be building low-cost modular houses for first-time buyers who lost out in the mortgage crash. We're calling it Home At Last."

"Wow. That is different."

"It's nice to be on the ground with a project, actually building something tangible. Not numbers on paper."

"I imagine that must take a lot of time. Starting something like that." How could he manage the mall, too?

"My partner Chet handles the day-to-day stuff. My job is getting the investors, which means evening meetings, some showings, phone calls. It shouldn't interfere with what I do here if that's what concerns you."

"Oh," she said. "If you're sure then." Now what? She wanted to hide somewhere to lick her wounds, but the mall came first. "So, exactly how do you figure we can work this out?"

Chase looked at his watch, then grimaced. "We'll go over it all tomorrow. I've got to meet with my partner."

"You're leaving? On your first day? This isn't a job you can just pop in and do for a few hours, Chase. We need a lot more than you gave us last time." She stopped short, sucking in a breath at what she'd done—conjured up Starr's illness.

Pain washed across Chase's face.

"I'm sorry. That was the wrong thing to say."

He managed a smile that didn't reach his eyes. "We'll start fresh in the morning," he said. "In the meantime, I need you to get me detailed revenue reports for the past two years, all your notes from the consultant's visit and her full report, along with anything else that will give me a clearer idea of the mall's status and revenue potential. Can you have that ready by the morning?"

"Easily," she said. Did he doubt her? Was he double-checking her work? *Don't say it,* she told herself, gritting her teeth. It was too soon to pick a fight with the man.

But she wouldn't let him off easy, either. "If you can wait a moment, I can make you a copy of my presentation to go over tonight. Also, you might want to read through the mall policy manual. I have a great book on mall management you should dig into. You know, to get yourself up to speed."

"Tomorrow," he said on a sigh. "We'll get into that in the morning." He looked suddenly weary, as if he'd rather be anywhere but there.

He doesn't want the job.

The idea blasted through her, leaving hope in its wake. Maybe Chase would see that this responsibility was too much to juggle with his new business. Maybe he'd bail and Sylvie would be where she belonged, fully in charge of the mall she loved.

Right. And maybe the mall Santa gave good little girls what they wanted for Christmas.

PULLING INTO THE PARKING lot of the high-rise that held McCann Development, Chase left the BMW convertible Fletcher had loaned him and strode inside. He buzzed up the elevator, breezed through the glass-and-brass door and burst into his brother's office, mad as hell.

Fletcher looked up from the papers on his desk. "It's customary to knock," he said. "That's why we put in *doors.*"

"It's also customary to get your facts right before you send someone to do a job for you." He dropped into the leather chair opposite his brother's fancy mahogany desk.

"What are you talking about?"

"That was utter crap about Sylvie moving to Seattle. Worse, she wants the GM job, which, by the way, she's qualified for. Wait until I tell her we're considering selling the—"

"Sylvie's not getting married? Really?"

"No, she's not." Chase eyed his brother. That was an odd detail to focus on. "Why? Are you interested in her? Still?"

"No. Of course not." But Fletcher's face had turned I-lied red. After all these years. Hmm.

Though who was Chase to talk? He'd felt sparks the moment he saw her again. And gotten that whole hold-still-and-be-here vibe stronger than ever. Not to mention how good she smelled.

But he was human and they had history.

A screwy history, but history nonetheless.

"That's what Mary Beth told me and she tracks the social stuff pretty damn close. So Sylvie's not going to Seattle?"

"She's staying right here. Now she wants me to hire a new operations manager and make her general manager."

"We can't afford a new hire and you know it. Believe me, once we tell the tenants we're selling, she'll be glad you're taking the heat instead of her."

"That is far from certain, Fletch. Sylvie's report was impressive. A mall consultant says we've got a solid niche as a destination mall. We've always made good money out there."

"We're developers, Chase. We don't belong in retail."

"Diversity gives us legs—flexibility and range, too." He wasn't about to make a knee-jerk decision or act on assumptions. "Dad might not be so crazy to want to hang on to the profit center."

"Come on. You and I both know that for the General this is about Mom. He treats the mall like her shrine." Pain flashed in his brother's eyes. A pain Chase knew well himself.

"That's not the whole story, Fletcher."

"Oh, yeah? He was into the photo albums the other day, Mom's music on the stereo, moping around, drinking whiskey. Mom's gone and he's got to get past it. Selling the mall will help."

"He won't see it like that."

"He will when you present the numbers."

"Numbers can tell different stories."

"So tell the right one. I'm counting on you, Chase."

Chase stared at his brother, as immovable as their father, who seemed to think once Chase convinced Fletcher to keep the mall, Chase would stay on as manager. The General had never forgiven him for going off on his own.

But no way would he stay.

Chase gathered investors, did deals and moved on. He needed challenge, variety, new horizons. A mall manager was a glorified landlord. Frankly it puzzled him why anyone as smart and talented as Sylvie would settle for something so small.

"I'll do a complete analysis, Fletcher. As I told you."

"Wait until you talk to the broker. Now is the time to sell. I'm talking a bidding war here. You'll see."

"He could be blowing smoke to get our business."

"We split the proceeds three ways, remember," Fletcher pressed. "Don't tell me that after Nevada you don't need the cash."

The jab hit home and Chase flinched. "I don't need the mall proceeds to survive." Though the failure of Home at Last in Las Vegas had hit him hard in more ways than financial.

"I realize that," Fletcher said, softening his tone. "How's it going for you here? You're out in the far west valley?"

"Yeah. There are the usual hassles, but Chet's managing the day-to-day operation. I'm getting investors." The pieces had come together quickly, considering all the McCann Development connections.

"You trust him? After what he pulled?"

"He didn't *pull* anything. We were both swindled." Chet had accepted the builder's word on permits and clearances and Chase had let it slide. The builder skipped town with half their capital and they lost the rest when inspectors forced them to raze what had already been built. They'd trusted good intentions, when they'd needed hard proof. Chase had learned his lesson—never let his heart override his business sense. This time they were crossing all t's, dotting all i's.

"The lawsuit's been called off?"

"Yes." Only Chase's negotiations skills and firm commitment to repay them had kept the furious investors from filing suit. He and Chet would have won—there were no guarantees in this business—but it would have been a waste of time and money for everyone involved.

"Good, because the last thing we need is legal bills." Fletcher looked suddenly bone-weary.

"What's up with you?" Chase leaned forward. "The truth now."

"Nothing." Fletcher blew out a breath. "I'm leveraged is all. We'll be okay." He searched Chase's face as if deciding whether or not to confide in him. "See, I bought into an assemblage in Chandler right before the bubble burst— without getting the General involved. I've been scrambling to make up for it, but so far no luck."

"I know a limited partnership looking for property near high-tech plants."

"Not the guys who want to sue you, I hope."

"Hey, play nice. No. Different group. I pitched Home At Last to them, but it's too slow-growth. I might talk your property up…that is, if it's not too bone-headed."

Fletch smirked at the return jab. "You've got enough on your plate already. I'll work it out." He sounded more discouraged than Chase had ever heard him.

"Let me help. This *is* what family does."

Fletcher tapped his pen against his blotter. "Okay. Yeah, I'd appreciate you putting in a word. The General takes it better if I have a solution when I break a problem to him."

"Hell, you're partners. Equals. Don't let him second-guess you."

"Easy for you to say. You don't deal with him every day." Unlike Chase, Fletcher had stayed on to fight the losing battle for their father's approval.

"If you hate it, leave. You don't have to stay with the company to prove you love the guy. Even if that's what he expects."

They locked gazes again, the old resentment hanging like stale smoke between them. Chase took off. Fletcher stayed. Fletcher believed Chase got more slack with the General because he was first born.

The bitter truth was that no one got slack from Marshall McCann.

Fletch broke the gaze-lock first. "I don't hate it. I run most of the operation."

"He could bring someone else on board, if you wanted to do something on your own."

"He'd never trust anyone outside the family. We have enough trouble with him second-guessing our contractors. I'm not going anywhere. I have no secret unfulfilled dreams." *Like you.*

Chase chalked the sarcasm up to his brother's financial worries. "I'll help where I can. I'm here now."

"Yeah, you are." Fletcher managed a faint smile. "You being around has cheered him up, at least."

"Not so I've noticed."

"That's the General. He can't let on he's pleased to the one who pleased him. You know that."

They both shrugged, regarding each other with the familiar sense of being comrades-in-arms against their difficult father.

"If it helps, tell him the Chandler buy was my idea," Chase said with a half smile. "He'd be pleased to have another example of my poor judgment. He hasn't let up about Nevada once. He somehow thinks that screwup will finally scare me back home."

"Will it?"

"No way. As soon as this is over, there's a limited partnership investment deal in Portland they want me in on."

"Yeah?"

"Meanwhile, I've got Sylvie to handle. She's hurt and angry and I need her cooperation to do this right." Far from being relieved to have Chase's help, she seemed to doubt his competence based on those bad months three years ago.

"You'll work it out, I'm sure. Frankly it wouldn't hurt her to move on. Mary Beth says she lives and breathes the mall. She needs a personal life." Fletch shifted in his chair, clearly uncomfortable that he'd said all that about Sylvie. He'd obviously been doing some thinking about her.

"Like you should talk. All you do is work, Fletcher. You're just like Dad before Mom humanized him."

Fletcher shrugged off his words, so Chase poked at him some more. "The Seattle guy's out of the picture with Sylvie now. Maybe you should ask her out."

"That's ridiculous." Fletcher's brows shot up. He looked like someone had splashed his face with cold water.

"You *do* still have a thing for her."

"Are you nuts? That was years ago…almost a decade." But Fletcher was getting redder by the second.

"Did you even ask her out back then?"

"Once, yeah. She wasn't into it." He looked down at his desk.

"Things change. Feelings change."

"Not Sylvie's. Not about that."

"If that's true, get out there and find someone else. Fall in love, get married, get yourself a picket fence."

Fletcher regarded him steadily. "You first, big brother."

"You're hopeless."

"Right back at you. And I date plenty. Not by your standards, but who could keep up that pace?"

"My reputation far exceeds my deeds, trust me."

"Whatever. Anyway, I've got work to do here."

"So do I. I'm heading out to Home at Last."

"Watch the photo radar with my car. It's easy to speed with that much horsepower. They'll mail the ticket to me."

"If they do, I'll pay for it."

"Oh, you bet you will." Chase was glad to see the edge back in his brother's attitude. He hated to think that money troubles and the General had him so beaten down.

"I'm impressed you bought a convertible, dawg. Pretty impractical for Arizona. Maybe there's hope for you yet."

"Say hello to Sylvie for me," Fletcher said, ignoring the tease.

"Yeah?" Chase lifted a brow.

"We're friends, Chase. I can send greetings to a friend. I haven't seen her in a long time."

"Stop by the mall and say hi yourself. You'll be impressed…with what she's done with the mall, I mean." He gave an exaggerated wink.

"Same old Chase." Fletcher shook his head. "I'll see you at supper. Nadia's cooking your favorites as a welcome home."

"My favorites? I didn't know I had any." Chase shrugged. "Tonight's no good. Or tomorrow. I'll ask her to push it forward."

"You're a busy guy."

He was, but once he got in the car, Chase found his thoughts gravitating to Sylvie.

She was as sexy as ever, trim and curvy, with all that *energy*. Her hair had deepened from a light corn syrup to a dark honey, and her voice held more authority, but her eyes threw the same green sparks.

Her mouth was still built for sin, with a plump bottom lip and a dip in the top one that created a heart-shaped pillow he wanted to rest his mouth on for hours.

Maybe days.

She smelled good, too. What was it? Fruit and spice? Cherry? Something edible anyway.

She had more self-confidence these days. She knew what she wanted. Like the mall job, for one.

How about in bed? Oh, yeah. He'd bet she knew exactly what she wanted in bed. Unlike that long-ago night.

Forget that night. It was old news and wrong even then.

Wrong because of the tequila, wrong because it was Sylvie's first time, wrong because Chase never stuck around, wrong because Fletcher wanted her, too.

Growing up, she'd been like a little sister—big-eyed and eager, warm and sweet, quietly busy and always thinking.

If only he'd left that alone.

But it had been her twenty-first birthday and she'd been so sad when her mother didn't show. He'd had to cheer her up. And if it hadn't been for those damned peach margaritas she kept ordering he would have kept his hands to himself. He knew better. Hell, he was six years older.

Somehow, before he knew it those lips of hers were in kissing range and he was a goner. He just wanted to wrap her in his arms and make love to her all night.

He'd hurt her feelings when he stopped. But better she

know he was a jerk up-front than find out later when he left, which he always did. Chase moved on.

Sylvie stuck around.

Hell, she was still at the mall.

As soon as he settled this crisis and got Home at Last off the ground, he'd be out of here. He could hardly wait.

Being home made him feel suffocated.

Tomorrow, he'd do his best to show Sylvie he wasn't such a bad guy to work with. He'd keep the possible sale of the mall to himself until he had preliminary data and a sense of the real estate market. No point breaking her heart again if selling was out as an option.

Hell, maybe they'd enjoy working together.

He pictured her on that ladder, flailing around, flashing those lacy stockings at him. He'd have preferred bare legs…nothing between his hand and her soft skin….

A horn honked and he realized he'd slid lanes.

Down, boy.

He'd better keep himself in check around her. He doubted there was any danger from her side of the sexual fence. At the moment, Sylvie saw him as the enemy. And depending on what he decided in the next few weeks, she just might be right.

CHAPTER THREE

WHEN SYLVIE STEPPED into the mall at seven-thirty the next morning, "Don't Worry, Be Happy" filled the air with its cheerful advice. The words hit home.

That was exactly the attitude she would take today. Like she'd told Marshall, she would do what was best for the mall. And what was best for the mall was Sylvie in charge. All she had to do was prove that to Chase and she'd be home free.

Don't worry, be happy.

Standing there, the feeling of home like a hot bath of Heaven Scent lavender salts, Sylvie surveyed her domain. Starlight Desert was small for an enclosed mall, just three hundred thousand square feet, floored in homey Saltillo, not glaring marble, the ceilings impressive, but not echo-cold.

In the center island, the banana trees, palms and bright flowers gleamed due to the careful care Betty's crew gave them. As a teenager working maintenance, Sylvie used to pretend she was in a jungle when she watered and dusted them.

As she headed down the mall, a prickle of awareness made her look up to find Chase watching her from the second-floor landing to the office. She forced a smile and a wave, annoyed that her body automatically went all tight and warm and interested, despite the misery the man was causing her.

When she reached the top of the stairs, she smiled again, determined to stay cool and breezy, even though being near him made her tingle. "I wanted to apologize for any harshness I showed yesterday," she said.

"I understand. You were shocked and hurt."

"I was surprised," she corrected, uncomfortable with her reactions being laid out so boldly. It made her sound weak and not very managerial. "Caught off guard. Especially since the decision was based on a misunderstanding about my plans."

And the fact that Marshall thought her only capable of pouring coffee and making PowerPoint presentations.

"I can't do my job without your help, Sylvie. So, how about a fresh start?"

"I'm sure we both want what's best for the mall."

"Of course." Something flitted behind his eyes, a difference of opinion, a doubt that raised the hairs on the back of her neck.

He held out his hand. "It's good to see you, Sylvie. It really is." The confession seemed pulled from him against his will.

"It's good to see you…too," she said, taking his hand. His fingers were warm and strong, making her feel safe and desired and turning her knees to noodles….

Was she holding on too long? Not quite sure, she released her grip.

"I won't leave you hanging like before," he said.

"That was thoughtless of me to say, Chase. Starr was so sick. You had her on your mind and—"

"Let's not," he said.

"Okay, but I just… I would give anything if she hadn't… I just miss her." They'd lost so much when they lost Starr. Her gentle ways, her big-as-life smile, her kind words that hugged them close.

"Hey, hey, fresh start now," Chase said, but she caught the flash of sadness before he blinked it away. "This could be fun, you know," he said, giving her his charming grin. He had perfect teeth, white and straight except for a tiny crossover in front she'd always loved. A single flaw in all that perfection was really quite sexy.

Sylvie forced herself to focus. "Fun? I suppose so. If you enjoy twelve-hour days, troubleshooting that never ends and checklists on top of checklists, especially with the Black Friday promotion coming up."

"Lead the way," he said, motioning her ahead of him down the hall. She took him into Mary Beth's office, then stopped cold. She'd forgotten the personal items she'd brought here when she'd assumed the job was hers—photographs, a gold pen set thank-you award from the Retailers Association, her leather planner and her Christmas cactus plant.

Hot with embarrassment, she gathered the plant and pen set. "Let me get these things out of your way."

"Hang on." Chase picked up the tri-fold photo frame and studied the pictures. "Graduation?" he said, looking at the one of her in cap and gown with her grandparents. They'd been killed in a car accident a few months later.

"Yep." She reached for the frame, but Chase was now studying the middle picture—her and Desiree on Sylvie's birthday four years ago, just after Desiree returned to Phoenix for good.

"Your mom, right?" He lifted his gaze to Sylvie's face. "Same eyes and nose. Not the mouth so much. Your lips are…" He looked at them, licking his own, as if he wanted a taste of hers.

"Mine are…?" she prompted, getting that tingle again, her knees giving way just a little.

"Uh...different." He blinked and it was over, like a light had been snapped off. "And this one's the big party."

"Starr took that shot." Starr had set up Sylvie's twenty-first birthday party at a restaurant, always doing what she could to fill in for Sylvie's missing family.

"That was some night," Chase said, shaking his head.

She cringed. Chase had caught her crying outside the ladies' room after her mother called to say she'd missed her flight. "I don't know why I was so upset. Desiree is Desiree. She came the next day with the handmade shawl she'd ordered for me, which was what made her miss her plane." She shrugged.

"You wanted your mom there on your birthday. Of course you'd be upset." Chase's dark eyes held her, told her to let herself off the hook, something she rarely did.

"Anyway, that was a long time ago."

"The dancing was fun," he mused, dragging her back there. *Let's keep the party going,* he'd said to ease her distress. At the club he took her to, she'd drunk more peach margaritas. They'd been dancing close, teasing each other, when their eyes met and locked and Chase had kissed her.

Desire had struck like the flare of a match, so bright it hurt. She'd felt unstoppable drive and aching need and triumph. Chase wanted her as a lover, not a kid sister. Hooray.

She'd wanted it, all of it, naked bodies sliding together, sex and more sex. Her first time for the whole glorious act of love, though she wouldn't tell him that embarrassing detail.

Later, at her apartment, she'd been only halfway out of her dress when he somehow figured it out. Like there was a big red V on her forehead.

He'd stopped, then lifted her sleeves back onto her shoulders, zipped her up and patted her. *Patted* her.

She'd felt exactly like what she was, a nervous virgin. The memory made her shudder.

"The drinking not so much." She closed the frame with a sharp snap, then added it to the pile of belongings she hoped she'd soon be setting up in here for good.

Chase looked thoughtful, when she turned back, as if he was still thinking about that night. "Did you see the reports I sent you?" she asked, sticking to business.

"Did I…what? Oh, yes, I did."

"You're after net operating income?"

"Exactly."

Unlike in residential real estate, where value was based on comparable sales, commercial property value was based on cash flow. Every dollar of increased revenue meant ten dollars in increased value due to the capitalization rate.

"There might be one final report on Mary Beth's system," she said. "She has all the material I sent you, as well."

"That's great, except I can't make sense of her computer files. Any clues?"

"She had a quirky setup. I planned to organize it better. Back when I thought I had the job."

"For now, save me some time and show me what you know."

"Sure." She dropped into the chair that should have been hers, moving the seat lower, since her legs were much shorter than Chase's, which were long and muscular and…

He leaned over her, not quite touching, but making her aware of him. He smelled of a spicy cologne and laundry soap. Very nice.

"Here's where she keeps the sales reports and the operations budgets I send her." She clicked her way to the folders he needed, then found the file she wanted to add.

Abruptly, Chase crouched beside her, eye level, his hand on her chair arm, way too close, making her skin prickle. She explained when the monthly sales data came in from the stores and what Mary Beth did with the various spreadsheets. "Wait, here's a directory. Let me print it for you." She turned to the printer and caught Chase with his eyes half-closed, a faint smile on his lips.

"Chase?"

His eyes flew open. "Hmm? Oh. I was just… What do you wear that smells like a cherry pie? You're making my stomach growl."

"Probably my lotion. It's from Heaven Scent. You want me to wear something less appetizing?"

"No, no." He leaned in to inhale. "I'll just have to get used to being hungry whenever I'm around you."

The word *hungry* came out low and he suddenly wasn't discussing pie anymore. Gone was the asexual, big-brother amusement in his gaze. She felt them both sink into the physical moment, their nearness, the longing they'd once shared back full force.

The air seemed to tremble between them, like heat off a summer sidewalk. Caramel sparks flashed in Chase's coffee eyes.

The moment stretched out, brimming with inappropriate possibilities. All good sense fled in the face of this electric pulse. There was something about Chase.

Maybe the way he looked at her, really looked.

Whatever it was, she felt the same wild yearning. A first crush hits hard and locks on, but to feel the same eight years later? She'd had boyfriends. She'd had good sex.

Some people just ignited each other, right? This kind of

thing didn't happen every day, did it? It was startling and remarkable and she could see Chase was struggling, too.

He snapped to abruptly. "Anyway, you smell good, kid!" He rubbed the top of her head, then backed away and stood, wearing the goofiest look she'd ever seen.

Kid? He'd called her *kid?* And ruffling her hair was somehow worse than patting her back, the way he had so long ago. What a jerk.

She grabbed the printout, stapled the pages and headed over to where he'd gone—the old gray steel file cabinet. He pulled open the top drawer. "God, I typed these labels when I was in high school. I used to file for Mom after school."

"Yeah. I remember seeing you. Starr used to let me play with the adding machine."

"You hung around here a lot when you were little." He turned to her, his arm on the top of the cabinet, fingers skimming the file tabs of the open drawer.

"Sure. I always loved the mall. We even have the same birthday. April 15, 1980. I was born at eight thirty-five and the mall opened at nine."

"You know the exact date and *time?*"

"Desiree figured it out."

"You call your mom Desiree?"

"She asked me to. After she'd been gone a while. Because of all her craft shows, she left me with my grandparents when I was seven. She used to bring me here while she hung out with Starr."

"They were childhood friends, right?"

"Yeah. Desiree and I had our best times here, visiting all the stores, making little purchases, snacking at the food shops."

"I remember you in the candy store one day. I was a freshman, so you must have been what…?"

"Eight. I remember." Vividly, but she wouldn't tell him that. Not after he'd called her *kid*.

"You were spending your allowance, I think."

"Not allowance. Income. I earned that money emptying shoe boxes at Tracer's Department Store."

"Yeah? Anyway, I remember you had a fishtail sticking out of your mouth and your lips and teeth were bright blue."

"Gummi sharks, right. You laughed at me."

"Of course. You were this feminine little thing in a lacy dress brutalizing that poor fish." Chase grinned. "You asked me to hand you down a lollipop that was as big as your head."

"It was the best value. More candy per penny."

"That's pretty shrewd for an eight-year-old."

"I had fifteen whole dollars and I wanted them to last."

"So strict. Didn't I try to buy it for you?"

"I couldn't let you. Starr kept giving me things she claimed were discards and Grandma didn't want me spoiled."

"Knowing my mom, she meant you to have whatever she offered. She loved to give away stuff. That was part of owning the mall to her—sharing what she could."

Sylvie's throat tightened as she thought about Starr and those lovely days. "In a way, we grew up here, you and I."

"This was always Mom's place." The words came out flat and he shoved the drawer closed with a sharp clang, like a jail door slammed between them. "Anyway, I hated filing. Mom would tell me even dream jobs have boring parts. I never bought that. I still don't."

"Yeah? Your work is exciting every day?"

"Always something new. That's how I like it."

"I can imagine," she said, hoping he found mall work as dull as dirt. "And your project here—Home at Last—that's exciting, too?"

"Very much so. The architect, builder and lenders are donating their services or cutting their rates to make this work. If all goes well Nadia's son will be one of our first clients."

"Nadia? Your housekeeper?"

"Yep. Her son Sergei and his wife and two little girls have been living with Nadia since they lost their home in the crash."

"Wow. So it's great that you can help them."

"If it works out, yeah." There was a light in his eye while he talked about this. He clearly would rather be there than here. That was a good sign for Sylvie, too. "So how about breakfast? Can I treat you to one of Sunni's cranberry scones?"

"We should go over the Black Friday promotion, which I had to skip yesterday." But Chase had a boyish, eager look that Sylvie couldn't ignore. "I guess we could start with rounds."

"Rounds? What, like in a hospital?"

"Exactly. The manager is kind of like a doctor. You keep your finger on the pulse of all the stores, triage the problems, offer cures. You'll want to visit every tenant at least twice a week, maybe more, depending on what else is going on."

"Twice a week for a checkup? That's a lot."

"Early diagnosis is crucial. If we keep the tenants happy and successful, they stay on. As the manager, you're their friend, priest, therapist. Sometimes even parent. The owners will want to confide in you."

"And complain?" he asked.

"That's mostly my department. The AC's not cool

enough, the roll-up gate is sticking. All the building issues are mine. Utilities, maintenance, security. Capital requests, too, since I do all the budgets."

"My job is handholding?"

"Sure, but you do need to be educated." She picked up *Mall Management, A-Z* from Mary Beth's bookshelf and held it out to him. "Bedside reading."

"Maybe later."

She set it on the desk. "I'm serious, Chase. You should know sales strategies, how to analyze market niches, assess advertising profiles, everything, really. The stores always need ideas for increasing their conversion rate."

"The conversion rate?"

"Converting shopper to buyer. Mall lingo. No store makes money if all it gets is lookie-loos, so we have to turn shoppers into buyers to survive."

"Makes sense."

"There's a lot to this, Chase. I want you to know what you're in for."

"Oh, I'm afraid I do." Something about the way he said that gave her a pinch of concern.

"So, breakfast and rounds?" She grabbed the two boxes of red umbrellas with their cheery promise and felt a pang.

"What are those for?"

"A morale boost." Sylvie opened an umbrella. "With Mary Beth leaving so abruptly, I wanted to reassure everyone. There's one for each tenant. You can hand them out when I introduce you. I doubt everyone's read my email about you being the new GM, so expect some startled looks."

And each one would break her heart all over again. She'd expected today's rounds to be a triumphant tour, a chance to reassure everyone that life at the mall would only get better with her in charge.

Don't worry, be happy, she reminded herself, leading the way to the mall floor.

Their first stop was Jumpin' Juice. "Hey, Theo," she called to the owner.

He turned from one of his blenders, "Just who I needed to see," he said, lifting the counter pass-through and joining them.

"I'd like you to meet Chase McCann, our new GM."

"Yes, you mentioned that in your email," he said coolly. Theo had wanted to circulate a petition of protest, but Sylvie had talked him out of it.

"Nice to meet you, Theo," Chase said.

Theo looked him dead-on. "Just so you know, Sylvie is the glue that holds this mall together."

"That's what I hear," Chase said.

"Do you have a minute to try some new combos?" Theo asked her. "You were right about the star fruit, by the way. Pear is cheaper and tastes just as good."

"That will cut your costs. Would you bring Chase a Berry Blend protein shake? It's my favorite," she said to Chase. She led him to a tiny table, where they sat altogether too close, though she'd sat here many times with Theo and not thought twice about the intimacy.

She felt all too aware of Chase's broad shoulders, muscular chest, the strong planes of his face and those dark eyes of his, which locked on to hers as if he never wanted to let go.

Was he this way with every woman? He confused her. One minute he looked like he wanted to eat her alive and the next he was giving her a noogie.

"When you laid out my duties you didn't mention taste testing." Chase tilted his head, teasing her.

"I do whatever they need me to do," she said.

Theo returned with three juice mix samples, along with Chase's shake, which he grudgingly slid across the table. Sylvie sipped each flavor, one at a time, savoring it against the roof of her mouth.

She pushed two of the cups toward Theo. "These two are great." She tapped the third. "This one, the flavors clash too much."

"You have the best taste buds," Theo said with a sigh, along with that wistful look they both pretended didn't exist. "Thanks, Sylvie."

"This is for you," Chase said, holding out an umbrella.

Theo took it, carrying it at arm's length as if it smelled bad as he headed back to his booth.

"You have the best taste buds?" Chase whispered to her.

"He likes to get opinions, okay?"

"He's hot for you, Sylvie."

"We're friends."

"Not if he had his way, trust me."

Theo was sweet, a good listener and an interesting man. If they didn't work together, she might even consider going out with him. He'd be easy to spend time with. She kept her dating habits orderly. No more than two nights a week and nothing intense. She wasn't ready for intense. She wasn't sure she ever would be.

That awful crush she'd had on Chase was her first lesson in how crazy she might get. Her mother was the second. Desiree was impulsive and romantic, treating her heart like a throw pillow, tossing it to a guy way too early. Then, when he failed to catch it or threw it back, she sank into depression. Sylvie did not have the resilience for that much misery.

She needed a stable life with no roller coasters.

"You've probably got every unattached man here and half the married ones drooling over you," Chase mused.

"That's ridiculous."

He tilted his head. "You still don't know how hot you are, do you? It's probably better that way. You might be tempted to use your powers against us and we'd be putty in your hands."

"That line work for you with the women?"

"Gotta call it real, dawg." His rapper imitation made her smile. "That's how I roll."

"Even if that were true, I don't date people from work."

"Plus there's your boyfriend in Seattle."

"Not that again."

"Sensitive subject?" He leaned in.

"I didn't appreciate Mary Beth mentioning him to Fletcher. I went to Seattle for a visit. Not to move there. Finish your drink so we can get going."

"Not sure I dare, with the evil eye Theo gave me." He sniffed the shake. "Doesn't arsenic smell like almonds?"

She had to laugh. "He knew I wanted to be GM, so he's upset for me. He wouldn't poison you—not without my say-so anyway."

Chase laughed, then removed the straw and took a gulp. Sylvie watched, mesmerized by the swell of his neck muscles as he swallowed. He slammed the empty cup to the table. "There. If I'm going to die, at least I'll go out with something tasty on my tongue."

Tongue. The word alone gave her an inner twinge. Ridiculous. Sylvie grabbed her box and they set off.

"How was Mary Beth as a manager?" Chase asked as they walked.

"She worked hard. She cared. She was a bit disorganized,

as you saw from her computer, and maybe too social. I filled in where I was needed. We made a decent team, I think."

"You'd be good on any team, Sylvie."

"I try."

He stopped in front of her and touched her arm. "I'm serious. Despite what my father said about loyalty, no one would blame you if you wanted to move on. We'd give you a strong recommendation, of course."

"What are you trying to say?" A chill shot through her. "Are you telling me to quit?"

"I'm just saying you have options beyond Starlight Desert."

"I love it here and I intend to stay."

"Got it," he said, hands up at her vehemence.

She introduced him to more shop owners and he handed out umbrellas. When they reached the space Marshall had rented to his golf buddy, the jai alai booster, Chase stopped. "Jai alai?" He turned to her.

She shrugged. "This spot's tough to rent and the president of the booster club is a friend of Marshall's. They want to bring a professional team to Phoenix, I gather."

"Sounds bizarre to me. Jai alai's a big betting game in Florida, right? Those big high stadiums—frontons, I think they're called."

"I guess. This is just an office. They hold meetings and making fund-raising calls…. This is Free Arts," she said, nodding at the space next door. Two heavily tattooed boys in muscle shirts were airbrushing a Virgen de Guadalupe onto the window. She recognized one of them. "Nice work, Rafael."

He turned, puzzled. "You know me?"

"I saw your b-boy crew perform for Cinco de Mayo. You organized the group, right?"

"Yeah." He nodded, pleased, but acting cool about it.

"Tell your guys there's a gig here the day after Thanksgiving. We can't pay, but there will be tons of people in the mall that day."

"'Scool." Rafael strutted a little, then turned back to his work. His friend hissed out, "dawg" to embarrass him for talking to the *gringa mujer*.

"What's rent on that space?" Chase asked as they walked on.

"It's a token amount since that's a difficult section to keep tenants in. It's part of our effort to support the community. Starlight Desert is a good neighbor."

"I noticed a lot of For Sale signs driving here. Lots of boarded-up shops. Is the neighborhood going down?"

"There have been a few problems, but nothing that has affected us. People love Starlight Desert."

"*You* love Starlight Desert, Sylvie. Everyone else just shops here. A mall is where you spend money or get a smoothie to escape the summer heat. People aren't that loyal."

She felt a stab of outrage. "You haven't been here long enough to know. Read our surveys and the consultant's report, talk to our tenants. You'll see I'm right."

The man who had stolen her job was trash-talking the place she loved. She would just have to give him the full picture right this minute.

CHAPTER FOUR

CHASE'S HEAD SPUN. The moment he mentioned that the mall was a business not a place of worship, Sylvie went crazy on him. The simple tour of the mall shops to introduce him to the tenants became a lecture on the Wide World of Retail Malls.

He listened as patiently as he could while she explained door-busters, per-foot kiosk rental charges and how Starlight Desert interspersed food venues among the shops to increase the shopper-to-buyer conversion rate due to "improved shopper eye scans," which evidently was much better than the food-court ghetto at most malls.

In between speeches, he handed out those stupid umbrellas to the store owners, who clearly adored her. Face after face registered disappointment that Sylvie wasn't the new GM.

Rose of Rose's Hobby Hut thanked her for locating a cheaper supplier for dollhouse furniture. He gathered Sylvie built dollhouses in her limited spare time. She'd evidently loaned money to the camera store owner and mediated a fight that would have ended the Toy Town owners' partnership.

Business peaked on Saturday, she informed him. Monday was decently busy due to the weekend's lookie-loos. Tuesday was the quietest shopping day of the week.

She described the daily changeover: seniors walked the mall in the early mornings, moms with strollers arrived

midmorning, followed by serious ladies-who-lunch shoppers. Kids washed through after school, working women
breezed in to pick up cosmetics or panty hose after five.

As she talked, he amused himself by taking in her flashing eyes, her kissable lips wrapped around a torrent of
words, her energetic gestures, the way she filled out that
white blouse, and, of course, her fresh-baked pie scent.

Ya smell good, kid. He couldn't believe he'd said that,
then rubbed her hair like she was ten or a puppy. What
a jerk. He was normally pretty easy with the attraction
dance.

Sylvie had thrown him. Because of their history? Or
maybe just her. She sort of sucked him into her swirling
energy, put him in a trance until he acted like a teen with
no control over his urges whatsoever.

At least she was no longer pissed at him.

Until he told her about maybe selling the mall, of course.
He dreaded that exchange. He'd tell her as soon as he knew
enough to confirm the possibility.

After rounds, they headed back to the office where
Sylvie buried him in printouts and minutiae about "A
Starlight Desert Christmas," the Black Friday event that
evidently was the GM's responsibility.

Nearby schools would present performances and an art
show, stores would give discounts for parents, and there
would be raffle prizes and a hidden-coupon scavenger
hunt. Chase was impressed with the plan. Even if they decided to sell, banking higher revenues would be smart.

"Sounds good, Sylvie. You've put a lot of effort into it."
He started to stand.

"Wait. We still need to discuss the tenant party
on Thanksgiving afternoon, when we prep for Black
Friday."

"Okay." He sat down again.

She explained that the tenant party consisted of food, of course, plus a white elephant exchange. Then the employees shopped in the mall for gifts for a needy family, which they placed under trees decorated to represent each store's merchandise.

It all sounded nice, but Chase's brain was jammed already. Sylvie wasn't helping, hypnotizing him with her cherry-pie smell and the way her breasts shivered whenever she gestured, which she did a *lot*. The generic khakis and simple white blouse she wore started to seem like something a stripper might wriggle out of.

Sylvie didn't seem to mess much with her appearance— her nails were plain, she wore next to no makeup and her honey hair was a mass of curls held back by two clips—but with her natural beauty she didn't need to fuss.

Then he'd seen her bra. He'd been innocently standing over her at the computer when her blouse gaped and there it was. Pink and lacy, cupping the soft rise of her breasts, and he'd wanted to tear it off with his teeth.

To escape the urge, he'd dropped to a crouch, only to get trapped in a close-up of her face in all its appealing detail—her snapping green eyes, edible mouth, that hint of a dimple when she smiled, right next to a beauty mark—pretty punctuation for her face—and her breasts close enough to—

"How do you want to handle it, Chase?"

"Handle...huh?" Had she read his mind? He whipped his attention to her words. She was looking at him impatiently.

"The work. The prep party and Black Friday itself. Officially both are GM duties. I've handled the prep party the past two years, though, since it was my idea, but it's up to you."

"Why don't you keep doing that, then?" he said.

"All right. Black Friday is new and a lot of work as you saw. We have Olive, our marketing assistant, but she's about to have her baby and has cut back her hours. Cyndi will do what she can, but she's stuck on phones, so—"

"This is your plan, Sylvie. You know it inside out, so you should be in charge of it."

"I'd love that, of course," she said with a sigh, "but that was when I expected to be the GM. I've got operations to manage. This is *your* job, Chase. And it's crucial. Black Friday revenues are make-or-break for our shops. I'll help as much as I can, but it will take all of us working as hard as we can to pull this off. I'm not kidding." Her eyes flashed at him. "You said you wouldn't leave us hanging."

"I won't." But he sure as hell wasn't ready to throw the kind of energy at this stuff that Sylvie was. She was clearly worried, chewing her lip like mad. She'd already put so much work into this project, he wanted her to see it through.

"What then?"

She clearly doubted him. She had a point. "Okay, I get it. I don't know a door buster from a loss leader, while you could do this job in your sleep."

She went pink. "I wouldn't have put it so bluntly, but basically, yes." She lifted her chin to emphasize the point.

"So, here's what I propose. You manage the Black Friday extravaganza and the tenant prep party. You know the plan, so that makes the most sense. I'll fill in where I can with what I can."

"But what about—?"

"Your operations job, right. It's full-time and you already work twelve-hour days. Got it. I want you to hire someone short-term to get us through the holidays. Divide up the duties between the three of us however you think will work best. Just keep me informed."

"Oh." Sylvie looked startled. "Really? I can hire some-one? We don't have the budget for that, Chase."

"Take it out of my salary line. No sweat."

"Really? Oh. Well, okay...." He could see ideas flying behind her eyes, how this changed her goal, which had no doubt been to let the door hit him on the ass on the way out.

"Let me see if I understand," she said slowly, her expression deadly serious now. "You're telling me that you and I will share GM duties and I can hire someone to fill in the gaps as I see them? On a short-term contract, hourly wages. And it's up to me who does what?"

"Within reason," he said. "I have veto power and you and I need to stay in close communication."

She beamed. "Then that's great. That will work, I think. Thank you for being reasonable." She was trying to restrain her excitement, he could tell. He liked seeing her eyes light up like that. One bright spot in an exhausting and irritating day.

"There's one more thing I need from you," Sylvie said, scooting forward, leaning toward him.

How about sex? Right here. Right now. The thought came unbidden and he leaned even closer. "Anything you want, Sylvie."

"It involves costumes," she said, her voice low and hon-eyed, her expression all sex kitten.

"Oh, I'm in."

"I'm glad to hear that. How about Marshall and Fletcher? You think they'd be in, too?" She licked her lips slowly.

"Eew." He sat up straight. "Forget it."

Sylvie laughed her musical laugh. "Relax, I just need you three to dress up like Santa and his elves."

"Are you nuts? Now, you and me, French maid and butler, would be great. But that...too kinky to even picture."

She laughed. "I'm serious. It's the perfect publicity stunt. Holiday shopping news stories are a dime a dozen, so we need a fresh angle to get TV coverage. Starlight Desert is a family-owned, homegrown mall. That's our hook. How better to illustrate that than to have Marshall McCann be Santa Claus and his two sons Santa's elves?" She grinned like Christmas morning.

"You *are* nuts," Chase said faintly.

"You and Fletcher would lead the kids to Marshall's lap and take their photos. I know TV would eat that up. Chase? Your mouth's hanging open."

"You want my father to be Santa Claus? I can't imagine anyone less jolly. And Fletcher in green tights and pointy slippers with bells?" He burst out laughing.

"He could wear a blazer and a tie if he wants."

"Business Elf, right. I'd love to see that."

"Don't laugh too hard. You'll be in green tights and bells, yourself, Chase."

"I don't see either of them agreeing to that."

"It would just be for the opening weekend. We'd promote it on Facebook and Twitter."

"The mall is on Facebook?"

"I created a persona—Bright Star. She's a personal shopper who posts deals from our shops along with general shopping tips and tidbits."

"Very smart."

"So what do you say?" she said, her big eyes drilling him. "You can talk them into it, Chase. It's important. They'll have fun, too. And the store owners will love it."

"I don't know. I'd have to talk to Fletcher."

"So call him." She whipped out her cell phone.

"Jeez, you're relentless, you know that?" He waved her away and pulled out his own phone. Sylvie had somehow made the most ridiculous idea sound vital to the mall's survival.

He did like her. He surely did.

"Fletcher, listen. I've got a proposition for you," he said when his brother answered.

"Uh-oh. First, I'm supposed to remind you about the big dinner tomorrow night. Nadia's afraid you'll forget."

"I'll be there, no worries. Listen, I've got Sylvie here with me and we're talking about Christmas at the mall and—"

"Sylvie's there? Yeah?"

"She is. And—"

"Put her on, would you?" Fletcher interrupted, his tone abruptly determined, as if he had a job to do.

"Okay...." What the hell? "He wants to speak to you," he told Sylvie, shrugging as he handed her the phone.

Sylvie looked as puzzled as he felt. "Hi, Fletcher," she said hesitantly. "I'm fine. How about yourself...? So far, so good. I'd say I'm giving him just as hard a time as he's giving me." She shot Chase a look. "Would I want to what...? Oh, I'd be intruding.... If you think so, I'd be happy to... All right. Sounds delicious. Sixish it is."

Sylvie shut the phone looking bewildered. "Fletcher invited me to your homecoming supper. Nadia's making pierogies."

"So *that's* my favorite. Hmm."

"He said it's been too long since I've been at the McCann table." She frowned. "What's this about, Chase?"

Uh-oh. Had their talk convinced Fletcher to fire up that torch for Sylvie again? "Your name came up when we were talking about the mall and he mentioned he hadn't seen you in a while."

"And…?" She held his gaze. "I can see in your face there's more to it."

"And…well, I sort of jerked his chain about being into you."

"You *what?*" Her eyes went wide.

"From years back."

"You knew about that?" Her cheeks colored.

"He let it slip once, yeah. Yesterday, he told me you turned him down, though."

"It sounds like you two had quite the heart-to-heart. The whole McCann family seems to be entirely too interested in my love life. First you think I'm moving to Seattle to marry Steve and then you goad Fletcher into asking me out."

"I was just joking around."

"I'm not amused."

"I don't blame you, but my intentions were innocent, I swear. I wanted him to get a life. I told him to move on, find someone else."

"He's not going to ask me out, is he?"

"I can't imagine he would, but I'll make sure."

"And how exactly will you do that?" She planted her hands on her hips, irritated as hell at him, he could tell.

"I don't know yet. I'll play it by ear. Trust me. He won't ask you out."

"Whatever you do, don't make this worse. I don't need another embarrassing moment with your brother."

Chase was dying to ask what had happened back then, but he didn't dare when she was this riled at him.

"I'll be subtle."

"Before tomorrow night at dinner?" she demanded.

"I swear." He crossed his heart.

He was startled to realize he was glad that Sylvie didn't

want to date Fletcher. Which was completely nuts. It wasn't like Chase was going to swoop in on her now.

Would she even want that? She'd felt something, he knew. He'd noticed the flicker in her eye, the softening of her body when they were close, a huskiness in her voice when the vibe zinged between them.

But Sylvie had discipline and restraint and had practiced self-denial since she was eight, calculating the best candy value instead of gobbling up whatever looked good. So even if she did want him, she wouldn't act on it.

"Good, then. I haven't been to supper at your house in a long time. Four years, I guess."

"You used to come for holidays. I remember the first one. Thanksgiving, I think, with your grandparents?"

"Yeah. The year I moved in with them."

"You sat so straight in your chair." Her eyes had been wide with wonder at all the utensils, china and crystal. "Your grandma showed you what fork to use and how to scoop your soup."

"And you shot a rubber band at me!"

"I wanted to see what you'd do. You gasped. It was perfect. Why'd you stop coming anyway?"

"When Desiree came back, I thought she and I needed to start some holiday traditions of our own."

"It'll be nice to have you back." He smiled at her. "Maybe having you there will help the rest of us behave better."

"Good grief. How bad can it be?"

He shrugged. "Hard to say."

"Great. You forgot to ask Fletcher about being an elf."

"Let's save that for dinner and you can ask him and the General yourself."

"You want *me* to do it?"

"They could turn me down, but you? One shot of those big green eyes and they won't be able to climb into their costumes fast enough."

"Oh, please."

"What do you mean? It worked on me, didn't it?" He couldn't wait to see it happen. Way more fun than shooting rubber bands.

THE NEXT MORNING, Sylvie was pretty darn happy. She was more or less in charge of the mall. Chase had promised to support her and she could hire an assistant to fill in the gaps. She'd bet it wouldn't be long before Chase stepped out of the picture altogether and she'd have what she wanted after all, just a little later than she'd expected.

Maybe it was better to have to fight for the job. A battle made the reward sweeter. That could only make her a better manager, right? Oh, she was feeling good this morning.

Parking her sturdy Volvo, she climbed out, clicked the key to lock it, then turned for the mall.

And stopped dead, staring with horror. All up and down one of the gold-painted turrets were the words *F**K this mall*. Over and over and over.

Again. It had happened again. Someone hated Starlight Desert enough to vandalize it twice.

Dread poured through her like ice water, followed by hot waves of anger. She fisted her hands, wanting to punch whoever had done this. She could hardly breathe.

Randolph and Betty rounded the corner with Chase, who was putting away his phone. Sylvie marched to meet them at the damaged columns, decorative pebbles crunching beneath each step.

"Looks like we'll need that graffiti buster again, Betty," she said.

"Not until the police see this," Chase said. "I called

them out here so we can make a report. Maybe there are vandals working the area they know about."

"It's those delinquents at Free Arts," Randolph said. "They have too much time on their hands and plenty of art supplies."

"They're not allowed aerosol paints," Sylvie said. "And they love the mall. Whoever did this has a grudge against us."

"We did what we could with the manpower we have," Randolph said. "Leo and his crew doubled their rounds and changed up the schedule. We need more guards to catch these creeps."

Sylvie surveyed the damage more closely. "This looks different than the first message. It's all capital letters and they used the *F* word. No toilet paper or dumped trash, either."

"Different kid on the trigger is all," Randolph said, "and they ran out of time to toss trash. Maybe they saw Leo coming."

Chase joined her at the wall, studying the letters. "There are lots of blots and drips here."

"I had that problem when I stenciled the umbrellas. It takes a while to get the spray right."

"So maybe they're new to graffiti?"

Chase bent down to the nearby hedge and pushed back the branches. "Looks like they left something." It was a spray-paint can and when Sylvie got closer she noticed black thumbprints forming a perfect heart on the yellow label. She gasped. "I think that's my can."

"How can you tell?"

Sylvie crouched beside him. "See the thumbprints? I noticed I'd made those when I was stenciling." She blinked and looked up at him. "But I put it back in the supply room with the stencils."

"Let's check," Chase said.

They went together to the supply closet where Sylvie found the stencils where she'd left them, but the paint can missing. "Who would know there was spray paint here?" she asked.

"Who gets supplies? Mall employees, right?"

"But the office is unlocked all day except when Cyndi goes to lunch. If she was on the phone or making copies or in the bathroom, anyone could wander in and look around."

"Are there any angry employees? Anyone we've fired? An evicted tenant who would want to make trouble?"

"I can't imagine anyone that mad. We rarely lose a tenant. We had a midnight move-out a few months ago and we've sent them to collections for back rent, but they left the state." The possibility of a member of the mall family attacking them rocked her to her core.

"Maybe the police will know more," Chase said, leading the way downstairs. Outside, a patrol car was pulling in at the same time as a silver Mercedes, from which emerged a familiar woman.

"Surprise!"

"Mary Beth? What are you doing here?"

"I'm back, can you believe it? I wanted to surprise you." Her former boss gave her a bruising hug. Over her shoulder Sylvie watched Chase lead the two officers toward the vandalized wall, her mind whirling.

"But your mother? Is she better?"

"I brought her here. Much better weather than Michigan and plenty of services for seniors. Right now, she's in a care facility for physical therapy, but once her strength's back, she'll move in with me. Isn't that great?" Her voice held less enthusiasm than her words. She seemed very jittery, too.

"That's wonderful news, Mary Beth, but I need to talk to the police right now." She motioned toward where the male officer was crouched with Chase looking at the paint can, while the woman cop took a tool kit from the trunk of the cruiser.

"Damn, I leave and the place goes to hell." Mary Beth elbowed Sylvie. "Just kidding. Hey, is that Chase McCann?"

"Yes, it is. Marshall made him general manager." Resentment rang in her words, but Mary Beth seemed oblivious.

"But I've only been gone two weeks. Don't you think that's hasty? I mean, you could have held down the fort for the time being, even with Seattle in the wings." Did the woman think she'd pop right back to her job?

"That was a mistake, Mary Beth. I never intended to move."

"Oh, I didn't realize."

"Why don't you go up to the office and we'll talk when I'm finished here." Mary Beth had dropped out of the sky into Sylvie's lap, which was already full of trouble.

"Sure, sure, you bet. See you upstairs." She turned for the mall and Sylvie joined Chase and the male officer. The woman was taking photographs of the graffiti.

"Is this happening anywhere else?" Sylvie asked the cop.

"Not that we've seen. We'd like to get elimination prints from you to confirm the prints on the can are yours. We'll check for any latents, but…."

"You don't have much hope?"

"This is pretty much a needle-in-the-haystack deal, I'm sorry to say. A detective will talk with your night security people and the manager of…" He looked at his notepad.

"Free Arts, is it? Your day security man seems to suspect some kids there."

"That's very unlikely, but you're welcome to check, I guess."

"We'll have a patrol swing by at night for a while, too, see if that acts as a deterrent."

"We appreciate anything you can do," she said.

"Let us know if anything else occurs to you, any suspicious behavior you recall." He handed her his business card.

The sound of a vehicle pulling up made Sylvie turn just as City Councilman Reggie Collins and a young man, an assistant, no doubt, jumped from the car. Worse, with them was a woman she recognized as a reporter.

"Oh, no," she said to Chase. "That's our city councilman and a writer from the community newspaper. The guy must have ears at the precinct."

Meanwhile, the male officer disappeared into his cruiser, no doubt to avoid press questions. The female officer was peeling tape from the wall. A fingerprint maybe?

Collins strode toward them, hand extended. "Reggie Collins, your representative on the city council."

She let him shake her hand. "Sylvie Stark, mall operations manager. And this is—"

Collins cut her off, patting their clasped hands. "I'm so sorry you've experienced this attack."

"It's just a prank," she said, tugging her hand out of his grip. She glanced around for the reporter, but she was snapping shots of the officer getting fingerprints. Great. A dramatic photo for the newspaper.

Collins noticed the reporter's absence, too, and nodded for his assistant to fetch her. He didn't speak again until the reporter stood close by, pen poised over her pad. "This is exactly the kind of incident that calls for the urban renewal

I've been demanding. This will only get worse. Once the gangs move in—"

"This is not a gang tag," Sylvie interrupted. "It is an isolated incident and hardly newsworthy." She nodded at the reporter, who did not react. "For all we know this is leftover Halloween mischief." She managed a smile. A long shot, but worth a try.

"Our troubled community needs more for our young people to do," Collins said, still politicking. "This is why I have called for more jobs, job training, and other programs to…"

Chase shot Sylvie an eye-roll. *Blowhard.*

But she knew this story could hurt them, so she jumped in. "Excuse me, Mr. Collins, but I want you to know that as a member of the community Starlight Desert Mall stands ready to help."

"That's good to hear," Collins said, clearly irritated at being upstaged. "The problem is much larger than a single business can address, so that's why—"

"That's why we'd like to host a neighborhood meeting to discuss any concerns residents have," she blurted, pleased with the idea. "We're all family here, after all."

"That's very kind of you," he said, flummoxed, but not for long, she was certain, so she pushed ahead.

"So, I should contact your office to arrange it, then?"

"That would be fine," he muttered. The reporter was scribbling away, so Sylvie hoped her offer made the paper.

When the excitement was over, Collins and the police gone, Chase finished a phone call and came over to Sylvie. "I hate to do this to you, but I've got to put out a fire at Home at Last. You okay from here?" His warm eyes held hers.

"I'll be fine," she said, a little annoyed he was leaving.

"Nice move with Collins, by the way. You blunted his hysteria perfectly. At the latest, I'll pick you up for the dinner." He was gone before she could tell him that Mary Beth was back and, likely, after the job Sylvie and Chase now shared.

Upstairs, Sylvie found her former boss at Chase's computer. "Just skimming email, seeing what I missed," she said, motioning for Sylvie to sit in her usual spot for their updates. "Just like old times, huh?"

"Not quite, Mary Beth. This is Chase's office now."

"I know." She sighed, suddenly deflated. "I should have taken vacation instead of quitting. I had no idea how things would go with my mother and I guess I panicked."

She paused. "But maybe Chase is just filling in. You think they'll take me back?"

"Actually, I'd hoped you would recommend I take your place, not tell them I was leaving town."

"I'm sorry about that. I assumed that with Steve…I mean, when you went up there… I don't know. I wasn't thinking clearly. I'm an idiot. I quit a great job because I thought my mother would never leave Michigan and now I'm stuck with her and no job. What a mess."

"I'm sorry, Mary Beth."

She raised her eyes and gathered her dignity. "It's not your problem, Sylvie. To be honest, I can't work full-time at the moment anyway, not with Mother like this. It wouldn't be fair to the mall. I'm sorry about the Seattle mix-up. Fletcher knows you're my right hand. He always asks about you."

Because of wanting to date her? Sylvie hoped not. "At the moment, Chase and I are sharing the work and—" She stopped, realizing she had a solution to both their problems. "He okayed me to hire an assistant. It would be part-time and just through the holidays, but…if you want it, the job's yours."

"Really? That would be a switch for us, huh? Me working for you." Mary Beth gave a weak smile. "I'll take what I can get. Will I be back on salary?"

"You know the budget. It's a short-term contract at an hourly rate. The money's coming out of Chase's pay, by the way."

"That's generous of him." She paused, seeming to think it through. When she spoke, she seemed resigned. "Okay. Where do you want me and what do you need me to do?"

Sylvie assigned her to share space with Olive, set her up with the spare computer and gave her the Starlight Desert Christmas Action Plan, highlighting tasks Mary Beth could start doing.

It was strange giving her boss orders, but Mary Beth took the switch humbly enough. For now. Later on, who knew? Mary Beth might make the situation better…or so much worse.

CHAPTER FIVE

THE HOME AT LAST headquarters consisted of a sleek Airstream trailer on two acres a few miles from the land they'd purchased to build their homes. When Chase drove up, he saw what Chet had warned him about.

The model Chase had promised to show investors over the weekend hadn't been finished. The walls were up, but there was no roof, no electrical, no plumbing and no more time.

Bounding into the trailer, Chase found Chet on the phone, giving someone hell, blueprints spread on the small table. "Unacceptable," Chet snapped. Catching sight of Chase, he nodded in welcome, his expression frustrated.

While he waited, Chase looked over the scale model on the acrylic drafting table. Jake Atwater, their architect, had nailed Chase's vision—a trim, modern-looking structure built as inexpensive modules using recycled materials whenever possible. If IKEA built houses, they would look like this.

Chase had majored in architecture for a while and working out the blueprint with Jake had reminded him how much he'd wanted to make that his career at the time.

"Next week is too late," Chet said to his caller. "We're all under pressure.... Let me know." He clicked off the phone. "The builder's stalling. He's got high-dollar jobs waiting. We're small fry."

"We don't want to lose him. He does quality work. Let's see if your call gets us any action."

"I'm afraid we're screwed, Chase." It wasn't like Chet to panic so easily.

Chase's gaze swung back to the model. "What about the prototype? Why can't we use that?"

"The one at Jake's place? It'd cost a fortune to flat-bed it here from North Scottsdale."

"Better than nothing." Chase was already punching in the number and in twenty minutes he'd arranged for delivery.

Chet knocked fists with him. "Since Vegas, every time something goes wrong, I feel like we're doomed."

That failure had shaken them both. "Nobody gets through this business without getting stung at least once," Chase said. "We can make this work. We're doing our homework. We've got solid people on the project. We're on target."

Chet shook his head, half laughing. "You could sell me a glass eye just in case I poke out one of mine, I swear to God."

"We're close, Chet. We'll get there." Chase wanted this project to succeed more than anything he'd done so far. It meant so much to so many people. Thinking about it lifted a weight off his shoulders that he hadn't known was there.

For the rest of the afternoon, he and Chet worked through plans and what needed to be done, finishing in time for Chase to pick up Sylvie for his homecoming dinner.

He'd almost forgotten his promise to Sylvie to clear things with Fletcher about dating her, so when he'd called to tell Fletch he would be bringing Sylvie to supper, he'd slipped in an offhand remark about how there was a new guy in her life. Not the best solution, but it was too late for a heart-to-heart, not that he and Fletch had many of those. Fletcher took the news quietly, which was no surprise. The McCann men kept their hearts to themselves.

Stepping through the door into Starlight Desert to get Sylvie, the hollow dread hit him again. This was Day Three. Shouldn't he be more comfortable by now? He shook his head. The sooner he escaped the place, the better.

In the office, he found Sylvie on the phone. It sounded like she was talking to someone about the school event.

He smiled. There was something about Sylvie that got to him. She was fierce, smart and energetic as all get out, but it was more than that. The way he felt around her, as if he should slow down and just be. Content. Enough as he was.

She hung up and noticed him staring at her. "How long have you been standing there?"

"Long enough to figure out someone was thanking you for giving them more to do."

She smiled. "I was pinning down details with the school PR person. Do you want an update?" She scooted her chair in and pulled a yellow pad closer.

"Tomorrow maybe." His head was full enough. He'd asked for a meeting with Fletcher's broker and he would block off some time to do a deeper analysis of Sylvie's numbers, which he'd just skimmed. If a sale seemed at all viable, he'd let Sylvie know.

"Before the tenant meeting at ten, then," she said. "We need to be in synch or this plan won't work."

"Got it." He checked his watch. "You ready to take off?"

"Not quite." She held up a stack of phone message slips, some papers and folders. "These are urgent calls, invoices to sign and some decisions we need to make. How do you want to handle them?"

He sat backward on a chair, resting his chin on his fists. "Hell if I know, Sylvie. Do what you can and run the rest by me later. How's that?"

"So I have full authority to act?"

"Is that a problem?"

"Not for me. I should tell you I went ahead and hired Mary Beth Curlew on a part-time contract as our assistant. You okay with that?"

"Mary Beth? She's back?"

"Yeah. She brought her mom out here with her. I think she wishes she hadn't quit her job."

"That's a hell of a thing."

"She seems perfect for what we need…." Something flickered in her eyes.

"But you have doubts?"

"She's a wild card. She was my boss and now I'm hers. She loves the mall, but she loved being in charge, too. My approach to the job will be different, which means she might undercut me or resist what I ask her to do."

"Sounds like you've identified the pitfalls. That's half the battle, isn't it?"

"I hope so."

"You have my support, Sylvie, if that helps. If you want me to run interference, I'd be happy to."

"I appreciate that, Chase." Her eyes softened with gratitude. "It means a lot that you trust me."

"I have no reason to doubt you."

She beamed. He loved that. "So you can announce the new arrangement at the meeting in the morning. I think it should come from you. Also, we should probably reassure everyone about the graffiti," she suggested.

"I don't know how reassured I feel. It might have been one of them. That paint was stolen from our office."

"The shop owners are happy here. What reason would they have to do that?" Sylvie said.

"What about Randolph? He's pretty eager to hire more guards. Maybe he faked the vandalism to prove his point."

"Not in a million years. Randolph is too protective of this place. I hope it was just a stupid stunt and it's over."

"The newspaper story won't help us." Chase sighed. "Collins was sure quick to declare the neighborhood crime-infested." Negative press could damage revenues and harm the mall's value as a commercial property, too. Bad news all around.

"So in the tenant meeting tell them to expect the story and mention the community meeting I want to set up." She wrote notes on her pad.

Chase glanced at his watch again. "We need to roll, Sylvie. Nadia gets cranky when her food gets cold."

"Okay. Right." She scribbled one last note. "You and I can meet at nine to finalize the agenda." She pushed to her feet, heading toward him. He wished to hell she wouldn't wear her blouses so snug. Or maybe if she just wouldn't *wiggle* so much in them. He had to laugh at himself.

"What's funny?" she asked.

"I don't know. Human nature, I guess."

She smiled uncertainly and he got the feeling she'd picked up on what he meant.

After she stopped in at the bakery for a loaf of the bread Sunni had told her Nadia liked, they headed for the exit. As they passed the pet store, Sylvie tapped on the window at the puppies inside. "Hey, Dasher."

"You know their names?"

"I named them for fun. That's Rudolph. There's Dancer."

"Reindeer names?"

"They make perfect Christmas gifts, don't you think?"

"You should buy one."

"I work too much to have a pet."

"You and Fletcher. You both need a life."

"Randolph says the same thing. He thinks I need to settle down and get a dog."

"And a boyfriend, no doubt. Him. Any day now, I expect Theo and him to duel at dawn over you."

"Oh, please. Randolph's lonely since his divorce and Theo is a nice guy, but I don't date anyone from the mall."

"You heartbreaker, you."

"Cut it out." She gave his arm a playful slap.

They reached the exit and he held the door. Before she stepped out, she turned to look at the place. When she turned back, she was smiling quietly.

It hit Chase with a jolt. His mother used to do that—look over the mall and smile with pride. He felt a sharp pain, remembering how impatient he would get. *Come on, Mom, let's go.*

"What's wrong?" Sylvie asked him.

"Nothing. Just hungry, I guess." He started to move forward, but Sylvie blocked his path.

"It's more than that. What?"

Looking into her concerned face, he realized he wanted to tell her. He rarely confided in anyone, but this was *Sylvie.*

"The way you looked around reminded me of my mom. Like she wanted to be sure the mall looked okay for company to arrive." He shrugged, not liking the emotions coursing through him.

"I hope I do my job the way she would want it done."

"I'm sure you do," he said, his throat tight.

"Is it hard to be here...because of her?"

He nodded.

"I miss her, too," she said softly.

For a moment, in the mall parking lot, Sylvie seemed to share his pain. He felt an abrupt connection to her and the release of a knot in his gut he'd lived with since his mother's death.

"Whenever I came to your house, she welcomed me with arms open wide, like family."

"That's how she felt," he said, forcing himself to lighten his words. "Hell, Fletcher and I weren't that huggable." He paused. "You didn't have to quit coming. We'd have been happy to have your mother join us."

"Yes, I did. It was too easy for me to slip into thinking I was one of you, when I wasn't. Not really." She shook her head, stubborn and independent and alone.

Like him. He'd always felt apart, even with his mother. Of course it was that emotional distance that allowed him to survive her death, thankfully numb, made him able to hold up his father and brother, handle the funeral arrangements, manage the mall as best he could. Cold to his bones, he'd moved through the fog somehow.

"We missed you on holidays, that's all I'm saying."

"I missed you, too," she said softly.

The family or him? Not that it mattered. "Nadia's going to give us hell for sure." He shook off the old sorrow and led the way to the BMW. "Top on or off?" he asked, nodding at the cloth roof.

"Off is nice."

"Yes, it is," he said, thinking of Sylvie's top, not the car's. He smiled.

"Human nature again?"

"Oh, yeah. Human nature for sure."

HUMAN NATURE? That's what he called that raw look he'd just given her? It was a jolt after their talk, but Sylvie felt it, too—like someone had set off sparklers in her bloodstream. Tender moment over, sex drive firing.

Chase held the door for her, sending his gaze on a slow trip down her body. "My jacket's in back if you're cool."

"Not at all." The sparklers had set off a bonfire in her chest. She slid into the seat and Chase joined her.

She picked up his musky cologne, the clean cotton scent of his sky-blue shirt, the laugh lines around his mouth, the flash of gold in his dark eyes. They were unbearably close, the air between them thick with unspoken need, as if something important had happened without either one noticing.

Like a sudden whisper in her ear, an abrupt kiss, a hug from behind.

Around them, sunset's streamers of gold, pink and purple stretched across the sky. Sylvie gripped the leather seat with both hands to ground herself. Butt in seat, feet on floorboards. She wasn't floating away. "Nice car," she said to drag her thoughts back to earth.

"Fletcher loaned it to me." Chase's voice started out husky and he seemed to be pulling himself together, too.

"Fletcher owns a convertible?"

"Yeah. Shocked me, too. I thought it might be a sign he'd started to live a little."

"Like dating me? Did you get that fixed, by the way?"

"Yep."

She caught a cringe. "How?"

"Okay, here's the deal. I kind of told him you were seeing someone."

"You're kidding."

"I know, so high school, but I was running out of time and that seemed simplest."

"For you maybe. What if he asks me about my new boyfriend? What did you tell him?"

"He won't ask. But I gave no details. It's entirely up to you. He can be tall, dark and handsome or short, blond and brilliant. I didn't mention a name. He could be Travis... Monroe...Rusty...Thor."

"Thor?" Sylvie had to smile. "Let's go with Thor. He sounds tall, blond and handsome."

Chase glanced at her, clearly intrigued. "Thor, huh? So what's he like? The strong, silent type? Maybe kinky? I mean, with that horned hat and a sledgehammer, hmm-boy."

She laughed.

"Nah, you're not into kinky so much, I bet."

"You never know."

"I'd say Thor is steady and successful, with a solid income. Serious, totally committed to a stable marriage."

"You're sneering, I can tell."

"Maybe. What about passion? Don't you want a guy to sweep you off your feet, adore you, promise you all the happiness you can hold?"

Of course she did. She wanted a man who would treat her like the sun rose and set in her eyes, a man who'd bring her flowers for no reason, share every pain and joy, and be her rock in every crisis.

But that sounded like her mother, who went through heartbreaks like tissues. Sylvie would not permit wild impulses to rule her. Passion burned out and you were left an empty shell. Sylvie had hated seeing her mother that way. She would never fall into her mother's trap of believing the dreamy fantasy of true love.

"That's all very romantic, Chase, but marriage has to be based on shared values and goals. Like anything good, you have to work at it." You earned love, day by day, proved yourself through actions, not sweeping emotion and overstated sentiment.

"Sounds like Thor could be best buds with Fletcher. They could go out for a beer and discuss pension plans together."

"Or convertibles. Don't underestimate either of them."

Sylvie glanced at Chase as he drove, one hand on the wheel, fingers strong and easy on the leather. He looked so sexy in that shirt, bright against his tan, his fashionably shaggy hair brushing the collar, his thin gold watch, subtly expensive, catching the dusk light.

Even his watch turned her on. God. As the moments passed, desire was dripping into her system like a slowly leaking faucet, the pressure building until she could see herself jumping into Chase's lap, kissing him wildly, forcing them off the road into a ditch where they could consume each other.

Yeah, right.

A perfect illustration of why she had to control her impulses. Chase was sexy and, no doubt, a fabulous lover. But was that all she wanted? Hell, no. She *did* want a Thor, a man who would stick around, content to sit home on a Saturday night to watch the baby coo and kick its legs.

Still, passion had its rewards. She took one last hungry look at Chase.

"What?" He'd caught her staring.

"Human nature," she said on a sigh.

"Ah." He nodded in a way that said he wouldn't mind driving into a ditch for sex with her, either. At least he wasn't calling her *kid*.

At the moment.

"What happened with you and Fletcher back then?" he asked her.

"Sheesh. It was so…awkward. A couple days after my birthday party, I came by to give Starr a thank-you gift and Fletcher was there. He offered me a drink and put on a CD I'd mentioned when we'd talked at my dinner."

"Yeah. I was with him when he bought the album. That's when he let it slip he liked you."

"You didn't say anything to him about…you and me…?" She felt a twinge of embarrassment, remembering the even more awkward moment when Chase had tugged up her dress and patted her.

"Of course not. That was…between us." He cleared his throat. It would be satisfying to think Chase had backed off because his brother was interested in her, but she knew better. He'd seen her as too sweet and too young, neither of which had been true. She'd been twenty-one and had known exactly what she was doing, peach margaritas or no peach margaritas.

She wished she could tell him that. Maybe she would when the time was right. "So, anyway, Fletcher put on the music and we were talking about it and he leaned toward me. I thought he wanted the CD case, so I reached for it. But it turned out he was going for a kiss and when I moved his mouth landed on my nose."

"Ouch."

"I know. Awful. We laughed and I said it was nice talking to him and got out of there as fast as I could. I mean,

Fletcher was a nice guy, but I didn't feel that way about him."

"So that was it?"

"Yeah. The next time I was at your house, he acted normal, like it never happened. Until you dared him to ask me out yesterday, you jerk."

Chase winced. "My bad."

A block later, they turned into the McCanns' exclusive community and soon Chase had pulled into the curved driveway and parked. "Showtime," he murmured, taking her all in again, making her insides shimmy like tires on ice. "I can't wait to see Fletcher's face when you tell him about the elf suit."

"I just hope I don't have to tell him about Thor."

"I could run in and web search Norse gods, Photoshop out the helmet and print you a wallet snap real quick."

"You're shameless."

"You've known that about me for years," he said, low and sexy.

And she wanted him all the same. Now, possibly more than ever. Sylvie felt herself leaning closer. He moved toward her. What were they doing?

"You sit in car all night?" Nadia called from the door. "Come in! Time for party."

Sylvie took a shaky breath, grabbed the bread sack and jumped out of the car. Chase led her forward, a gentle hand on her lower back. Her knees were noodling like crazy.

Human nature again, dammit.

At the door, Nadia pulled Sylvie into a hug, managing to squash the bread between them. "So nice for you to be at special dinner for our boy who never is home." She tugged Chase's sleeve with affection, smiling up at him.

"Bread for you." Sylvie tried to fluff up the smashed

sack before she handed it over. "Sunni says it's your favorite."

Nadia sniffed the contents of the sack. "For French toast, yes. You are too kind to me."

Chase held the door and Sylvie followed Nadia into the familiar beauty of the McCann home, the front room's high ceilings, filled with Starr's tasteful furniture in creams and chocolates—warm and understatedly extravagant.

"Sylvie." Fletcher spoke from the bar at the back of the room.

"Fletcher." When she reached him, he leaned in for a friendly upper-body hug, nothing lingering. "If I recall, you liked peach margaritas?" He motioned to a frosty pitcher of pink liquid. Yikes, he'd remembered that from her birthday party.

"Sylvie's probably outgrown blender drinks, Fletch," Chase said, shooting her a look, clearly nervous about this stroll down memory lane. "We could crack that Malbec I brought."

"Actually, I'd love a margarita," she said, not wanting to hurt Fletcher's feelings. "Thank you, Fletcher."

Fletcher poured three salt-rimmed drinks and handed them out. "Salud," he said, lifting his glass. Sylvie and Chase echoed the toast and they all sipped.

Eesh. Sylvie grimaced. The drink was a drop of tequila in a sea of heavy syrup. How had she ever enjoyed this?

Chase made a face that only Sylvie could see, then reached into a silver bowl brimming with cashews. Nadia returned and slapped his hand away. "Not to spoil supper."

"Okay, okay," he said, dropping the nuts. "I wouldn't want to ruin my favorite dinner."

"The pierogies..." Nadia sighed sadly. "Not best work of mine. Not fluffy. Not tender."

"They're always perfect, Nadia, and you know it."

"Come...taste." She gestured for him to accompany her, beaming at his praise.

Chase shot Sylvie a look. *You okay without me?*

She smiled. She'd be fine. She had Thor for a shield.

"Whatever you do, don't ask Fletcher about the Copper Creek Business Park," he said. "He'll drown you in builder minutiae."

"We can manage a conversation without your advice," Fletcher said drily.

"See why I was glad when he left home?" Fletcher said once Chase had gone. "So. Here we are. On our own." He cleared his throat and fidgeted, clearly nervous, despite his claim of conversational finesse.

"Thanks for inviting me to dinner, Fletcher."

"It's like old times, having you over." He looked at her affectionately.

"It's been a while, for sure." They sipped their drinks at the same time.

"God, that's sweet," Fletcher said, making a face. "We should have gone for the wine. Don't tell Chase he was right. I'll never live it down."

"It was thoughtful of you to make them in my honor."

"I wanted to do something I knew you liked. You look... very...well." His gaze softened.

Uh-oh. *Please don't ask me out.*

"I am. You look well, too. Business is good?"

"We're managing." His face tightened slightly. "The market's difficult and construction has us over a barrel these days—" He stopped and smiled. "No builder minutiae. Sorry."

"Forget what Chase said. You love your work and I love mine. Of course we want to talk about it. Tell me about your business park."

"There's not much to tell. Things okay at the mall?"

"Once we got over that confusion about me moving to Seattle, yes," she said, thinking she could impress Fletcher with her professionalism. "Chase and I are sharing mall management. Did he mention that?"

"Not yet, no."

"That's working out nicely, I think, especially be-cause—and you probably don't know this yet, either—we were able to hire Mary Beth on a part-time basis to get us through the holiday crunch. She brought her mother here to Arizona."

"You hired Mary Beth?" Fletcher set down his drink.

"We're paying her out of Chase's salary, so there's no hit to the budget. I'm very cautious about spending, as I'm sure Mary Beth has told you."

"Certainly. She speaks highly of you. As well she should." He looked her over again. God, was he going to say something mushy?

"Starlight Desert is such a great place to work. I hate to leave at night and can't wait to get back in the morning." Meaning, *I don't have a moment to date.*

"But that's not good, Sylvie. You're letting work con-sume you. I'm the same way. We both need to change our ways."

"Please, no life changes until I get the mall through holiday shopping." She snorted nervously.

"Chase and I disagree a lot, but he was right when he got on my case about the rut I'm in. With work. With family. In my private life." Uh-oh. Not the find-a-girl-and-settle-down speech.

"I'm sure you know what you're doing, Fletcher."

"You would say that. You're in a rut, too. At the mall." He smiled sadly. "All I know is it's easy to get hung up on things that will never happen." Was he thinking about that awkward missed kiss? "So it's time we both moved on, don't you agree?"

"Um, do I want to move on?" Surely he didn't mean she should leave the mall. "I guess that depends. I'm ready to make progress, yes. I can say that."

"Good." He sound relieved, but she wasn't sure why. "We have to keep our eyes open for new opportunities, new challenges, you know?"

"Right," she said faintly. Was he talking about work or love or what?

"So, here's to forward motion," he said, lifting his glass.

"To that." Sylvie sipped more tequila-splashed peach syrup, wondering what they'd really been talking about.

CHAPTER SIX

"WELL, LOOK WHO'S HERE." Marshall nodded at her. "Glad to have you over after so much time."

"Thank you for having me, Marshall," she said.

"I'm afraid you'll find our supper table dimmer these days." He ducked his head, frowning as if to fight emotion. He meant without Starr. A look flashed between Fletcher and Chase.

Sylvie jumped in. "It's nice to be back. I surely missed your food the first Thanksgiving I had with Desiree. It was a disaster."

"What happened?" Chase asked, sounding relieved she'd lightened the moment.

"Desiree's stove must have blown a circuit, I guess, because the turkey came out almost raw. We ended up at a fast-food place."

"A Big Mac with cranberry sauce?" Chase asked.

"And a pumpkin shake," she said. "We had a laugh at least." The fiasco broke the ice between them, too, so it had all been for the good.

Chase laughed warmly, then caught her eye, thanking her for the help. It was strange, but standing here with him and his family, she almost felt as if they were a couple, looking out for each other, navigating the shoals of family interactions. Her with Fletcher. Both boys with Marshall.

"How is your mother these days?" Marshall asked.

Sylvie had heard him criticize Desiree to Starr years ago. He hadn't understood that Desiree had done the best she could.

"She's well," she said brightly. "She helps manage the mobile home park she lives in and she's got a kiosk at the mall where she sells her crafts."

"What does she offer?"

"Right now it's ceramic birdbaths and beaded pet leashes. Oh, and personalized anklets. Those are big sellers with the moms-with-strollers set." Except her mother was erratic about her hours and was currently behind on her rent.

"Pour me some of that pink stuff, son," Marshall said, nodding at the sweating pitcher.

"We're moving on to Chase's wine, Dad," Fletcher said, shooting a look at his brother, admitting defeat to a respected opponent. Chase opened the bottle and poured them all glasses.

"So Chase tells me you two make a good team out at Starlight Desert," Marshall said to Sylvie.

"We've worked it out," she said. "We have to, since this is our crucial season. The Black Friday promotion should really boost revenues."

"Starr always loved the mall at Christmas. Do the stores still sponsor needy children?"

"You bet. And we've arranged it so all the employees shop for the gifts in each other's stores, which is a nice way to help each other while also helping those in need."

"Starr used to get tears in her eyes over the thank-you cards, you know. She put them in a scrapbook. I've got it here somewhere." He started to head out of the room.

"Later, Dad," Fletcher said. "It's about time to eat."

"I think there were some pictures in there of you boys on one of your campouts. Remember those?"

"Campouts?" Sylvie asked, turning to Chase, who groaned.

"Ancient history," Fletcher muttered.

"We used to spend the night at the mall," Chase said to Sylvie. "I was twelve, so you were, what, eight, Fletch?"

"Starr would help them set up a tent and sleeping bags," Marshall said, his eyes shining with pleasure. "She'd give them Thermoses of hot chocolate and potato chips and red licorice and those graham cracker marshmallow messes...."

"S'mores," Chase said on a sigh. "They're called s'mores, Dad." He wasn't as irritated as he let on, she could tell. He was leaning toward her so that their bodies brushed as they swayed, which contributed to her sense of the two of them as a couple.

"It sounds like a blast," Sylvie said.

"Oh, it was," Marshall said. "Starr used to spy on them. They'd eat themselves sick and Chase would scare the pants off his little brother telling ghost stories."

"It wasn't the stories," Fletcher said. "He'd hide in the planter, then jump out at me. Anyone would freak out."

"I forgot about that," Chase said. "We used to slide down the promenade in our socks and holler for the echo."

"Not many kids have the chance for that kind of experience," Marshall said. "You should appreciate it more."

"You wouldn't have thought it was so great, Dad, if you knew we were also sneaking into the stores," Fletcher said.

"You what? You broke in?" Marshall's eyebrows shot upward.

"Through the old heating conduit," Fletcher said, "from when they changed to the overhead AC."

"All we had to do was unscrew the vent plates and go through the tunnel," Chase added, then turned to Sylvie.

"It's ground level, four feet high. The vents into the stores popped right out."

"Did your mother know about this? The shop owners would have been hopping mad," Marshall said.

"She might have known. But we were careful," Fletcher said. "We put back any sports equipment we played with at Tracer's."

"We'd fool around with the demo toys from Toy Town," Chase added. "We mostly played hide-and-seek."

"And we took candy, but only a few pieces—about what Mr. Morgan would have given us anyway."

"I'll be damned," Marshall said. "So, see, that old mall has lots of good memories for you boys. That's not something you throw away like that." He snapped his fingers.

"Times change, Dad," Fletcher said. "And so has the neighborhood. Has Chase told you we've had vandalism? Graffiti on the walls, trash thrown around. Twice."

"Is that true?" Marshall asked Chase.

"Minor incidents," Sylvie said. "Pranks, really."

"Bad enough to be in the paper, I hear," Fletcher said.

"Just the weekly and only because our councilman wanted to grandstand over it," Sylvie said.

"The area's clearly in decline," Fletcher said. "Mason Construction had plans for a condo development but they couldn't get the permits. Someone on the council blocked it."

"It didn't happen to be Reggie Collins, did it?" Chase asked.

"Might have been. Yeah, that sounds right."

"That's our guy. Interesting. Why would a politician stumping for funds to save a neighborhood fight a condo development?"

"I have no idea. What I do know is the last thing we need right now is bad publicity." Fletcher's tone was ominous.

"Sylvie handled the reporter well. She offered to host a community meeting for Collins, to show we're good neighbors."

"Excellent, Sylvie," Marshall said with a sharp nod. "Starr always made the mall part of things. That's why I gave James Abernathy some space for his jai alai club. A new sports team would bring in some tax revenue."

"Jai alai? What a ridiculous sport," Fletcher said. The men debated that idea for a few minutes, and Sylvie was relieved when Nadia finally called them to the table.

As they moved into the dining room, Chase put his hand on her back again. "You holding up okay?" he whispered near her ear.

"I'm fine, but what does Fletcher have against Starlight Desert?"

"Long story," Chase said, then smiled. "Did Thor come up when you were alone?"

"Not so far."

"Good." He gave her a quick hug at the waist.

She smiled at him, enjoying the shared moment.

In the dining room, Sylvie took her old spot across from Chase. She glanced at the foot of the table where Starr used to reign over her gracious table, welcoming each guest with a warm smile. The empty chair made her stomach jump.

Luckily Nadia distracted Sylvie from her sadness with the heaping tray of pierogies she placed in the center of the table, filling the air with the smell of baked pastry, pork, onion and garlic.

There was borscht with a dollop of sour cream and a half dozen side dishes—piles of cabbage salad, fluffy potatoes, corn on the cob, pickled mushrooms and thick sausages, a salad called "herring in sheepskin coat"— herring and boiled potatoes, with beets and carrots mixed in mayonnaise.

"Thank you, Nadia, for all my favorites," Chase said.

Nadia beamed, pink with pleasure. "All to you, Chase," she said. "Because of you, Sergei will soon to be leaving my house."

"It's too early to be certain, Nadia."

"I no count chickens while eggs they lay." She gave a definitive nod, then turned for the kitchen.

Sylvie watched Chase's face. She could see in his eyes how much he cared for Nadia and wanted to help her and her family. Chase was definitely one of the good guys.

They passed the food around and dug in, enjoying the delicious flavors with no sound but hums of pleasure, requests for dishes to be passed, the click of silverware and the ring of ice in water glasses. Chase's eyes sought hers throughout the meal, making sure she was enjoying herself, smiling at her. Once he mimicked shooting a rubber band at her. She felt herself slipping into her old self here, feeling almost like she belonged again, even though she never really had in the first place.

They were finishing the meal with groans about being stuffed, when Marshall balled up his napkin and leaned on his elbows, looking at Chase. "So I hear at the club you're still rounding up investors for your project. Is that right?"

"The more the merrier, Dad. Yeah."

"I'd have thought you'd have the financing nailed down by now, after the last mistake." He reached for his wineglass.

"We're fine," Chase said, a muscle ticking in his jaw, fire flashing in his eye.

"Steady," Fletcher breathed.

"I think the project is a wonderful idea," Sylvie said to smooth the moment. "It's great you can help Nadia's family and so many others."

"Sounds like a house of cards to me," Marshall muttered.

"Not if you see the big picture," Chase argued.

"The big picture is one thing, but the devil is in the details. And the credit report."

Chase set his knife down hard.

Marshall glanced at his son, his eyebrows dueling, as if he hadn't intended his words to come out as they had. "I'm just saying look after the pennies and the dollars take care of themselves."

"That wasn't what happened and you know it," Chase said, locking gazes with his father.

Marshall broke off first. "Hell, I don't know. If it weren't for big-picture guys, we'd still be in caves, I guess." He lifted his wineglass. "To the big picture."

"And great credit scores," Fletcher added, which sounded like a dig at Chase.

Sylvie could see Chase was hurt, but trying to hide it. Marshall was tough to please and clumsy about showing his affection. The friction among them had to be long-standing judging from the sparks crackling in the air.

Sylvie had always envied the McCanns. She'd been lonely with her quiet, self-contained grandparents. Though they never complained, Sylvie knew she'd robbed them of the privacy they valued, so she tried to not impose too much or get on their nerves.

The McCanns had seemed so much happier. Relaxed and easy with each other. Normal. Both parents interested in their kids, lots of noise and celebration, games and parties and talk.

But no family was perfect. Filled with imperfect people, how could it be?

"We need big-picture and detail people at Starlight Desert, that's for sure," Sylvie said, wanting to ease the tension and advance her cause. "Take the Black Friday event. We've involved schools, which is big-picture community involvement, but there are millions of details to handle or it all falls apart."

"You say the schools are involved?" Marshall asked. He seemed relieved to switch topics. Sylvie ran through the basics of the promotion for him. "That's quite impressive," he said when she'd finished.

"It's Sylvie's baby all the way," Chase said. "We take our marching orders from her."

"We're a team," she said, blushing from his praise. "Team Starlight Desert, remember?" Warmth passed between them—they were in this adventure together. And there was something more that gave her a shiver inside—a sense of connection, of rightness.

There you are. At last.

"Not to rain on anyone's parade," Fletcher said, "but where's the money for advertising, liability insurance and everything else an event requires?"

"We have the stages and risers, the schools provide sound equipment and a lot of the promotion," Sylvie said. "The insurance rider is in the works and we'll piggyback ads onto our regular buys."

"Okay," he said. "But what's the plan for keeping all that confusion from getting in the way of the shoppers?"

"First off, many of the shoppers will be parents of the students performing. They'll have special discounts. And we'll ask mall employees to manage traffic flow."

"Sylvie's nailed it, Fletch. Leave her be."

"I'm sure that's true." He shot Sylvie a quick smile. "I'm just saying this isn't the time to color outside the lines. I hear you hired Mary Beth back."

"We're paying her out of my salary," Chase said in

a tight voice. "Let it go, Detail Guy." He was trying to lighten the mood, but he was clearly annoyed.

"I think it's a great idea, Sylvie," Marshall said. "And Starr would have loved the schools being involved."

"The mall is a business, Dad. We can't get sentimental about it," Fletcher said. "Mom's not here to care one way or the other." He stopped abruptly and a tense silence swelled like a dark cloud over the table.

"I know I sound harsh," Fletcher said quietly, humbly, speaking to Sylvie now. "I'm concerned because they're predicting a bad retail season this year. I don't want you to be caught short."

"Starlight Desert can weather the storm," Marshall said. "Tell them what that consultant said to you." He poked his fork in Sylvie's direction.

She summarized the report and Fletcher mumbled an *interesting* or two to be polite, but he clearly hadn't changed his opinion. Maybe it was about Starr, the reminders his father kept bringing up.

She looked at Chase and he mouthed, *Sorry.*

"Dessert!" Nadia announced, descending on the table with a pink Bundt cake with yellow frosting smothered in confetti sprinkles, silver balls, gumdrops and M&M's. "Favorite of Chase!"

They all looked at Chase, eyebrows lifted in question, while Nadia cut them each a huge slice. "Eat, eat," she said while they stared down at the gloppy mounds of sugar. "I get coffee."

"*This* is your favorite?" Fletcher asked when she'd gone.

"When I was five maybe." He picked up a fork. "Dig in or we'll hurt her feelings."

"*You* dig in. My fillings ache just looking at it," Fletcher said. "Where's a Great Dane under the table when you need one?"

"You'd send it into a diabetic coma," Chase said.

They lifted cake-loaded forks in salute to each other, the tension broken. Whew.

"Down the hatch," Marshall said, eating his bite.

They joined him, grimacing, then laughing at each other's expressions.

Nadia brought in coffee and they all complimented the cake, rearranging their pieces to make it seem they'd consumed more than they had.

The lighter mood seemed right for Sylvie to bring up Santa's Workshop, her goal for the evening. "There's a wonderful way you three can make 'A Starlight Desert Christmas' even more successful this year."

"Oh, yeah. Listen up." Chase grinned. "This is good."

Fletcher and Marshall set down their forks and Sylvie explained the plan to the two wide-eyed men, emphasizing the media potential, the likely boost to sales from the publicity.

When she finished, there was a stunned silence.

"You want me to be Santa Claus?" Marshall finally said. "With a suit and a beard?"

"You'll be perfect."

More silence.

"There's no budget for costumes," Fletcher said hopefully.

"I can get them donated," Sylvie said. "No worries."

"I would look pretty foolish," Marshall said, but his lips twitched into a half smile.

"You? Think about me and Fletcher with bells on our toes and little felt caps," Chase threw in.

"God." Fletcher gave a mock shudder.

"I say we do it," Chase said. "For Starlight Desert.

For Sylvie." He paused. "And for Mom. Mom would love this."

More silence, but this time the three men looked at each other, considering the idea.

"You're absolutely right," Marshall declared suddenly, banging his fist on the table so hard the cups rattled in their saucers. "I'll be Santa and you boys will be my elves. It's exactly what Starr would want."

Fletcher groaned. "This is insane."

"Come on, Fletch," Chase said. "Sylvie says you can add a bow tie and a blazer and be Business Elf."

Fletch looked at her. "Did you say that?"

"Sort of. We were joking around."

Fletcher's mouth twitched this time. He clearly wanted to laugh. "As long as the costumes are free," he said, "and you publicize the hell out of it and it's only for a few hours."

"Actually, all weekend would be better, so we catch all the press we can," Sylvie said.

Fletcher groaned. "Only for you, Sylvie," he said.

Soon after, Sylvie and Chase got ready to leave. Nadia loaded Sylvie's arms with leftovers, including half the cake, and Fletcher walked them to the front door. "I can't believe you played the do-it-for-Mom card, Chase."

"Anything to see you in tights, bro."

"Listen, I'm showing your investors that Chandler property tomorrow. If they bite, I'll owe you big-time."

"Pay me back by being the best elf ever."

"You first." He looked at Sylvie, his expression going earnest. "Think about what we talked about, Sylvie."

"I will." He wanted her to move on. That made her uneasy. Chase had told her she shouldn't feel trapped at

Starlight Desert, too. Were they both trying to tell her something?

That made no sense. Starlight Desert needed her more than ever.

CHAPTER SEVEN

"It's getting colder. Shall I put the top up?" Chase asked her when they stood at the car.

"It's such a nice night. Can I borrow your jacket?"

He reached past her for the leather coat, brushing her body, then held it while she slipped her arms into the cool silk lining. "Looks good on you," he said, patting her shoulders. "Kind of Biker Chick goes Gidget."

"That sounds pretty sad."

"Oh, no. Trust me, it's very sexy."

The jacket smelled of his cologne, a playful spice that suited him, and it felt as though he'd wrapped her in his arms.

Sylvie placed the leftovers at her feet and they drove off.

"What did Fletcher want you to think about?" Chase asked as they reached the street.

"He thinks we're both stuck in a rut."

"Is he right? Are you?"

"Not at all. I like my life and I love my job."

"Even though your life *is* your job?"

"I'm dedicated, but that's what's required. When you love something, spending time on it is no sacrifice and it's certainly not a rut."

"But what about marriage and kids? And a dog? You want those things, right?"

"You mean with boring Thor and his 401K? When the

time's right, sure. When I've built the proper foundation with my finances and career, I'll be ready to bring on a partner."

"Jesus, Sylvie, you sound like Fletcher starting a construction project. The idea is to fall in love and share your lives, not lay out footings and pour concrete."

"And you're an expert now?"

"Nah. I'm just hassling you. I'm not even in the neighborhood, let alone hammering up two-by-fours." Sadness flashed across his face like a streetlight reflection in the dark.

"But one day...?"

"Hard to say."

"I bet you've broken a few hearts."

"Nope. I don't offer more than I can give and the women I hang out with feel the same."

"And what is it you give?"

"A good time, a physical connection, interesting talk, friendship." He shrugged.

For all that Chase acted open and available, he was guarded. A person could wade only so deep into those dark eyes of his before hitting a reef.

"But what about passion, sweeping a woman off her feet and promising her the world?"

He glanced at her. "Hey...are you making fun of me?"

She held her fingers in a pinch. "A little bit."

Chase laughed his strong, low laugh. "Good for you."

"There was something else Fletcher said...that he'd been holding on to things that could never be. What do you think he meant?"

"You, of course," Chase said without question, his dark eyes locking with hers for a moment. "He's been holding on to you."

And she'd held on to Chase, too. For far too long. Spending all this time with him seemed to be making it worse.

"Anyway," she said to stop that idea, "he told me you were right about him getting a life."

"He actually said that? I should have heard the crackle of hell freezing over."

"Congratulations, Dr. Phil."

"Damn, I'm good." He drove for a few blocks, a big smile on his face. Then he glanced at her. "I hope the dinner wasn't too intense for you with us sniping at each other."

"There were moments I thought I'd have to hide the knives. Marshall has trouble showing you affection, doesn't he?"

"Showing affection? The man's impossible to please. He jabs at any weakness or error. We don't call him the General for nothing."

"He tried to pull back from criticizing you, at least."

"Yeah. There's history there. He wants the best for me, but only on his terms. In his mind I betrayed the family by not staying in the business like Fletcher. And Fletch plays the martyr role a lot."

"Fletcher envies you?"

"He thinks being the oldest gave me advantages. I don't know. Just hardwired sibling crap. Since Mom died, we've all gotten worse. She was our peacemaker."

"Is that why you've been so scarce around here?"

He shot a glance her way. "My work keeps me moving, but…maybe I look for excuses not to visit. Sounds like you're pushing for some Dr. Phil cred yourself." He reached over and squeezed her hand, his palm warm.

Electricity zinged, sparking and stinging along her nerves. Chase cleared his throat, released her hand and shifted gears through the intersection. They were quiet while the ripples between them settled.

"You sure charmed them into the Santa Plan," Chase said.

"I was amazed they said yes after all that arguing about the event. Why is Fletcher so hostile about the mall anyway?"

"He's focused on the bottom line is all."

"But our bottom line is fine. You saw that, right?"

"For now, sure…" He paused. "Could we leave the mall alone until tomorrow? Enough of that subject for one night?"

"Okay. Sure."

Too soon, Chase pulled into the mall lot beside her car. The evening was over. For some reason, Sylvie felt let down.

After all the fun and intimacy, it seemed sad to just part ways. What did she expect? Sex? That made no sense at all.

"Check this out." Abruptly Chase reached across her body, his arm brushing her breasts, warm across her middle. Was he going for it? Would he kiss her? Oooh, wow.

But he reached past her hips and pushed down on something. Her seat began to recline. A seat adjustment, not a wild sexual impulse.

"The stars are bright tonight." He lay back against his headrest and lowered his own seat beside hers. "Nice, huh?"

"Very." She released a breath. The stars were sharp sparkles in the velvet-black sky. "I don't spend enough time outdoors, I don't think."

"No wonder, living and breathing the mall as you do."

"At home I'm inside, too. I make my dollhouses indoors. I use my treadmill there. I'm an indoor girl, I guess."

"If you get that puppy—Dasher?—you'll be set. Nothing like a sad-eyed doggie with a leash in its mouth to get you out of the house."

"Forget the puppy, okay? Your Dr. Phil act is getting old."

He turned to her on the headrest. She turned, too, so they were like lovers engaged in pillow talk, close in the dark car. "I enjoyed tonight," he said softly. The moonlight made Chase's face gleam silver and his eyes glint bronze. A puff of a breeze ruffled a lock of hair onto his forehead.

"Me, too," she said, her pulse racing. Entirely too warm, she shrugged out of the jacket. Chase watched her upper body emerge like she was unwrapping something he couldn't wait to taste.

She settled back in the seat, still facing him, the leather creaking beneath her.

"I can't believe Fletcher remembered peach margaritas," she said after a few seconds.

"I'll never forget them," he said, keeping his eyes on hers. "I wasn't very responsible that night. I should have warned you tequila sneaks up on you."

"I wasn't that drunk, Chase. I knew what I was doing… and what I wanted. And I didn't want to stop."

"Yeah?"

"We never talked about what happened, you know." And at the moment that was exactly what she wanted.

"There wasn't much to say."

"So was it just a big-brother mercy mission? Cheer up the sad birthday girl?" She kept her voice light, making it a joke, though she'd been mortified by that possibility.

"Trust me, the last thing I wanted that night was to be your brother," he said, leaning closer.

"You stopped because you thought I was a virgin?"

"You *were* a virgin. You fibbed."

"Of course I did. What person with a normal sex drive wants to admit to being a virgin at twenty-one?"

"How did you last that long anyway?"

"I was waiting for the right guy."

"Me?" He looked alarmed.

"Relax, okay? The right guy for a first time." Though deep in her heart she'd wanted more.

"The first time should be special." He brushed a curl from her cheek. "Not a drunken mash-up."

"Neither of us was that drunk."

"I wasn't in town long. You would have regretted a one-night stand. I know you." He ran his gaze over her face.

"What, did you think I'd stalk you or something? You zipped up my dress and patted me like a kid."

"That was my most noble act ever. I wanted you so bad I couldn't see straight."

"Yeah?" She'd turned him on that much? That was nice to know. She wished they'd talked about this long ago. Her heart was beating so fast it nearly hurt.

"You were beautiful and funny and smart and so hot." He ran the back of his hand along her cheek, then twined a curl around a finger in a tender gesture that made her insides coil like her hair. "We always had such a good time just talking." She could hardly breathe. Everything in her waited to hear what he would say, what he would do.

"You were impossible to resist, with or without tequila." He cupped her cheek, his palm warm against the evening chill, his face so near his features blurred. "You still are. Ah, hell." He gave in and pressed his mouth to hers, holding motionless, as if waiting for the spark to flare.

And, oh, did it flare. Just like all those years before, pure desire poured through her. She wanted more of his lips, his tongue. His mouth pulled at her, but gently, pausing for her to indicate what she wanted. More or less.

More. I want more.

Immediately doubts rose. *What are you doing? You have to work together. You're in the parking lot, for God's sake.*

She broke away long enough to be sure the area was deserted, then returned to Chase's mouth. They were reliving a memory, fixing it. For once in her life, she was going for it.

Chase threaded his fingers through her hair, still holding her face, guiding her closer, a groan of pleasure vibrating his lips. He tasted of the sweet cake they'd eaten and of him, warm and human and very male.

The rasp of his evening whiskers was the only thing that reminded her he wasn't an extension of her own hungry mouth and eager body. Arousal sparked along her nerves, like strings of twinkle lights, except hotter. Much hotter.

Her body tensed and below the waist she was a twist of need. She tilted her head and extended her tongue a bit, telling him to take her deeper.

She pressed her torso against his, the friction of her bra against her nipples almost unbearable. She felt the hard length of him against her thigh, proof of his desire.

Their tongues shifted, tasted, dipped and teased. She felt light-headed and pulled back just long enough to take in a gulp of air. With their hands on each other's faces, their upper bodies close, the embrace was tender and hungry and wild all at once and she never wanted to stop.

Wanting even more, she climbed on top of him. A sharp blast of the horn made her jerk upright. She'd bumped it.

Chase startled out of his trance, too. "Wow. I hear horns."

Sylvie fell back into her seat, her heart hammering her ribs, and stared up at the sky, fighting for air. She'd never felt like this. Well, not since the first time with Chase. It had to be all the buildup, the history, the unresolved lust.

He turned to her, looking dazed, and slid his thumb back and forth on her lips. "You have an incredible mouth. Did you know that?"

"I didn't, but thank you." None of her lovers had been particularly chatty about favorite body parts. And none had the slow, simmering kiss down to a science like Chase did.

"What are we doing here?" he breathed.

"Making out in the mall parking lot." And she wanted to go somewhere private, get naked and finish what they'd started years before. "I vote you follow me home." That was bold, but what the hell.

"You think that's wise?" His voice steadied into his usual rational baritone.

"Why not? We both need to…um…blow off steam." That sounded right for Mr. Good Time Friendly Sex.

"Blow off steam? Come on, Sylvie.…"

"What? I'm a sexual being. I have needs."

"I don't doubt that. I'm just saying that—"

"Sex can be just sex. Satisfying fun. A release of tension, a clearing of the brain. Heck, it's good exercise."

"I don't see you treating sex like a Pilates class."

"Then it's like you said, a physical connection, a way for two people to share…um…a climax…. What am I saying?"

"You're saying we want each other. Badly, in my case. But we both know taking this further is asking for trouble.

We have a lot to get through together. Sex would complicate the situation."

"True." Now that Chase had invited reality into the car, her own fire faded fast.

CHASE WATCHED SYLVIE absorb his oh-so-logical explanation for not doing what he was dying to do—dive into that incredible mouth, take that arousing woman into his arms and not come up for air for hours, maybe days.

Sylvie just plain got to him. Her drive, her heat, her big, soft heart. She was a force to be reckoned with.

And he wanted to reckon a little.

But he was right. Sex would complicate things. On top of that, he couldn't keep Sylvie in the dark another minute about his job at the mall. He owed her the full story even if the real estate guy had been blowing smoke about a bidding war.

"Listen, Sylvie, there's something you need to know. I'm not just here to manage the mall."

"What?" Her green eyes went wide, startled.

"Here's the deal. Fletcher wants to sell Starlight Desert. Dad doesn't. My job is to run the numbers, check out the commercial market and break the tie."

"Fletcher wants to sell…? And you're going to…?" She took two deep breaths, her eyes searching his face, then she fell back against the headrest as if she'd been struck. "I can't believe this. That's horrible news." She sat bolt upright. "Why didn't you tell me sooner?"

"I wanted to talk to the broker first. If a sale was impossible why upset you unnecessarily? But I figured you'd rather know than not."

"You're right." She took another shuddery breath then jerked her head to face him. "So which way are you leaning?"

"I'm neutral at the moment. The consultant report and your projections look good, but the market might be right to sell."

"What would it take to get you on our side?"

"I don't know. No buyers, I guess. Or very low offers."

"How about if 'A Starlight Desert Christmas' breaks all revenue records? What if we make so much money even Fletcher will want to keep the mall?"

He studied her anxious eyes, wishing he wasn't the cause of her distress. "It depends. I can't promise, Sylvie."

"Give us a chance, Chase. You know how important the mall is to so many people. The owners, our shoppers, the staff. Me."

"Things change. Tenants move out. Managers go back east to take care of relatives."

"But some things are constant."

"If we do sell, you can count on a strong reference letter. I know you'll go on to bigger and better things."

"That's what you think? That I *settled* for Starlight Desert? You're wrong. About me and about the mall and I'll prove it to you."

He studied her face as determination began to take over despair. He was glad for that. "For now, keep this information to yourself. I don't want to alarm the tenants until we know where we stand."

"I won't say a word."

"If we do sell, they'll have several months to relocate."

"That's good, I guess."

"I know this is hard for you, Sylvie, but as much as you love the mall, it *is* a business. If it's better for McCann Development to sell, we have to sell."

Angry flames lit her green eyes. "Starlight Desert is

more than a business, Chase. I just have to make you see that." She got out of the car.

Chase handed up the sack of leftovers. "I'm sorry tonight had to end like this."

"We needed some kind of cold shower."

"As far as mall management goes, I want you to take the lead. Tell me what you need me to do and I'll do it."

"Don't sell Starlight Desert," she said. "That's what I need you to do."

"No promises. I'll do whatever else I can."

She bit her lip, worried as hell, and Chase wanted to take her in his arms and tell her it would be all right, that he'd *make* it all right.

But he couldn't do that. Besides, selling the mall might be best for her, too, though she wouldn't want to hear that. She'd get swept out of this little tide pool and into the larger career stream. One day she'd thank him. Maybe.

At least now sex was out of the question. Sylvie would never sleep with a guy who might sell her precious mall. For all her talk about *letting off steam,* she didn't take sex lightly.

Chase had the uneasy feeling that with Sylvie he might not either. And then where would he be?

CHAPTER EIGHT

SHAKING AND STRUGGLING to breathe as Chase's news sank in, Sylvie braked halfway across the mall parking lot to collect herself. She rested her head on the steering wheel and made herself take slow, deliberate breaths.

As much as you love the mall, it is *a business.* So cold.

She'd thought the worst thing that could happen was Chase taking her dream job, but this was far worse. It could be the end of all she loved. Any day now, they could up and sell Starlight Desert right out from under her.

What could she do about it? Nothing much beyond making the Black Friday event the best it could be. Would that be enough? Chase wouldn't promise anything.

For comfort, she looked back at Starlight Desert. It looked sleepy in the fall darkness. Evenly spaced security lights created triangles of orange along the back wall, making the place seem mysterious and beautiful. Except there was a gap, right in the middle, like a punch in the mall's eye. Had the light burned out? Or had it been smashed? And was that Dumpster usually against the wall that way?

Maybe she was being paranoid, but she called the security office just in case. The call went to the machine and she left a message. Leo and his crew must be on rounds. She hoped they weren't holed up watching TV at the information desk, which might have been how the vandals got away the first two times. On the other hand, she and Chase had been lucky no one had been patroling the lot in a golf cart while they were kissing like maniacs. What had possessed her anyway?

Chase had turned her down because he thought she'd make too big a deal of sex. She knew why. The first time with him, she'd been ridiculously dreamy, believing sex meant love and love meant forever. But eight years had passed and she'd matured. Sex wasn't necessarily that big a deal.

Certainly it wasn't with Chase, Mr. Easy Breezy in the Sack, and he'd made that clear. It was tempting to think a guy would change for love, that the right woman could "fix" him. That was how Desiree talked about the flawed men she chose.

Sylvie knew better. People didn't change. The trick was to accept them as they were.

And Chase was a guy who moved on—in work, in life, with women. He would do what he would do with the mall and then he would leave, no matter what happened between them.

Which would be exactly nothing now that the mall was at risk. There had to be more she could do to save it. If she could make Chase see that Starlight Desert was more than a business, if she could get him to side with Marshall, he wouldn't want to sell, no matter what anyone offered. But how could she change the mind of a hard-line business guy?

THE NEXT MORNING, Randolph met Sylvie at her car looking worried. "Don't panic," he said, when she stepped out, "but there's been another incident."

"What happened?"

"We took pictures for the police." He pointed to where

Betty was hosing graffiti from the wall. Black water ran across the decorative pebbles and along the gutter. "At least this time it's water-based paint. Brushed on, not sprayed."

Sylvie saw she'd been right about the Dumpster. It had been shoved against the wall. "Was the security light broken?"

"Yep. And there's more. Guess what's on the roof?"

"I have no idea."

"The batteries from both security carts. They climbed the Dumpster to get up there. Plus the cart tires have been flatted." He shook his head in disgust.

"Why would they vandalize the carts?"

"To keep us from catching them probably. But that's not the worst. That lock I keep saying needs to be replaced? Come here."

Sylvie followed him to the door.

"They tried to pry it open." He showed her the scrapes on the lock.

"Where was the night crew, Randolph?"

"See, that's where I take full responsibility." Randolph looked down at the ground for a few seconds before lifting his gaze to hers. "Leo called in sick and I couldn't stay because I had the girls, so it was just one guy on shift."

"So we were understaffed."

"If I had Leo's nephew on board, we wouldn't have been caught short. With more guards, we'll catch these clowns. I know they're just laughing at us." His jaw clenched with anger.

It was almost like the criminals *knew* the mall had been underguarded. They'd also taken her spray paint last time, so they knew the mall's inner workings to some degree. She didn't know what to think about that.

"Can you get the carts operational?" she asked.

"Maybe, but they belong in the junkyard. I can't do my job without staff and equipment." Sweat poured down Randolph's temples and he looked like he'd lost his best friend. No way had he faked these incidents as Chase suspected.

"I'll talk to Chase." She didn't look forward to revealing the new crime. More vandalism made the neighborhood seem worse, the mall like it was in trouble, which had been Fletcher's point at dinner and Reggie Collins's rant for the newspaper story.

Sylvie wanted to lock herself into her car and scream with frustration. Who was doing this? Why?

Chase would have to mention this at the tenant meeting, too. She dreaded the meeting now that she knew what the McCanns were up to. How could she act normal when the tenants might be booted out of their stores in a few months? She almost wished Chase had kept the secret a while longer.

At least he'd promised to be here early so they could go over the agenda before the meeting. She forced a smile so she wouldn't alarm Cyndi, Olive or Mary Beth, and headed upstairs.

The minute she entered the office, Cyndi thrust a newspaper at her. "I marked the story," she said grimly.

Sylvie didn't need the Post-it note to find the photo of a police car beside the ugly scrawl, carefully cropped to not show the first letter of the *F* word.

The headline was awful. *Councilman vows renewal funds and more police to end crime spree.* The story was even worse. Sylvie's calming quote about Halloween pranks was on the last paragraph and there was no mention of the community meeting she'd offered to host.

"Damn," she said. "Damn, damn."

"I know it's terrible," Cyndi said, "but Mary Beth has some ideas for you. She's in her old office."

Sylvie found her at Chase's computer. "Mary Beth, this isn't your office anymore," she started.

"I know, but the spare computer is so slow. I just borrowed this until Chase gets here." She waved at the guest chair.

"If that's the case, bring in your laptop."

"You're right. I'm sorry." She gave her old desk a sad look. "Anyway, you saw the story." She nodded at the paper in Sylvie's hand. "You should email a strong letter to the editor."

"I intend to. I'm waiting to hear back from Councilman Collins about holding a community meeting here."

"Did you call the scheduling secretary?"

"No. I called his office."

"That won't work, hon." Mary Beth's smug tone irked Sylvie. "I'll follow up on that for you, no problem. Let's offer Tuesday afternoon, since that's the slowest shopping day and we might make the six o'clock news."

"Okay…" Sylvie said slowly, glad of the tip, but not happy about the way Mary Beth seemed to be taking charge.

"Mention it in your email to the paper and insist they send a reporter to the meeting. They owe us that."

"I can take it from here, Mary Beth," she said firmly.

"Oh." Caught short, Mary Beth stared at her. "I'm sorry. Am I stepping on your toes? I didn't mean to."

"I appreciate your advice and I'll want you to read over the email before I send it to see if I've covered all the bases, but you have plenty to do already."

"Sure. Of course." Mary Beth blinked. "I just want you to be glad you took me onboard." She gave a hesitant smile.

"I am, but sharing the GM job with Chase is complicated enough, so you and I need to be clear on who's doing what."

"Absolutely. I guess I got too upset about the story. Plus, these attacks. Is it true there was a death threat?"

"No. Where did you hear that?"

"Around." She shrugged.

"Then I hope you'll clear up the rumor when you talk to the tenants. You'll be helping the stores get their coupons together for the scavenger hunt, right?"

"Right," she said, saluting Sylvie. "I'm on it, boss."

The phone rang and Mary Beth reached for it. Sylvie caught her eye. "Whoops," she said. "Sorry."

Sylvie answered the phone. "Chase McCann's office."

"Is he there? This is Chet Walker."

She recognized Chase's partner's name. "We expect him any minute." It was nine-fifteen, so he was already late for their premeeting session. "Can I take a message?"

"Tell him we need him out here in a hurry."

"I'll let him know." She wrote down the message, irritated. Chase had promised her his help, but he was late and now had his partner after him, too.

"A problem?" Mary Beth asked, clearly relishing the prospect.

"We'll work it out, I'm sure," she said. "I'll get started on my email." She opened the paper looking for the address for letters to the editor, then noticed a headline: *PriceLess Warehouse in market for new Phoenix location.* "Wow," she said.

"What is it?" Mary Beth leaned closer.

"PriceLess wants to build another store. We have all that open park space. Why couldn't they come here?"

"They could. Savings Club approached us a couple years back, but they decided on Tucson before we even started negotiating. There's a build-out, from what I remember, and they expect incentives. It's a lot of up-front cash."

"But think of the revenue potential." Sylvie scanned the article for the official most quoted.

Five minutes and a Google search later, she had Roger Munford, Business Development VP for PriceLess, on the line. In ten minutes, she had several possible meeting times to run past Chase.

"Great work," Mary Beth said when she'd hung up, offering a high-five Sylvie was delighted to slap.

This could be it, the solution to the threat to sell the mall. Chase said it would be a business decision based on revenues. PriceLess Warehouse was a revenue machine.

Sylvie almost did a happy dance in the middle of Chase's desk. They weren't finished yet. Not even close.

CHASE TOOK THE STAIRS to the mall office two at a time, late for Sylvie's tenant meeting because of his last-minute appointment with the commercial broker, then a lengthy three-way phone call with Chet and Jake Atwater.

The mall decision would not be easy, he knew now. The broker listed a half dozen potential buyers, including an amusement center, an indoor go-cart track, a physicians group and a charter high school.

No offer was on the table, and Chase had lots more questions, but the time might be right to sell. The cash would be welcome, he had to admit. Fletcher had been right about that. With his share, Chase could buy into the Portland venture instead of just brokering it, which meant he could pay back his Nevada investors far sooner than with Home at Last in Arizona.

Personal gain wasn't reason enough to sell, of course. Chase still had to thoroughly examine the data on the mall's revenues and potential. Black Friday income would be important, though a high sales price could easily trump that.

He'd hated how hard Sylvie had taken the news. He wished her the best. He did. But facts not wishes would rule his choice.

He slipped into the conference room, where the meeting was already underway. At the front of the room, Sylvie stood with one of the red umbrellas over her head, a newspaper in one hand. "Lately we've really needed our umbrellas, haven't we?" She wiggled the newspaper, offering a smile that trembled only slightly.

"This article grossly exaggerated the vandalism and I've submitted a letter to the editor saying as much. You'll be pleased to hear that next Tuesday we'll be hosting a community meeting for Councilman Collins to discuss neighborhood concerns."

"That's all nice, Sylvie, but what about the new attack?" The speaker was Talley Toombs, the manager of the department store, Tracer's. "Security carts wrecked, more hate graffiti, a break-in and a death threat."

"What break-in?" someone else said. "A death threat?"

"There was no break-in or death threat," Sylvie said over the murmurs of alarm. "Those are just false rumors. Randolph thought someone messed with the lock, but no one got in. We're working with the police to catch the mischief makers, so there's no need to panic, Talley."

"When people read that crap about crime they'll shop elsewhere," said Rose, the hobby shop owner. "What then?"

Heads across the room nodded.

"I know you're worried, but don't forget 'A Starlight Desert Christmas.' I'm sure that will reverse any possible losses."

Angry murmurs came from the tenants. They weren't buying it.

"We just have to be patient," Sylvie tried to assure them. "We're working with the police. We'll talk to reporters, speak at the community meeting and keep serving our customers the way we always have."

"But there is good news," Mary Beth said, jumping up from her chair beside Sylvie. "Tell them about PriceLess, Sylvie."

"That's really premature, Mary Beth."

"Oh, you're too modest. Sylvie found out that PriceLess is looking for a new locale, so she called them up and they're interested in coming here."

The group made sounds of surprise and approval.

"We haven't met with them yet," Sylvie said. "It's way too soon to say this will work."

"But it's hopeful?" Theo asked.

"Like I said, it's too soon to—"

"They're very interested," Mary Beth said. *"Very."*

Great. This was no time to float a development idea. Chase frowned at Sylvie, who shrugged.

"So just keep those umbrellas up a little while longer," Mary Beth said, waving the one Sylvie had put down.

The tenants applauded, the tension gone, and Chase made his way to the front of the room. "I apologize for being late, everyone, though you've been in excellent hands here with Sylvie." He smiled at her. "I bring greetings from everyone at McCann Development and thank you for your patience during this time of transition. We're so impressed with what Sylvie's planned for Black Friday, we let her talk us into being Santa and his elves for the weekend."

People laughed and smiled.

"I'm not looking forward to wearing pointy shoes and green tights, but I'm sure you know how hard it is to say no to Sylvie." There were groans and oh-yeah's. "Seriously, McCann Development is grateful to have Sylvie here. No one is better equipped to handle the job than she is and I'm sure Mary Beth agrees." He waited for Mary Beth to nod.

The group applauded and Chase joined them.

"Can Santa get us new air-conditioning?" someone called out.

"I'd settle for Santa bringing PriceLess here," someone else said.

"That's far too remote for even Santa to speculate about," he said. "Let's focus on doing all we can to make this holiday season our best." He sat down to applause.

Sylvie took over, going over the Thanksgiving Day staff party and Black Friday preparations. When the meeting ended, he caught her elbow. "Can I speak to you?" He pulled her into his office and shut the door. "What was all that about PriceLess?"

"It's new. The VP wants a meeting. Here are his available times." She pulled a paper from her pocket and held it out.

"We're in no position to start negotiations on something like this. You should have talked to me first."

"I wasn't the one who brought it up. And if you'd been here when you said you'd be, we *would* have discussed it."

"That couldn't be helped."

"Is this how you 'do all you can to help me'?"

"I got here as soon as I could."

"And Mary Beth was just trying to help."

"False hope is never helpful."

"Neither is doom and gloom," she snapped, her cheeks pink with anger. "If you're so neutral, you should be eager to meet with PriceLess. That changes the revenue picture dramatically. Have you written us off already?"

"Slow down, Sylvie." He stepped closer, wanting to soothe her somehow.

"*You* slow down." She backed away. "The newspaper story made us look awful. People are scared. You saw Talley fanning the flames. Mary Beth is no help. She spreads rumors with the best of them. I needed your help to settle everyone down and now you're quashing the one thing that gives us hope—"

A tap on the door made them turn to see Randolph, clearly embarrassed he'd interrupted their quarrel. "I can come back...."

"No, no, come in," Sylvie said, taking a deep breath, clearly trying to calm down.

"I know you don't need more bad news, but Leo can't work again tonight," he said. "They lost their daytime babysitter, so he's been watching the kids instead of sleeping."

"That's not good," she said.

"Worse that that, the other night guy has his bachelor party tonight, which he failed to tell Leo about. I've got my girls and I can't give that up, not with my ex-wife after full custody. I was thinking we could hire Leo's nephew and we'd be covered for tonight at least."

"I don't want an untrained person here alone. We'll have to call the service and hire some temps."

"It'll cost a fortune this last minute."

"I'll do it," Chase said. "I'll take the shift."

"That's not necessary, Chase," Sylvie said.

"I need to get a better sense of the place anyway." She studied him. "Are you sure?"

"Just let me know," Randolph said wearily, shaking his head, clearly not happy with the idea.

"What is this about?" she asked Chase when Randolph left.

"We seem to have guards asleep at the wheel whenever the attacks occur. Randolph will give me the rundown and I'll see for myself just how secure we are. Maybe he's right. Maybe we do need more guards. I'll find out tonight."

"I don't know, Chase…"

"I meant what I said about helping you. You want the tenants to know the McCanns care, right?"

"Maybe if you spend time here you'll appreciate it more." She smiled sadly and sank into a guest chair. "We have to stop these attacks, Chase. Our tenants are freaked that we'll lose customers, and frankly, so am I."

He pulled over a chair and sat close to her. "If it makes you feel any better, I'm worried, too. Lower revenues would hurt any sales offer we get."

"That's supposed to cheer me up?"

"The point is we both want to get to the bottom of this." She was so pretty, even with her green eyes cloudy with distress. "How are you holding up?"

"Not that well, judging from the way I jumped on you."

"You expected me to be here and I wasn't. And after what happened between us last night… I'm sorry that I—"

"Stop. Don't you dare apologize for kissing me. Besides, I was all over you."

"Don't I know it."

Her eyes lit as they had the night before and he felt the same urge to hold her, kiss her, fix what was upsetting her.

"You were right, though," she said. "Sex would have

been a bad idea even before you told me why you're here. We got carried away talking about old times."

"And we have needs?"

She grinned. "And steam to let off."

"Plus, think of the exercise."

She laughed, the sound musical and light. He really liked it when she laughed.

"And what did I babble? *A man and a woman going after a climax.* God."

"You were aroused. We both were. No one thinks straight when they're aroused."

"But that's all over." She spread her palms flat, definite. "We put it behind us and go on from here. Forget it ever happened."

"I'd hate to have to forget, Sylvie." The thought of never touching her again emptied him out inside.

"Anyway—" she shook her head, as if to clear it "—back to business. You'll still meet with the PriceLess guy?"

"The build-out would be a huge capital drain."

"Let me get some data from him and put together a proposal. There's no harm in talking, right?"

"Sylvie…"

"Pick a time and day." She shoved the note at him.

He read the options. "Okay. Set it up for Thursday morning. But don't get your hopes up. This is a long shot."

"Good enough," she said and bounded out of his office. At least he'd made her a little happier. For now at least.

On his way out later to talk with Fletcher about the broker meeting, Chase noticed the pet shop sported a big, new banner. "Puppies must go! Prices slashed! Impossible to resist!"

Hmm. He stood at the window watching the dogs play. Only three remained and they were damned cute. Sylvie was right. He could see one of these guys peeking out of a

Christmas stocking, like a fuzzy stuffed toy. He recognized the one Sylvie liked best. Dasher, right? Before he knew it, he was inside the store.

CHAPTER NINE

THAT NIGHT, SYLVIE SET UP her surprise for Chase, being careful not to be seen by anyone who might think she'd lost her mind. She finished and made it back to her office just before eight when Chase was due to start his security shift.

If everything went as planned, Chase would want to save the mall as much as she did. Or at least, he'd think of it as more than just a business.

"Hey, Sylvie." Sylvie looked up from finalizing the PriceLess proposal to see Chase in her doorway wearing a white security guard shirt tucked into black jeans, an official guard cap on his head.

"Look at you, all dressed up to protect-and-serve," she said.

"I catch anyone with spray paint and I'll nail his ass with my, uh—" he whipped his cell phone from his pocket "—phone? Randolph was disappointed I don't have a hand-gun permit. But don't worry, I was a brown belt in karate when I was twelve." He struck a pose and she had to laugh. "He ran me through the paces. Seems like a decent system if it's implemented the way he claims it is."

"Randolph is conscientious."

"What are you still doing here anyway? It's late."

"Finishing up the PriceLess proposal. And waiting for you, since I have a surprise."

"You do? Because I have one for you, as well. I was

going to show it to you tomorrow, but…what the hell. You go first."

"Okay." She came toward him, heading for the door, her gaze slipping over him, noticing how tall he was, how in charge he seemed. There was something about a man in a uniform.

Yes, Officer. Yes, oh, yes.

Her attraction hadn't gone away just because Chase had threatened her world. She half wished they'd managed to do the deed before coming to their senses. It seemed so unfinished, hanging in her head like a musical note held too long.

Stupid, of course. But that had been her reaction to Chase from the beginning—stupid. Far too much human nature involved.

She led the way down the stairs, fingers crossed that her plan would work.

"Where are we going?" Chase asked.

"You'll see." She took him to the plant island in the middle of the mall, hiked herself up onto the low tile wall, then waited while he joined her and took in the scene she'd set.

"You're kidding me."

"Nope." She'd placed a two-person tent between the banana trees, complete with a sleeping bag, a flashlight and a book of scary stories. Outside the tent, she'd set out two camp chairs, an ice chest with sodas and a basket with snacks.

She pointed at a hot plate plugged into one of the light outlets. "That's for making s'mores." She'd set her laptop to a screensaver of a crackling fire. "That's the closest I could come to a campfire without setting off the sprinklers."

Chase looked stunned.

"Bring back happy memories?" She was counting on

it. If Chase fell back in love with the mall, he'd think past the bottom line to what really counted, the heart and soul of Starlight Desert.

"I can't believe you did this," he said, turning to her, emotions flying across his face.

"Since you had to be here all night, I figured you'd enjoy it. Besides, I kind of wanted to see what those campouts were like. I borrowed the gear from Tracer's. Come on. Check it out." She dropped to her knees and crawled into the tent.

Chase took off his guard cap and crawled in with her. The tent seemed tiny with both of them inside, cozy and intimate, and way too personal. Sylvie hadn't counted on that.

"You're on duty, so you can't sleep, of course," she said, running her hand across the slippery sleeping bag, "but we needed something to sit on for this." She picked up the book: *A Dozen Spine Tinglers*.

"Plus, socks so we can slide down the tile." She showed him the two fuzzy pairs she'd bought.

Chase laughed. "You thought of everything."

"Oh, and this." She reached into her back pocket and held out a screwdriver. "So you can show me how you sneaked into the stores. Just unscrew the vents, right?"

"Yeah." He grinned. "That's how we did it."

She'd actually tested the entry by the restrooms, opened it and peeked inside. "That sounded so fun I had to try it."

"You're telling me you're spending the night with me?"

The idea spiked her pulse. "Just long enough to hit some stores, make s'mores and read a scary story or two."

"This doesn't sound like you, Sylvie." His gaze chased

over her, affectionate and intrigued. "Adventurous and downright silly."

"That's because you put me in a box labeled All Serious, All The Time. I know how to have fun, Chase."

"As long as it's at the mall."

"Tonight, sure. But not always. I enjoy my free time."

"I'm glad to hear you say that," Chase said with a new twinkle in his eye. "Considering my surprise for you."

She'd forgotten about that. "What is it?"

"Wait here and I'll get it out of my office."

Sylvie sat in one of the camp chairs to wait, looking out at her mall in the dim light from the orange security lights. The cross-hatched metal gates that blocked the store entrances made the place seem cold and lonely, not at all like it was during the day.

If the mall closed, these gates would never lift. She would miss it so much. Her stomach flipped at the prospect.

"Surprise." Chase's voice came from behind her. She took in a pile of gear, a shopping bag and Chase with a leash. A leash? She followed the leash with her eyes to the collar of a furry ball with scrabbling paws.

"You bought a puppy?" She jumped from the planter to meet them. "Is that Dasher?"

"He's on loan for now. One of those try-before-you-buy deals." He scooped up the tiny spaniel and held him toward her.

"Wait a minute." She froze, though Dasher wiggled frantically, trying to get at her. "He's not for me, is he?"

Chase shrugged, plopping the dog into her arms. "They were closing out the puppies and I knew he was your favorite."

"I can't keep him. I told you I work too much. He'd be

lonely. And I have dollhouse parts and screws and delicate things…no way." She held the dog out to Chase.

Chase crossed his arms so she was forced to hang on to the puppy. "Lots of workaholics have pets, Sylvie. Hell, bring him to work with you, make him the mall mascot."

Dasher was now licking his way across her cheek with his pink tongue.

"You go, little dog," Chase said in a low voice. "Is that not the softest skin ever?" He caught her gaze and heat flashed for a moment, slowing time.

"Chase…I…can't do this. It's impossible."

"When you love something, you find a way."

"That's romantic and sweet, but no." She looked down at the dog, trying to harden her heart against this canine maniac squirming against her and moistening every inch of her face. "You'll have to take him back."

"Give him a week. If you really can't stand it, then the McCanns will adopt him. It'd be good relationship practice for Fletcher."

"I don't know…"

"Don't deny yourself this, Sylvie. Look at him."

Dasher had locked his melting brown eyes on her like she was his entire universe. His little tail wagged his entire body. "You're milking it," she said to the dog who squirmed even harder at her words.

"He loves you," Chase said.

"That's not love. That's a crush. Love takes time."

"You have to start someplace," Chase said softly. "He wants you. You want him. Go with that." Chase's lips parted and his eyes held flickers of golden heat. Surely he wasn't going to kiss her again.…

She shifted away, afraid she'd lunge for his mouth herself. "I thought you didn't know how love works."

"I've seen a few movies, read some books." He was studying her as if she was the most fascinating woman he'd ever seen. Chase was always so present, so *there,* as if he would never leave. But of course he would. Chase always moved on. He was a heartbreaker, for sure.

Sylvie looked behind Chase and saw the items he'd brought with the puppy: a padded bed, a roomy kennel. "What's in the sack?"

"Bowls, food, chew toys. Puppy gear." He pulled out the things one by one to show her.

Dasher struggled to get down, so she bent and released him. He galloped off a few yards, trailing his leash, then turned back to yip, as if urging them to follow. When they didn't, he squatted and looked at them over his tiny shoulder as a puddle of liquid spread on the tile, shining silver in the orange glow of the security lights.

"He did that on purpose," she said, while Chase laughed his deeply pleasurable laugh. "I'll have to potty-train him, too."

"Guess that's part of the deal."

"Maybe I'll turn him over to you for that."

They mopped up the mess and settled Dasher in his kennel, with his bed, food and water. He set about gnawing a chew toy. "Pretty cute, huh?" She had to admit the little guy was darling.

"Very," Chase said, but he seemed to be looking at her.

"Ready to explore?" Sylvie produced the screwdriver again. "There's a flashlight on my key chain."

"Why not?" Chase was intrigued. So far so good. Soon enough, she hoped, he'd be in love.

SYLVIE WAS A WONDER, for sure. Her scheme to prowl the mall and fake a campout together was endearing. She figured dredging up fun memories would make him reluctant to sell. Simplistic but sweet. Chase would go along for the ride. This was Sylvie, after all.

He'd been right about the puppy. She plain lit up when she saw him. He hoped she'd give the dog a chance.

When you love something, you find a way. Big talk, of course. Could Chase ever make room in his life for someone else—a pet or a person? Most people managed to. They settled down, got married, had families.

But he wasn't most people and he knew his limits.

Pretty soon he was unscrewing the entry vent while Sylvie held the small flashlight like a pair of burglars. In seconds, he had the thing open and motioned Sylvie ahead of him. The ductwork looked the same—dusty, high enough to walk bent at the waist, but more comfortable on hands and knees, and nearly wide enough to move side by side.

He crawled inside. She turned back toward him, aiming the flashlight overhead so they wouldn't be blinded. "This is so cool."

He grinned at her delight. "Where do you want to go first?"

"The candy store's just over there, right?" She aimed the light down the duct, then headed in that direction. Together they pounded on the screen into the store until it rattled open. He jumped down, then helped Sylvie to the floor. They dusted off their knees and looked around at the fishbowl bins with brightly colored treats.

"This place always seemed magical to me," she said. "Like something out of Willie Wonka."

"True." He spotted the dish with blue-and-white gummi sharks and held one out to her. "Your favorite."

"We shouldn't take anything," she said.

"Come on. One little shark." He ran it along her

bottom lip. "You know you want it." He wanted her mouth even more.

"Just one," she said, taking the candy with her teeth. Her tongue brushed his finger and he sucked in a breath, a charge hitting his parts. That tongue.

She arranged the shark in her mouth with the tail hanging out. "This what you remember?"

"Chew it a bit."

"Right." She munched away.

"You make that look better than it could ever taste."

"Try one." She picked up a shark. He opened his mouth and she aimed and tossed it in.

He chewed. It was like a rubber eraser dipped in berry-flavored chemicals. "Must be an acquired taste."

"Color check?" She stuck out her tongue.

"Very blue."

"Gross." She scrunched up her nose.

"Nah. It's kind of cute." And what that tongue could do. Damn, Chase had only so much willpower.

As they wandered the aisles, Sylvie told him that the shop owner had inherited the store from his grandfather, that he donated stockings full of candy to homeless shelters each Christmas and loved to watch kids sample any new candy he found.

They compared notes on the treats from their childhood—the way Pixy Stix burned your tongue, whether Skittles or Starburst had more true fruit flavors and what a mistake it had been to add blue M&M's.

The entire time, Chase was aware of Sylvie's body, how she moved, the feel of her hair brushing his arm, and how damn good she smelled.

Once they were back in the tunnel, he said, "I choose the next store," then had to climb over her to lead the way, a move that required way too much contact with legs and breasts and backside. He groaned inwardly, hoping she couldn't tell how aroused he was. Reaching the store he wanted, he banged open the vent and jumped down, raising a hand for Sylvie.

She hit the ground beside him. "Heaven Scents?"

"This is where you get your lotion, right?"

"Yes. It's called—"

"Don't tell me the name. I want to see if I can find it." He leaned close and took a deep sniff of her skin, resisting the urge to rest his lips on her neck. "Okay, got it."

At the shelves, he sampled anything pink or red. "Not sweet enough," he said of the first, "sweet, but not fruity," of the second. A third and fourth missed the mark, too.

"Hang on. I need a fill-up." He turned to smell her again. She shivered beneath him. It might be wrong to tempt each other, but it was so much fun.

He stayed a little too close a little too long, so she pulled away. "Let's not drag this out." She marched across the shop to a row of red glass bottles with white flowers on dark tree branches and handed him a bottle. "Cherry Blossom Vanilla Bean."

He sniffed it. "Okay…that's the cherry and vanilla, sure, but the rest, that spice…" He breathed her in. "Must be just you. Your skin. Your own smell." He ran his eyes down her body, slowing at the other places he'd like to sample, to smell, and touch and taste. "Whatever it is, I like it."

She put the bottle back on the shelf with shaky fingers.

There was an alcove to the left and he stepped in, finding a massage table and shelves with oils, towels and lotions. "What do you know?"

"Yeah. The owner is trained in massage."

"Have you ever had one?"

"I don't have time really."

"For a massage you *make* time." He studied her. "It's not really about that, is it?"

She shrugged "It seems so...personal. I would feel lazy just lying there while someone worked so hard over me."

"Trust me, it's well worth it. People don't go into massage unless they enjoy it. A friend taught me some techniques."

"Oh, I'll just bet she did."

"It was completely legit, I assure you." He turned her back to him and pressed into her neck and shoulders, making gentle circles with his thumbs, the way Rachel had showed him. No woman had ever failed to dissolve into moans after a few minutes of this.

"Oh, wow, that feels so good." Sylvie sagged a little.

He smiled. "Your trapezius are pretty tight."

"Sounds like something I should slap you for saying."

"True. Your deltoids are aching for it," he said in a breathy, fake-sexy way.

She laughed, then moaned. "Ooooh, don't stop."

"If you lie down on the table I can do it right."

"I would just melt away." She sounded so dazed, not even joking anymore.

"I'd like to make you feel that good, Sylvie." He would. In fact, he was picturing it right now....

She turned around. "Time to go," she said firmly. "And to a store with no table."

Who needed a table when you had the floor...?

CHAPTER TEN

AFTER CHASE FINISHED with her, Sylvie's legs were so rubbery she could hardly walk, let alone crawl along the ductwork. *No stores with a table, indeed.*

As he'd squeezed her shoulders, she'd thought of what else those skilled fingers could do...slide across her bare skin, smooth her thighs, tease her breasts, cup her backside and so much more.

Somehow, she managed to move forward along the echoing tunnel. Knee, hand, knee, hand, aware always of Chase behind her. "What shop is this?" He tapped at the vent to their left.

"Lucy's Secrets," she said, pushing it open a crack to be certain. Chase moved beside her so their faces were inches apart as they peered down into the store.

"Look at all that sheer, slinky, fluffy stuff." Chase groaned. "Forget the massage table. I can see you in all of it."

A girlish giggle escaped her. She wasn't used to feeling irresistible and maybe it was silly, but she liked it.

"Is this where you got those stockings you were wearing when I helped you down the ladder?"

"You deliberately looked up my skirt."

"Not my fault. You flashed me when I was saving you."

"You didn't save me. I caught my balance fine."

"But I was there just in case. And the view was great."

They were close enough to kiss. Chase's breath brushed her face, warm and minty. "Though I figured you for a bare-legs girl." His eyes were golden-brown in the reflected glow of the flashlight. They were both breathing unevenly.

"Why was that?"

"Stockings seem like too much of a hassle. Sexy, sure, but…" He paused. "Bare legs makes it all so much easier…."

The words made her ache where she craved his touch. Who needed a table when they had this dusty tunnel?

Ridiculous. Again.

"Lucy talked me into the stockings," she said.

"How about that pink lace bra? She talk you into that?"

"My pink lace… When did you see my bra?"

"Accidentally, I swear. Your blouse gapped while I was leaning over you at the computer and there it was, pink and lace and you filling it out in nice tempting mounds. Mmm."

Sylvie burned with embarrassment and lust. "I like to support our stores," she croaked.

"That Lucy's quite the saleswoman." Chase's eyes twinkled with hot mischief. "Anything else she talk you into? Say a feather boa? Or one of those corset thingies you can tie…real…tight?"

"I'm not so much into costumes," she breathed, sinking into the low, slow sexiness of his tone.

"Are you forgetting Santa and his elves?"

"That's different. As a rule, I prefer to keep it real."

"Oh, me, too. Real and…raw."

Raw? Not so far in her sex life. With Chase, though,

judging from the open-air make-out session, where she'd been out of control enough to bang the horn and not care if Leo saw them, it might be just that. Real and raw and wild. "Completely off the hook." Her bold words aroused her further.

Chase whistled softly. "Now *that* I'd like to see." He clearly wanted her badly. He made her feel like a luscious dessert—a *tres leches* cake dripping with buttercream glaze, say—and he was desperate for a fork.

"How about the toy store?" Chase blurted. "How much trouble can we get into there?"

"Sounds safe enough," she said, tucking away her sexual impulses.

Once in the aisles of Toy Town, Chase handed Sylvie the demo Nerf shooter and grabbed a Nerf bow-and-arrow for himself.

"I'm not normally a violent person," she said, hitting him three times before he hid behind a counter.

"But I bring out the worst in you?" He fired an arrow that hit her shoulder, then ducked back.

"Something like that." When she reached for one of the arrows that had missed her, she spotted an open carton of Silly String cans. The box was marked *defective*. She read the label on one can: "No stain, no stick, cleans up easy." Perfect for what she had in mind.

She pulled off the lid and squirted a small amount into her hand to see how defective it was. The string came out fine, except it was a sickly green color, so that must be the problem. Best of all, the store wouldn't be out a dime if they emptied a can or two before putting them back.

A sponge arrow shot past her head. "You missed! But I won't." She jumped up, and sprayed a wad of string into Chase's hair and across his white guard shirt. He looked utterly startled and she burst out laughing. "Gotcha!"

He dropped behind his counter, then popped up beside her a few seconds later.

"Hey," she said as he went for his own can. She tried to hold him back, but failed and soon he was on top of her, pinning her to the floor.

The green web dangling from his hair did not detract one bit from how manly he seemed in his uniform leaning over her, holding her down. "What do you know?" he said. "We're in trouble in a toy store."

She raised her chest, as if trying to escape, then licked her lips, which had gone dry.

"Ouch. If that move isn't against the law, it should be." He squeezed his eyes shut as if trying to get control of his lust.

She loved that, so when he opened his eyes, she did it again, even slower, watching him the whole time, deliberately teasing him.

She was aware of his hips pressing down on hers, his thigh nudging between her legs. She wanted to kiss him, slide herself against him. All wrong. They were supposed to be having fun, enjoying the mall, not stirring up sexual urges.

"How about a duel?" she said. "We stand back to back, walk ten paces, turn and fire."

"I'm in," he said.

"So let me up." She struggled against his grip.

"Promise you won't shoot me."

"You'll just have to see, won't you?"

He let her hands go and sat back on his heels. She grabbed her can and planted a blob right in the middle of his forehead.

"No fair," he said.

"All's fair in string wars," she said, aiming again.

He blocked the shot with his palm, then scooted to a counter.

"Truce," she said, waving a stuffed white rabbit in the air. "I'm standing up now. Don't shoot."

They both rose slowly, watching each other, cans at the ready. Fully upright, they relaxed, then met in the middle of the store, backs together. Sylvie's head rested against Chase's strong shoulders. She felt his ribs expand and contract with each breath.

"Ready?" he said, the word vibrating against her body.

"As I'll ever be," she said.

"I'll count the paces," he said. "One...two...three..."

At ten, they both spun and squirted. Sylvie yelped as his green string hit her in the chest. She'd gotten him in the shoulder. They kept spraying until they'd emptied their cans, laughing the entire time, string drooping in big loops from everywhere.

"You're a mess," she said, peeling the fibers hanging from his hair and shirt.

"You, too." He removed strings that had caught in her curls and brushed more off her shoulders. They were close now, nearly embracing, and his fingers were warm as they teased her cheek, her arms, her ribs. He ran his hands down the sides of her shirt, almost touching her breasts, lingering as they moved, coming to rest on her hips. He never took his eyes off her.

"I think I've been clean for a while now," she said shakily, everything in her wanting to throw her arms around him and kiss them both into a mindless frenzy.

"Who knew toy stores could be so sexy?"

Anyplace would be sexy with Chase, she realized in dismay. They kept circling each other, closer and closer, as if pulled by a powerful magnet.

"This was fun, huh?" she said.

"Yeah, it was...fun."

And far too tempting. Fighting the urges was wearing Sylvie down, like struggling against a rolling ocean. But she had to stick it out a while longer, get Chase talking about the good times he'd had here, cement his enjoyment of the mall.

"I should make my rounds," he said with a slight smile. "Randolph was very firm. *Every two hours, but change it up. Inside and outside.* Want to ride along? We can take Dasher outside to pee while we're at it."

As they drove the length of the mall, Dasher cozy between them, Sylvie got Chase talking about his childhood campouts—the time Fletcher got the rubber raft from the camping display stuck in a stairwell, the time the iguana got loose and they had to trap it with a fishing net, playing hide-and-seek among the wooden furniture in Captain Bean's Wood Wonders, the time they'd brought skateboards and nearly killed themselves trying to jump the low planter wall.

Outside, the night was clear, the stars bright, the air mild. At the edge of the park area, a police cruiser stopped and the officer asked them if everything was all right. They thanked him for the extra attention.

Back inside the mall, Chase helped her from the cart and she swayed against him, enjoying the closeness too much. She had to get out of here soon. "How about s'mores and a ghost story before I head home?" she said a little too breathlessly.

"Sounds good," Chase said.

Back at the tent, they stuck marshmallows onto the chopsticks she'd brought for that purpose and held them over the hot plate to roast.

"Mom always made the s'mores in advance," Chase

said. "No way she'd let us use a hot plate here. This is much better. You get that toasty smell." He brought his light brown marshmallow to her nose.

"Mmm. I'll make yours." She tugged the blob from his chopstick and dropped it onto the chocolate-covered graham cracker on a paper plate she'd prepared, then licked the melted marshmallow from her finger.

"I thought I warned you about that tongue," he murmured.

"Sorry," she said, but she wasn't. She handed him the plate, then assembled her own treat. The laptop fire crackled romantically beside them.

"Mmm," Chase said after the first bite.

"I know. Yum, huh?"

"You've got marshmallow on your chin," he said.

She started to lick it off.

"Uh-uh-uh," he said. "Allow me." Holding her chin with one hand, he carefully thumbed away the sticky goo.

"Thank you."

"Oh, my pleasure."

When he'd finished his s'more, Chase wiped his mouth with a napkin. "This takes me back, for sure. Thank you, Sylvie."

"Oh, I'm having fun, too."

"No, I mean it." He looked suddenly serious. "The first couple of days here, stepping into the mall was like a punch in the gut. Now it'll be better. I can tell." He looked out at the closed gates, the orange-lit tile floor. "Now it's a place, not a reminder of Mom being so sick."

"I'm glad, Chase." Sylvie felt abruptly awful. She'd been so busy trying to get him to love the place, she'd forgotten about all the sadness he associated with Starlight Desert.

A rustling inside the tent made them both turn.

"Uh-oh, Dasher's digging," she said. "I can't give the tent back damaged." She dove after the dog, pulling him away from the zipper he was worrying with his teeth.

"You little pill," she said, putting him on her lap.

Chase joined her inside the tent, lying on his side on the sleeping bag, his head braced on a palm. "You two look like you belong together."

"Don't push it, Chase," she said, but she was enjoying holding the puppy like this. She picked up the book. "So, one scary story before I go?"

"Get comfortable, first." He opened the bag and motioned for her to stretch out alongside him.

She did and positioned the flashlight so she could read without holding it. With a sigh, Dasher curled up on the book.

Laughing, she started to move him, but Chase stopped her. "You don't need to read to me, Sylvie." His eyes focused on her. "It's late. If you want, you can sleep here."

"You know that's not what would happen if I stayed. I might attack you like I did last night."

"We attacked each other, Sylvie. Mutual combustion. And I can't get it out of my mind. I was late today partly because I missed my exit thinking about you."

"You're exaggerating."

"Jesus, Sylvie. I just confessed that you put me in a daze. No man gives up that kind of intel easily. I'm talking serious wimp factor."

"I can't stop thinking about you, either."

"Yeah?" They were together in the dark again, horizontal this time. Much easier. *Why was this wrong again?*

"How about I make you a s'more to go?" Chase pushed himself off the sleeping bag and out of the tent.

"Great." But she realized she was disappointed. She didn't want to leave yet. She'd had more fun than she remembered ever having with a man. In the middle of the vandalism mess and the Black Friday promotion, with her job in limbo and the mall at risk, Sylvie had had a full-out blast.

And she wasn't done yet, dammit.

She wanted the man who was busily making her a treat for the road just outside this tent.

Why not? He wanted her. She wanted him. Why couldn't they see where it went from here? Even as she tried to be sensible, to think this through, her desire became a river rushing toward a waterfall, swirling and spinning, picking up speed, taking the big leap.

She slipped out of the tent. Chase turned to hold out the paper plate and she lunged at him, pushing him into the redwood bark, kissing him hard.

He still held the paper plate in one hand, so she took it from him and set it on a chair, going for him again.

He grabbed both her arms and held her away from him. "What are you doing?"

"Attacking you. Can't you tell?"

"But we agreed this was a bad idea." He looked so confused.

"Denying ourselves makes the sex too important. We both have needs. Let's meet them. Simple." She leaned in to kiss him again, but he held her off a little longer.

"What about…protection?"

"I'm on the pill. Are you healthy, sex-wise?"

"I'm good. But you're not thinking straight, Sylvie. You—"

She laid a finger to his lips. "My thoughts are crystal clear. This will be good for us, like—"

"Please don't say Pilates. I know you're a woman with needs and all, but the thing is, I don't stick around and I don't get serious."

"You think that's news? Let's stop thinking and just do this." She grabbed the hem of her shirt, whipped it over her head and flung it into the banana tree. That was *so* not like her. She sat there, breathing hard, hoping Chase would take it from here before she embarrassed herself to death.

Chase focused his attention on her breasts. "Okay. I've officially stopped thinking." He made short work of his uniform shirt, tossing it up with hers into the tree, then pulled her against him. "Sylvie," he said into her hair.

He unlatched her bra and removed it, holding her close, as if to protect her modesty, clearly sensing that whipping off her shirt had exhausted her vixen side.

He kissed her, then looked at her. "You sure about this?"

She nodded, so weak with lust she feared she'd faint and fall on her face in the decorative bark.

"Good. Because if you weren't, I'd have to change your mind."

THANK GOD. When Sylvie threw herself at him Chase had never caught anything more welcome. Now her lips were wet and welcoming, her nipples tight as beads against his palm, her breasts a soft weight.

He wanted her so much, this determined woman with her womanly *needs*. He felt like a semi speeding downhill with no brakes. He knew he would crash, but it was worth every injury to be with this woman, to give her pleasure and take some for himself.

She'd gone for him the same way she went after her job at Starlight Desert, with everything she had. And right now he was all hers.

He hauled her back into the tent and got them both

naked on the sleeping bag. She lay there, her skin pale and pretty, nearly glowing against the dark fabric.

"You're beautiful," he said, examining every inch of her—the delicate rise of her collarbone, the soft mounds of her breasts, the ridges of her ribs, the dip and swell across her hips, the soft blond curls below.

He ran his fingers over a spray of beauty marks near her sternum, then traced a circle around her navel, her skin trembling beneath his fingers.

She watched his hands, her breathing ragged, her fingers digging into his forearms. Every few seconds, she would lunge up to claim his mouth, as if to be certain this moment was real.

Chase felt the same. This was like a shared dream he hoped would last all night. Her fingers found him, wrapping tight, sliding, squeezing, teasing.

He released a shaky breath, then leaned down to take one nipple into his mouth, running his tongue over its peak, relishing her gasp and the way her shivers came in waves.

"Oh," she said. "This is so nice."

"Nice? I'm going for mind-blowing here." He wanted to spread her legs and enter her, go after the sweet relief she'd made him burn for.

"Yeah," she said breathlessly, "that, too." She shifted her body, led him to her center. She was so slick he slid inside easily, as if he belonged there. As if he were home.

Her eyes widened with pleasure and she gripped his backside with both hands, urging him deeper. In her eyes, he caught flashes of light, a private electrical storm just for him.

He stilled to let the pressure build, to let them feel how they were together, connected, the same current flowing through them both.

She bent her knees and heaved her hips upward, asking for more. He pushed deeper and she inhaled. "Again," she said on the exhale. "Do that again."

So he did. Again and again.

She met each stroke and they began a sweet rhythm that built the heat between them like a bonfire that would incinerate a million marshmallows to ash.

Braced on his elbows so he wouldn't crush her, he lifted her upper body with his palms, reveling in the slide of her breasts against his chest. She tightened around him, powering forward, racing toward release.

He raised his hips and plowed deep, urged on by her cries and gasps, hungry music that asked for all he could give.

He'd had intense sex before, but this was Sylvie.

Sylvie.

Who knew his history, his family.

Sylvie, who got it.

Maybe he was carried away by the moment, but so what?

"Chase," she breathed in his ear, the sound full of relief and joy, as if he'd been away too long and finally returned.

He smiled against her neck, feeling like he'd found the place he needed to be.

He felt Sylvie quicken her pace and knew she was about to climax. He matched her speed, going after his own release. She shivered and gave a sharp cry, bucking up again and again, pulling him over the edge with her. He surged inside her, once, twice, and again.

Spent, he collapsed onto his back, pulling her on top of him, holding her as he fought for air.

"Your heart is pounding so hard," she said, her eyes wide, her fingers against his chest.

He pressed his palm against her sternum. "Yours, too. Feels like an entire *Stomp* performance going on in there."

She laughed.

"You have the best laugh. It's like liquid music." He ran his fingers along the side of her body, tracing the slope, pausing at a patch of beauty marks.

"My moles." She made a face.

"Beauty marks. They're pretty. So are you, all rosy and glowing like that."

"You mean blotchy and sweaty?"

"You look freshly laid," he said. "And that's beautiful."

"You're being kind." She pushed back her hair. He loved how her curls haloed her head.

"Why do women pick on their appearance so much?"

"It's in our DNA, I guess."

He loved the things women seemed to dislike about themselves—the way sweat made curls frizz, the bump on the bridge of a nose, the swell of extra flesh on the hips, freckles sprinkled like stars, one breast slightly smaller than the other.

The differences charmed him.

Women charmed him. He loved that their bodies were so soft, their skin so silky. He loved how their minds worked, how much better they navigated emotional turmoil, wading in with buckets to bravely bail away, sure it was the right thing to do.

"That was amazing," Sylvie said.

"It was."

"Eight years later, I finally know what sex with you is like. Worth the wait."

"Oh, yeah," he said, chuckling. "Well worth it."

Sylvie looked happy at the moment.

What about tomorrow? When doubts and questions filled the space where heat and drive had been? Lust was worse than booze for encouraging shortsighted thinking. He knew better....

"Relax, Chase." She lifted her head and studied him, her green eyes crackling, not missing a twitch. "We had great sex. We enjoyed each other. It's fine. It's all good."

He hoped she was right. He never wanted to hurt her. The idea made his gut bottom out. For now, he had her naked in his arms and it was great. Her body softened into him, her breath warm on his chest. "You sleepy?" he asked.

"You should do the security circuit again," she murmured, cozying into him, one leg between his.

"In a minute," he said.

This was nice. Very nice. He wanted more of this. Which was odd, since he'd always been content with the present, its pleasure and its passing. For the first time, he was thinking ahead, planning the next encounter.

She was fading now, her breathing slower. He would close his eyes for a moment, until she was so far under his leaving wouldn't awaken her.... Just a minute more....

CHAPTER ELEVEN

SYLVIE WOKE WITH A START to find Dasher licking her face. She sat up, remembering abruptly that she was lying naked in a tent in the mall's greenery with an equally naked Chase.

Yikes. How had *that* happened? Her watch said it was 3:00 a.m. She'd slept about two hours. Chase's uniform shirt still hung from the banana tree branch next to her top, so he clearly hadn't made the rounds. So much for the security protocols.

Dasher whined. Chase seemed dead to the world, so she decided to take the dog for a walk and check on the mall herself. She pulled on her underwear and pants, crawled out of the tent to take her bra and shirt from the banana tree.

Hooking Dasher's leash to his collar, she looked back at Chase lying in the tent, his hair tousled, his manly face softened by slumber. It had been so lovely to be tangled up with him.

Maybe when she returned, they would go again. It was just sex. She'd meant that when she said it, thank goodness. They'd enjoyed each other physically, broken the tension, and it had been wonderful.

Would more ruin it? Was sex with Chase like frosting? Too much and she'd feel like she'd had two bites of Nadia's tooth-zinging cake?

She hadn't felt this close to Steve or any of her other

boyfriends. That had been deliberate, she knew. They might expect more than she had to give, which, now that she thought about it, was pretty much how Chase had described his own relationships with women.

She'd always thought of herself as too busy to get serious, but maybe it was more than that. Maybe she was afraid to get close to anyone.

If she ever expected to make a life with a man, she'd have to let the guy in, risk getting hurt. The idea scared her. She had a great life, friends and coworkers. Sure, she got lonely now and then, but didn't everyone?

Dasher squirmed so she set him down and started after him. She'd be exhausted when she returned for work, but she didn't regret one minute of lost sleep.

She looked ahead and yelped in horror.

Someone had spray-painted red words across three of the store gates: *This is a Dead Mall.... Get out or this gets worse.... Starlight Desert out of our hood... Starlight Desert is scum.*

The hairs on the back of Sylvie's neck stood straight up. This was so much worse than before. This vandalism was on the *inside*. Someone had broken in and defaced the place while she and Chase slept. She lunged back into the tent. "Wake up, Chase."

"Huh, what?" He jerked to a sit. "Are you okay?"

"I'm fine. It's the mall that's in trouble." She gestured for him to come out with her.

"Wow," he said, when he saw the mess. They walked over to examine the damage more closely. She knew the graffiti couldn't be more than a few hours old but she ran her fingers over the letters. "It's dry," she said.

"We didn't hear a sound."

"Did they know we were here? What if you and I were... you know...when they did this?"

"Then they were pretty damn bold."

Sylvie called the police and she and Chase checked all the entrances, finding the door with the lock that had been messed with wide-open. "Randolph said we should have replaced this."

"Randolph again. I don't know about that guy."

"No way would he do this." She shook her head, aching with outrage over the crime.

The police got no fingerprints, but made a troubling discovery. The lock had not been broken. There were no more scrapes than the last time.

"This means they had a key," Chase speculated.

"They could have picked the lock," the officer said.

"If they had a key, we're talking an employee or tenant," Chase said.

"Unless the key was stolen, borrowed or copied," Sylvie corrected. "This handwriting is different from the other three attacks. It's more threatening and the paint is red this time."

The officer promised to have Alan Lawson, the detective assigned to the case, call them when he was on duty later in the morning. After he left, Sylvie headed for the maintenance room.

"Where are you going?" Chase asked.

"We should have gray enamel left from when we repainted the railings. I want this covered up before any tenants arrive."

They worked together, painting side by side, using brushes not rollers to cover every crack.

"This attack is aimed at our tenants," Sylvie mused. "*Dead Mall* is an industry term, too."

"Yeah?"

"It means a mall with high vacancies, low traffic or one

that's dated or deteriorating. Usually without an anchor store. Like if we lost Tracer's, we might go dead."

"So this could be a tenant who wants an excuse to weasel out of a lease? Talley Toombs seemed pretty eager to complain."

"But she wouldn't want to lose her job." She covered up another ugly sentence. "Someone wants to scare our tenants, make them think the mall's going downhill or is no longer safe."

"What if it was Leo? He was off-shift for the last attack and he called in sick tonight."

"But he's in charge of the night crew. This happened on his watch, so blame would obviously fall on him. I know he feels terrible about it."

"One of the other guards?"

She shook her head. "I don't see it. I keep racking my brain. It's not any of the Free Arts kids, no matter what Randolph thinks. Even if they did do the first graffiti, which I doubt, this continued assault is like a vendetta."

"One new factor is Mary Beth," Chase said. "She returned just as this began. You said she wants her job back. Could she think this will make you look bad?"

"She's not a vindictive person and she loves Starlight Desert. If she wanted to make me look bad, all she'd have to do is criticize me to you or Fletcher."

"True."

"As far as that goes, you arrived when this started, too. Give me your hand." She studied his fingernails. "No red paint, so I guess you're innocent."

"I appreciate your confidence in me. This damages the mall's reputation in the industry, as well. It hurts our value."

"What about a possible buyer? Maybe they want to make

a low offer." She put down her brush. "*Is* there a possible buyer?" Her heart jumped into her throat at the idea.

"I met with the broker yesterday morning. He says some businesses are definitely interested."

"Really?" Her heart sank. "What businesses exactly?"

"An indoor go-cart track, some doctors offices, a charter school, one or two others." He shrugged.

Sylvie stared at him, worry filling her.

"We have a million questions and no one's made an offer."

"But there's interest."

"I still need to analyze our revenue picture, remember?"

"You'll allow for Black Friday income, right? And we have that meeting with PriceLess. That could change everything."

"Don't panic, Sylvie. Nothing's going to happen overnight."

She blew out a breath. "True." Her shoulders ached from painting and her heart was heavy with dread.

"We've got this covered for now," Chase said. "Go home and get some sleep. I'll fill Randolph in when he comes on shift."

"You were supposed to be on duty. Are you going to tell him you fell asleep?"

"I certainly won't tell him what I was really doing." He smiled, taking her by the arms, pulling her closer, trying to lighten the moment.

But Sylvie couldn't smile back. "If we hadn't…um… done that, we might have caught them."

"We had a great night. I'm only sorry I fell asleep afterward." He kissed her softly. "Please don't regret it."

"I don't," she said with a small smile.

"I'm going to tell Randolph to rent more security cameras for inside and out. Extra eyes for now and they might act as a deterrent."

"That's a good idea. It'll make him happy, for sure."

"I want you to forget all this for a few hours." He searched her face, concern in his eyes. "I'll handle the mall for the morning, meet with Detective Lawson, hold down the fort. You just sleep, Sylvie."

"This is a crucial time, Chase."

"And that's why you need good sleep. Take Dasher home, close the curtains and sleep. We'll handle everything just fine without you for a bit."

She was too tired to argue, so Chase carried the dog gear out to her car and she headed home with Dasher in his kennel.

At her house, she shut the door to her workroom to keep him out of small-item mischief, poured him food and water and watched his whole body wiggle as he ate and drank, looking up at her happily, as if he couldn't believe his luck.

"I don't believe it, either," she said, dropping to the floor to pet him. She ached with exhaustion, her eyes were gritty and her mind was fuzzy as a cotton ball.

Maybe Chase was right. Sleep would help her and the mall would be safe in his hands for a few hours.

Until he sold it, of course. The idea sent a zing of worry through her. Then she thought of the spray-painted threat of more harm to come. Wouldn't the store owners wonder why she hadn't come in?

She squeezed her eyes shut. *Calm down. Get some rest. You'll do a better job.*

Dasher pounced on her hand and began to nibble at her fingers the same way worry chewed at her brain. She sighed. Between Dasher and her racing thoughts, she doubted she'd sleep a wink.

CHASE LOOKED UP AT ELEVEN to find Sylvie entering his office with the puppy at her feet.

"What are you doing here already?" he said, going to her, wanting to take her in his arms. "You're supposed to be sleeping."

"Not with this little beast bounding all over the bed," she said. "He whined so I let him out of his kennel. Big mistake."

"You're worried," he said, reading the truth in her face.

She nodded and dropped into the guest chair, lifting the dog into her lap. "Catch me up."

"I'm glad to see you." He had to say it. She'd stayed in his head for all these hours. The smell of her skin, the way she'd said his name, her soft cries. "I missed you." What an idiot he was.

"Oh." Color splashed her cheeks and Chase could tell she felt the same.

"I have one question for you."

"Yes?"

"White lace or pink?"

"Chase!"

"Tell me or I'll have to find out for myself."

"White, okay? And don't do that. This is not the place—"

"If we lock the door it is," he murmured, enjoying the flicker of alarm in her eyes, the way her blush had spread to her neck. She was so fun to tease. Though he wasn't quite teasing. "We've got the desk or my chair if the arms come off...."

He rolled his chair to the side of his desk, as if to come after her.

"Cut it out!" She looked completely shocked.

He chuckled. "Just kidding. I can wait until tonight. Barely. Your place after work. Six-thirty?"

"I usually stay late," she said faintly, looking dazed.

"We have to get an early start so you get plenty of sleep afterward. Trust me, I can be a really, really good sleep aid."

She sighed. "Okay...."

He wanted to kiss her right then, just to see if she tasted as good as he remembered, but he forced himself back to business.

"So, catching you up, Randolph got a good deal on renting a closed-circuit system. I'm holding a meeting for all the security staff this afternoon, ostensibly to talk about that, but maybe something will come up that gives us some leads."

"Sounds good," she said, but her gaze flitted away.

"You okay?" he asked. "With us?"

"I guess. What happened was so..."

"Amazing," he finished for her.

"I was thinking crazy, insane, out of control."

"Why do you think I can't wait for tonight?"

SYLVIE AND DASHER had barely gotten into the house when Chase arrived. The minute he stepped inside, he started taking off her clothes. "I've been thinking about doing this since this morning."

All day long, she'd gotten little thrills when the night before passed through her mind. Now she held on to Chase to keep from slumping to the floor in a jelly-girl heap.

Chase kissed her, long and slow, firing her blood,

making her heart pound in her chest. She pressed herself to him, rocking her hips against his.

"Keep that up and we'll go right here. How do you feel about rug burns?" he said.

"The bed's not far," she said, though it felt miles away. Inside, her sterner self wagged a finger. *Have some control. It's just sex, not life itself.* She didn't care. She wanted to be naked with Chase *right now.*

Chase yanked her against him. She felt the scrape of his belt, the soft fabric of his shirt, heard his hungry breathing and her own as she walked him backward into her bedroom, kissing him all the way, both of them so frantic they bumped noses and teeth as they fought to get at each other everywhere at once.

She didn't bother with the covers, just pushed him onto the bed and went after his shirt and jeans while he finished undressing her.

Vaguely, she wondered what mischief Dasher could get into and how long before he'd need to go out, but she wasn't capable of doing anything but be with Chase at the moment.

Warm and naked at last, they looked at each other in shared wonder for a long moment. Then Sylvie lifted her hips and Chase entered her, making her gasp for air…and more of him.

Much more.

Her senses on overload, Sylvie took in sights, sounds and scents. Warm skin, soft gasps, tightened muscles, pushes and pulls, their smells, sweet and pungent and lovely. She felt so alive with Chase, wanting all he had to give, and giving him all she had, too.

Afterward, they lay wrapped in each other's arms, legs entwined. Dasher yelped from the floor, so Chase lowered a hand to heft him onto the bed. He licked both their faces and snuggled between them.

"If you want to head out, Chase, no problem," Sylvie said. "If you sleep better in your own bed, I mean."

"You need me gone?" He braced himself on his elbow, studying her, his eyes twinkling.

"I'm fine, but I don't want you to feel obligated to stick around. I know a lot of men prefer to leave."

"I want to stay. If you'll have me."

"That would be nice. Sure." Which was kind of a fib. She loved stretching out alone in her big bed, not having to worry about kicking or crowding a partner. "Though we should be clear about what we're doing here. This is just, how did you put it, *a physical connection, friendship and fun?*"

"Something like that, I guess." There was hesitation in his voice, as if he wanted to object, but she pushed onward.

"Above all, we can't let it interfere with work. Like all that talk in the office was highly inappropriate."

"No, we can't."

"And we can't let it get complicated."

"Check."

"And when either of us loses interest, we're done. That way no one gets hurt."

"Exactly." He paused before he added, "And if we fall in love with each other?"

"We can't," she said, fearing she might already be headed down that path. She bit her lip. "But if we do, then we just ignore it."

"Ignore it?" He grinned.

"That's really all we *can* do, don't you think? I mean,

you're fun to spend time with, Chase, and you're sexy and charming, but you're not…um…"

"I'm not your Thor. I get it." Sylvie couldn't quite read his expression, but he sounded almost hurt.

"I'm not your kind of woman, either, right?" She felt a funny pinch in her chest at the thought. "What would you look for? If you were looking, which you're not."

"I guess she'd be someone who kept me on my toes. She'd be restless like me, into travel and new experiences. Spontaneous, too. That's important. Someone happy to dance all night, then skydive at the crack of dawn."

"You skydive?"

"Not yet. But I fully intend to."

"I see." She tried not to laugh.

He tilted his head. "You think I should grow up, huh?"

"You are who you are, Chase."

He laughed, low and rich. "Maybe I'm full of crap. Maybe I'll find a place I want to stay, get married and have kids and a 401K and a damned picket fence."

"Why wouldn't you?"

"Because I could change my mind on a dime and break the poor girl's heart. I should come with a warning label."

He had a point, but he sounded lost when he said it, like he wished he were different. She wished he were, too.

"Like you said, you never promise more than you can deliver." She pressed herself against him. "And, boy, can you deliver."

He chuckled and she could tell he was grateful that she'd shifted the subject to something more comfortable.

She liked Chase even more for his honesty, but that almost made it worse. She could become attached, start making more of what was between them than could ever be. She knew better. Chase would leave. Whether he decided to sell Starlight Desert or keep it, he wouldn't stay. He'd move on to the next project and the next woman. Sylvie had to keep that firmly in mind, or stay out of Chase's arms for good.

CHAPTER TWELVE

WHEN SYLVIE WOKE IN the middle of the night she was alone in her big, roomy bed. Instead of luxuriating in the space, she felt lonely. Not a good sign.

Where were Chase and Dasher?

She got up to investigate, reaching for her serviceable brown terry robe. Nope. Not tonight. Instead she pulled out the sexy silk thing she'd bought from Lucy's Secrets for Steve, but had never worn because it seemed too silly.

The fabric was slippery and smooth, tickling her skin as she put it on. She felt pretty damned sexy at the moment.

She padded barefoot down the hall and found Chase in her living room, naked, looking at the books on her shelf, Dasher against one shoulder.

"Hey," she said softly.

"Sylvie." He gathered her into his arms, the puppy cuddled between them, and kissed her. "Dasher whined so I took him out. I didn't want to disturb you."

"You didn't." What disturbed her was missing him.

"Those shelves have to be from Captain Bean's Wood Wonders," he said, nodding over her shoulder.

She turned to look. "Yep."

"And that stuffed bear is from The Teddy Stop." He nodded at it. "You do support the stores."

"With every purchase I can, yeah."

"And this thing…mmm." He stroked her body through the silk. "One of Lucy's secrets?"

"I don't know what I was thinking when I bought it."

"You were thinking how easy it would be for me to take it off." He tugged at the tie so it released the bow, then slid one hand around her bare waist to cup her backside.

"Mmm," she said, softening against him. "If that wasn't what I was thinking, it should have been."

Dasher wanted to get down, so Chase crouched to let the puppy go. Sylvie retied her robe.

"The place looks like you," Chase said, looking around the room. He seemed so large and male, her living room tiny and feminine and far too orderly by comparison.

"You mean girlie? Scary neat? Boring?"

"No. Peaceful, everything where it belongs. Just so." He leaned over to tip a pillow onto one corner. "That make you crazy?"

"I can handle crooked pillows. Just don't mess with my dollhouses. You'll limp for a month."

"Show me. I promise I won't move one tiny chair without permission."

She led him to the second bedroom, her workshop. She'd ringed the room with shelves and compartments to hold the finished houses and the ones in progress, along with her supplies of nails, screws, varnish, paints and fine brushes, as well as small pieces of paneling and plywood.

Chase zeroed in on the shelf with her latest finished houses—a Victorian, a log cabin, a Tuscan villa and a fairy-tale cottage. "These are amazing."

"I'm pretty pleased with them. I'm thinking of giving the cottage as a prize for the Starlight Desert Christmas raffle. What do you think?"

"I think you do a lot for the mall. And for the people— all those gifts and loans and taste-testing favors. You know everybody's birthdays—hell, when their kids graduate. Not to mention the fortune you spend in the shops."

"Of course. We're family."

"Not exactly," he said slowly. "I know you love the place, but—"

"You think I'm too attached? It's good business practice, Chase. Happy tenants stick around even when times get tough…like now with the vandalism."

"I guess so…." She could tell it still bothered him. But she wasn't up for arguing about it now.

"These are so beautiful," he said, looking back at her dollhouses. "Have you ever thought of selling them?"

"You sound like Desiree. She wants to create a website for me and market them."

"But you don't want that?"

"Desiree gets lots of ideas."

"And you don't want to get let down again."

"Again?" She jerked her eyes to his.

"She left you."

His words were three matter-of-fact punches to her solar plexus. "It wasn't like that. Desiree was selling her crafts at state fairs and shows, so she was on the road a lot. She knew I adored my grandparents. I had a room of my own there and the school was better, since our neighborhood was kind of sketchy."

"You have every right to be hurt, Sylvie. Angry, too." He held her gaze, not letting her escape. "She let you down."

"What's the point?" she said, a bitter taste in her mouth. "Desiree did her best. Why expect more?"

"You don't think people can change?"

"Not that I've seen, no."

"I'd like to hope they can." His eyes seemed distant.

"I used to wish for more, but…" She shrugged,

remembering with sudden clarity waiting in her grand-mother's needlepoint window seat for *Mommy* to pick her up that last time.

She must have fallen asleep, because the next thing she knew it was morning and she was in bed in her room at her grandparents' and they stood over her with fake smiles and told her how, guess what, she would get to live with them for a while and wasn't that so lucky and such a gift?

Which it had been. Truly. But it didn't change the fact that her mother had left her. She swallowed the emotions surging inside her. "It's better not to get your hopes up. Then you don't get disappointed and you don't make people feel like they've failed you."

"So you step back from people, right? Keep your distance?"

"I guess."

"We're alike in that way. We're both surrounded by people, but no one really gets in." Chase's dark eyes drew her closer. His words poked through her defenses. She preferred to skim painful realities, work around them or ignore them altogether.

"Maybe. I just make the best of what I've got and go forward. Why get overwrought about it?"

"You feel how you feel, Sylvie. And that's okay." Hearing him tell the truth so clearly made her emotions snarl and twist. She turned to her dollhouses with their precise beauty. "Building a dollhouse is like a meditation to me. All my focus narrows to varnishing this tiny chair or attaching these curtains to the fragile toothpick rods."

Her words rushed out and she picked up a Victorian hutch with tiny pewter dishes and a pitcher. "For the furniture, I buy the crude imports because the wood is better, then sand them down and paint and upholster them myself."

She rattled on, breathless, her throat tight. "It's all to one-inch scale. My favorite part is putting all the pieces in place, like a delicate puzzle, where everything fits just so."

"Sylvie..." Chase turned her toward him and pulled her into his arms, tucking her head under his chin. "I didn't mean to upset you. God knows I've ducked plenty of tough moments, but seeing you, with your heart so big, I just want more for you."

She pulled back. "I don't *need* more. I'm fine."

"I want more for me, too," he said, sudden determination clear in his dark eyes. "You make me want more."

She looked up at him, startled, and he kissed her with so much tenderness, it frightened her a little.

They went back to bed, arm in arm, then whispered intimacies and touched each other gently, staring into each other's eyes the entire time. Something was happening here. Something more than friendly sex. Silver threads of hope flew between them, binding them closer. Hope for more for each other and maybe, just maybe, for more for *them*.

Afterward, Chase ran his fingers lazily up and down her arm. "The other night at dinner, I remembered that one Christmas you spent with us."

"Yeah. I was nine. Starr was so insistent when she knew Desiree wouldn't be home and my grandparents figured I'd enjoy the bigger fuss you guys made. I was thrilled. You had eggnog and hot chocolate and homemade cookies and you played games and decorated the tree together."

"And fought the whole time."

She shrugged. "That tree was like a skyscraper to me."

"I remember in the morning, you ran downstairs and

when you saw all the presents under the tree, you gave out this huge squeal and threw your arms around my mom."

"I remember that. Yeah."

"Then you pushed away from her like you'd been electrocuted. What happened?"

She smiled. "I felt you all staring at me and I knew I'd overdone it."

"Are you kidding? We loved it. We're guys. We don't shriek and jump up and down, even when we want to. I was a teenager. I was perfecting my sulk. And Fletcher never was much of a hugger. Mom was thrilled. It made me sad to see you back off like that."

"I got carried away. I was your guest. Plus, it felt like I was being disloyal to my grandparents after all they'd done for me. It was complicated."

"You deserve so much more than you allow yourself, Sylvie," he said, kissing her forehead, his breath warm on her face. "You're standing at an all-you-can-eat buffet afraid to fill a spoon."

"What makes you so sure there will always be seconds?"

"Maybe that's my problem. I figure whatever I want will be there when I'm ready for it."

"Who's to say who's right?" she said. Was life an everlasting buffet or a single meal to be enjoyed spoon by spoon? She didn't know. What she knew was that she was falling in love with Chase, despite all her attempts to be sensible.

"I need to go out to Home at Last early in the morning," he said. "Want to come with me? See the place for yourself? We'll leave by six and be back to Starlight Desert by nine."

"I'd love that, Chase. I would." And she hugged him hard, shutting out all the doubts and questions.

DRIVING SYLVIE OUT to Home at Last, Chase felt as eager as a kid showing off a new toy. As he drove, he kept glancing at her smiling, Dasher in her lap. When she caught him, her smile would broaden and so would his. It was like they had some great secret they were bursting to tell.

What the hell was going on here?

You are who you are, Chase.

Those simple words from Sylvie had set off a change in him. The instant she accepted him as he was, he wanted to be different—better somehow.

He wanted to tell her more about himself than he'd ever told a soul. Somehow, her steady gaze, her close attention, her curiosity made him want to answer every question, explore every aspect of his life. Around her he felt like someone had dropped a bucket of ice into a pot of boiling soup. Instant calm and smooth, cool peace.

He'd always been content with women as short-term bedmates and good friends. With Sylvie he wondered about more. What would it be like to settle down with one woman?

Say, a woman like Sylvie.

Maybe constantly traveling, doing deals, meeting new people wasn't what he wanted anymore.

Could he change? Sylvie sure didn't think so. He had to wonder himself. He was thirty-six. If he had it in him to be a settle-down guy wouldn't he have made the switch by now?

When you love something, you find a way.

Yeah, but what if staying put was just an experiment for him? A fleeting idea he'd get bored of soon enough? Where would Sylvie be then? Hurt. And he never wanted to hurt her.

"What's going on in your head, Chase?" Sylvie asked.

"Nothing." Nothing he could share anyway. They were passing through one of the West Valley towns hit hard by the housing crash. "Let me show you why Home at Last is needed." He took the exit ramp, headed for a neighborhood of modest tract homes.

"Check out the signs," he said, nodding down the street when they'd reached it. Everywhere they looked were for sale signs, bank auction signs, trashed yards and boarded-up windows.

"These were starter homes—first-time buyers going for their dream, getting in over their head on payments for loans they shouldn't have qualified for."

"How terrible," she said. "This is so sad."

"Very. That's what happened to Nadia's son and his wife. They came away bewildered and ashamed. How did Nadia put it…? 'They fail at doing dream of America.'" He drove them back onto the freeway, heading for Home at Last.

"I think it's great that you can help them."

"Like Nadia says, I'm not chickens counting before hatching. We're being very cautious this time."

"This time?"

He'd forgotten she didn't know about his failure. "We started Home at Last in Las Vegas last year. It failed because we trusted a builder without verifying what he'd promised. We lost a lot of money."

"That's awful."

"Yeah. I've never screwed up like that before. We'll pay back our investors, no question. Every dime."

"You had a partner, too. Chet? It wasn't just you."

"I took the lead. I knew better."

"And you're trying again here. Is that why Marshall said it was a house of cards?"

"Oh, yeah. He loves the fact that I made a mistake. He thinks I've learned my lesson and I'll finally join McCann Development. He'd love it if I kept managing Starlight Desert."

"But you've had your own company for years."

"That means nothing to the General, Sylvie."

"He wants you to stay on as the GM?"

"Don't worry. If we keep the mall, the job's yours if you still want it."

"Of course I do. You know I do."

"I'll be in Oregon as soon as I can get there. There's a new project in Portland I want in on." He paused, feeling his enthusiasm wane just a bit.

"That makes sense," Sylvie said, though she seemed a little sad about it.

He pulled into the gravel parking lot of Home at Last.

"Wow." Sylvie was looking at Jake's prototype resting next to the nearly completed model. She got out of the car and set Dasher down, holding on to his leash.

"Come into the office. I'll introduce you to Chet, go over a couple things, then get the key and show you inside."

Soon enough, they were in the prototype. Dasher wandered the rooms while Chase explained the modular aspects of the design, the precision required by Jake's blueprints, the use of glass to give openness and recyclables to keep costs down.

"Inexpensive doesn't have to mean ugly or boring," he said. "You have to be smart about materials, use every scrap, be savvy about angles and tolerances."

"This is lovely." Sylvie ran her hand across the recycled cork countertop in the kitchen, which gave him a jolt. If they didn't have to be at the mall in an hour, he'd make good use of the futon in the bedroom.

"I'm glad you like it. Come on, I'll drive you to the acreage where we'll build."

She grabbed Dasher and they set off, going slowly on the dirt road.

"Back there you sounded like an architect," Sylvie said.

"That was my major for a while. That's probably why I spent so much time on the Home at Last plans." At the drafting table with Jake, he'd felt the familiar joy. He'd been focused, synapses firing away, completely at home, absolutely present.

"Why'd you change majors?"

"I'd already had a string of them—mechanical engineering, environmental biology, even industrial design for a semester. I'd run through too much of Dad's cash, so I gutted out a finance degree, which led to a great internship, which meant I could pay back the General right away." He figured it would help get his father off Fletcher's case, too.

"He didn't expect that, did he?"

"I wasn't about to owe him a dime." His mother had told him the General had been offended by the payments. "Mom used the money to set up a college account for her future grandchildren."

"That sounds like her, planning ahead that way. So was architecture your dream?"

"Everything's a dream until you start living the details. What I regret was believing anything I did would make things right with my father."

"That sounds pretty harsh. He clearly loves you."

"Maybe, but he's always backing up."

"What does that mean?"

"You ever watch a parent teach a kid to swim? He stands

a couple feet from the side and coaxes the kid in. 'Just swim to me. That's all you have to do.' The kid thinks, that's not far, he could almost jump there, so he takes the leap, heart in his throat, terrified, but trusting his father. He dogpaddles like mad and it seems to take forever to get there, so long his lungs nearly burst and he's scared as hell. Finally his father catches him up into his arms. The kid gasps for air and looks back toward the side of the pool and realizes his dad's been backing away the whole damn time."

She chuckled. "So you think there's no pleasing Marshall? Whatever you do, he'll want more?"

"Exactly. Fletcher still hasn't figured that out and keeps trying. But like you said about me, the General is who he is."

"That's true of all of us, I guess."

"What about your grandparents? Did they back up on you or were they easy to live with?"

"They were wonderful. But I knew I had disrupted their lives. I tried my hardest so they never had a reason to regret taking me in."

He could picture her doing extra chores, tiptoeing in from a date, always smiling, a guest in her own life. "No family is easy, I guess."

"Funny you should say that. I used to envy you guys. You seemed so normal—two loving parents, two great kids—dinners together every night, all that. I had no dad, a missing mom and I lived with my grandparents."

"Now you know the sad truth." He grinned.

"We do the best with what we get." Sylvie smiled at him, a warrior in the same battle.

He realized she had him dusting off memories for a

second look, appreciating things he'd taken for granted and loosening his grip on some old resentments.

He stopped at the edge of the enclosed acreage in view of the White Tanks Mountains and led her over. Dasher raced up and down the wire fence, yipping, trying to get the horses and goats lazing beneath the wooden ramada to race him.

"We're in escrow now. Before long, we'll be planting a big sign—Home At Last." He shaped a billboard with his hands.

"Wow." Sylvie wrapped an arm around his waist and rested her head against his chest, surveying the fields that used to grow cotton and alfalfa. "I can see it now. Those beautiful homes with all those big windows laid out in neat streets. Kids riding bikes, neighbors talking over the fences, everyone happy and proud."

"Yeah," he said, letting the picture she'd drawn take hold inside him. "I've been so focused on getting the ducks in a row, I haven't let it sink in what we're about to achieve, how really great it will be."

"It's important work, Chase."

"This project is different for me. It's not just about making money and pleasing my investors or building a reputation, or even proving it can be done. I don't know...."

"You love it. This one hits your heart."

"Yeah. That's right." His heart had been hit, all right, and not just by Home at Last.

He was falling in love with Sylvie.

Not very smart at all. They were on different paths, devoted to careers in different cities at least for the foreseeable future. Maybe one day, Chase would settle down the way he'd begun to imagine. And maybe it would be in Phoenix.

But by then, Sylvie would have found her Thor and there would be little Thors and Thorettes running around her yard.

That would be Chase's loss.

He'd just begun to realize how big.

CHAPTER THIRTEEN

"Is that what I think it is?" Fletcher nodded at the plastic sack Chase carried.

"It's our Christmas costumes. Sylvie wants us to make sure they fit. Black Friday's just a week away, you know." He pulled out an elf cap and plopped it onto his brother's head. The bell gave a little jingle and the red feather stuck out crookedly. "Green's your color."

"Holy crap," Fletcher said, looking at himself in the mirror over the bar. "I look ridiculous." He did.

Chase put his own elf hat on. "Yeah, me, too."

"I hoped this would fall through."

"You know Sylvie. Once she gets an idea in her head, it's tough to argue with her."

As a matter of fact, she'd managed to convince Chase that keeping the mall had merit. The meeting with Price-Less that afternoon had impressed him. The capital draw would not be as bad as he'd expected. He needed to talk to Fletcher about that now. It wouldn't be a happy chat.

"I can't believe she talked you into that campout in the mall." Fletcher shook his head, amused and puzzled.

The evening after his adventure with Sylvie, Chase had handed Fletcher a shot of Bushmills and a leftover s'more and told him the whole story of Chase and Sylvie, starting with her twenty-first birthday party and ending with the campout.

Fletcher had accepted the news that Sylvie and Chase

were together—sort of—with a quiet nod. He'd been touched that Chase had backed off when he learned Fletcher was interested in her. *I had no idea you were that honorable,* he'd said.

Now he gave Chase a sideways look. "What's with the goof-ass grin? It's Sylvie, huh?"

"It might be." Every day that passed seemed to bring them closer. Chase had the nagging feeling this would not end well, but he didn't know how to stop seeing Sylvie.

"I hope she knows what she's doing," Fletcher said.

"Meaning?" Even though Chase felt the same way, he wanted to see how Fletcher would put it.

"Does she know you'll be out of here as soon as the mall business is over?"

"She's okay with it." So far.

"She knows we're selling?"

"Hang on. *We* don't know we're selling. In fact, I want you to look this over." He took the two copies of the Price-Less proposal packet he'd brought for Fletcher and Marshall out of his messenger bag and set them on the bar. "Sylvie ran the numbers from our side, too, and it looks really good."

"PriceLess? You want to lease to them? A build-out would require major capital and a huge time commitment."

"Not as bad as you'd think. And their positive revenue impact is remarkable. I've seen their data. It would be a major boost in property value."

"We need to sell, Chase. Your investors turned down the Chandler deal, by the way. The margin was too tight."

"I'm sorry to hear that, but I told you I would consider the whole picture, not jump into a decision."

"Okay, so why is it that the real estate broker can't get you on the phone?"

"Relax, I'll call him tomorrow. I've been swamped."

"Swamped with what?" Marshall asked, entering the room. "Good Lord, what are you boys up to?"

"Just mall business," Chase said. He pulled out the red-and-white fur Santa hat and put it on his father's head. "Merry Christmas, Santa."

The General frowned at himself in the mirror. "We're not really doing this, are we?"

"Yep, next week. Sylvie wants you to be sure the suit fits. She got news coverage, too, like she promised. She's booked us on the top morning show in the state."

"God almighty, no," he grumbled, flipping the pointed end of the hat from one side to the other, studying the effect in the mirror. He was loving this, Chase could tell.

Chase poured three shots of Bushmills, knowing this conversation would be rocky. He pushed the other copy of the PriceLess proposal toward his father.

"What's this?" The General glared at Chase from beneath his Santa hat.

"It's a proposal to bring in a PriceLess Warehouse to Starlight Desert. I think it's worth considering."

"It would cost far too much and take too much time," Fletcher said, slapping his copy onto the bar. "These deals collapse halfway through construction all the time and we'd be out a lot of cash."

"This your idea?" the General asked Chase, bearing down on him, clearly suspicious of his motives.

"Sylvie's, actually. She's looking for ways to make the mall more valuable."

"Sylvie? Oh. Well, that's admirable." His eyebrows did a complicated dance of wary surprise.

"Meanwhile, we have strong interest from buyers and McCann Development could use the money," Fletcher said. "And so could Chase."

The General turned on Chase. "Is that what this is about? You want to cash out and leave?"

"Believe it or not, I want what's best for McCann Development," Chase said, his jaw tight.

"Since when?"

Fighting the urge to explode, Chase tossed back his drink and slammed the glass on the counter. "Ask the son you trust. Fletcher, fill him in on Chandler."

"Dammit, Chase." Fletcher threw back his whiskey, too, making a face at the burn. "Okay, Dad, here's the thing. That assemblage in Chandler I bought hasn't worked out. Selling the mall would give us cash flow to make up for that."

"I warned you against that property, didn't I? I saw what was coming, how overdeveloped the technology parks were. And why am I just hearing this now?" The General's face now matched his hat. "This is unacceptable, irresponsible and—"

"And you're overreacting," Fletcher interrupted, anger making his red feather shiver. "Which is exactly why I didn't tell you earlier. You second-guess every move I make. I thought this was a good project and I stand by my decision. It's not my fault the market caved when it did." The jingle bells on Fletcher's cap rang cheerfully as he jabbed at the bar.

"I've been in this business a hell of a lot longer than you. You should value my experience."

"I've got experience of my own, though you'll never admit it. If I hadn't jumped on that contractor offer we'd have spent three times the money we have on Copper Creek, but do you acknowledge that? No! You wait to pounce on any screwup you—"

"Hold on," Chase said, resisting the urge to laugh at the sight of them arguing business in their jingly hats. "Before we get too far afield, here's what I suggest. Both of you take a look at the PriceLess proposal. I'll get the details on any viable sales offers from the real estate broker and we'll make a decision after the Thanksgiving weekend. Black Friday profits will tell us a lot about revenue potential. How does that sound?"

"Like you two are plotting against me," Marshall growled. "Do what you want, like you always do." He was speaking to Chase alone and it grated on him. "Go ahead and treat your mother's dream like your personal piggy bank. She wanted you two to carry on the mall in her name, you know. I'm just glad she's not here to see how little you care about it."

He tossed back his drink. "I'm done here." He stalked off, jingling away, then yanked the Santa hat from his head and brought it back to Chase, before resuming his angry march out of the room.

"That went well," Chase said, pouring a second drink for himself and his brother.

Fletcher took it with shaking fingers, clearly furious. "What do you mean, the son he trusts? He treats me like I'm some college intern. He thinks you walk on water."

"Didn't you notice that when cashing out came up he assumed it was my idea? The General cuts no slack." He paused. "Sylvie says he has trouble showing that he loves us."

"Oh, yeah? Well, I say he's a stubborn, sentimental old goat. How's that?"

"Not far wrong." Chase couldn't help grinning.

"What's so funny?"

"It's hard to take you seriously with that thing on your head."

Fletcher grabbed the cap and shoved it at Chase's chest. "You look just as stupid."

"I know. Believe me." Chase took off his own hat. "Dad is who he is, Fletch. He's never going to hug us and tell us he's proud. We have to read between the lines."

Fletcher rolled his eyes. "Since when have you gotten so philosophical about the guy?"

Since Sylvie. But Chase just shrugged.

"You know he thinks if you joined McCann Development all our problems would be solved."

Chase laughed. "He gives me nothing but grief."

"Yeah? You don't get the 'in my day' or 'haven't I taught you anything?' lectures."

"He worked out the script on me, remember?"

His brother managed a wan smile. "At least he knows about Chandler now. Though I'll never hear the end of it."

"Who knows? Maybe dressing up like Santa will give him some Christmas spirit."

"Let's hope so," Fletcher said. "It won't look good to have Santa and his elves duking it out on morning TV."

IT WAS MIDMORNING when there was a tap on Sylvie's office door. She looked up to see Chase standing there, his face split in a grin so big she almost laughed.

She could feel her smile get ridiculously huge, too. He'd stayed home last night to talk with Fletcher and to let her rest up because of the community meeting to be held this afternoon. She'd missed him.

Dasher, who'd been chewing a toy under her desk, ran to Chase, whining to be picked up. Chase obliged.

Resisting the urge to go to him, she said, "What did Fletcher say about PriceLess?"

"He didn't break out the champagne, but he'll look it over. No decision either way until after we get the weekend numbers."

"I guess that's the best I can hope for."

"You catch up on your sleep?" Dasher licked Chase's chin, then yipped at him.

"Not with Dasher having to go outside every twenty minutes. I think he missed you."

"I missed him." Chase lowered his voice. "And you. I missed you, Sylvie."

"Me, too, Chase."

"I'm sorry you didn't sleep."

"It's all right." She'd been annoyed as hell, shivering in her robe outdoors half the night. Keeping Dasher would mean endless hassles. But once she was back in bed, with Dasher curled up on the second pillow, his warm, wheaty puppy breath in her face, she was happy she had him.

When you love something, you find a way.

With Dasher, maybe. How about Chase?

She had no idea. They'd grown so close in the time they'd been sleeping together, sharing feelings, hopes and hurts they'd always kept to themselves.

Chase spoke about his mixed feelings about his father, his regret over leaving Fletcher to deal with the man on his own all these years, about the huge hole their mother's death had left in his heart and between the three McCann men.

He talked about Home at Last, how much the project meant to him and how badly the failure in Nevada had hurt.

Sylvie told Chase how confused she'd been when Desiree left her with her grandparents and about her grief when they were killed in the car wreck, how afterward the world seemed more undependable than ever.

These were topics she avoided thinking about, but, somehow, in bed with Chase, the words floating in the dark between them, she felt ready to sort out the lessons from the losses.

She didn't know what to make of her and Chase anymore. They were impossibly close, scarily close. No matter what they'd agreed to in the beginning of their affair, not even a week ago, she knew someone could get hurt. Badly.

"If I'd known you were awake, I'd have been there in a heartbeat," Chase said. "In fact, I want you right now."

"Me, too. I want you." Her pulse pounded in her ears. She could lock her door, clear off her desk and they could make love right in her office. What was wrong with her? She was at work, for God's sake. Had lust completely clouded her mind?

As if to prevent the rash act she was contemplating, her office door flew open, banging Chase in the back.

It was Cyndi and she looked terrified. "There's a bomb in the mall. A man called just now. We have one hour, he said, before it goes off."

"My God!" Sylvie said, her brain shifting instantly into emergency mode. "Tell Randolph to implement emergency evacuation procedures."

"I'm calling 9-1-1," Chase said, already at the desk phone.

Mary Beth burst in wearing the Emergency Captain billed cap and a whistle she'd been given at the formal fire drill arranged by the fire marshal a year ago. She and Randolph, the other captain, were in charge of ensuring everyone got out of the mall safely. "I hope all the store employees remember their exits."

As soon as the police dispatcher assured them a bomb squad was on its way, Chase and Sylvie headed downstairs to help however they could. The crowd was noisy and jumpy. Mary Beth wasn't helping with her frequent blasts from her whistle. Even so, Randolph and his crew managed to herd everyone quickly and efficiently all the way out to the park.

Sirens wailed as emergency vehicles neared and Sylvie's heart skipped a beat. "What if there really is a bomb?" she asked Chase, who took her hand.

"We'll handle whatever happens." He looked so grim she knew he was worried, too.

"Even if it's just a stunt, our stores lose money every second we're out here," she said.

Soon bomb-sniffing dogs had been deployed and there were squad cars and police, some in SWAT gear, everywhere. Officers erected barricades all around the mall and yellow tape shivered in the breeze.

Shoppers, who couldn't leave until they could get their cars from the parking lot, were joined by neighborhood gawkers. News helicopters hovered overhead and news trucks dotted the area. Chase answered questions from reporters, saying he believed this was a prank call and that safety was the top concern of mall management.

Randolph had called in all the security guards and she spotted several in uniform sprinting across the parking lot to offer their help to the police.

Leo arrived in a noisy truck driven by a young guy, who jumped out, slipped under the yellow tape and ran toward the mall.

"Jesse! Hold up!" Leo yelled. "He thinks he's going to defuse the bomb himself, I swear," Leo said to Sylvie, then hurried after his gung-ho nephew, who'd been stopped by a police officer. No wonder Randolph kept urging her to hire the guy.

Store owners and employees gathered around Sylvie, Mary Beth and Chase. "I have to tell you, I'm getting scared," easygoing Sunni Ganesh said. "I've been ignoring all this stupid crime wave business, but now I don't know. We've been broken into, threatened and now maybe a bomb? What's happening?"

"I wish I knew, Sunni," Sylvie said. "We're working with the police to solve this. This is our highest priority." She looked at Chase for his agreement.

"We'll be hiring additional guards," Chase said, which made the tenants nod in relief, but they looked as grim and worried as Sunni.

A few minutes later, Detective Lawson approached with a smile to tell them the mall was clear. No explosives had been found. It had been a prank. Sylvie released a breath she'd been half holding since Cyndi had burst into her office.

Back upstairs, Sylvie and Chase found Mary Beth on the phone in Chase's office still wearing her cap and whistle. She hung up the phone. "Sorry, Chase. The phone rang so I had to answer. That was Peter Anderson from Reggie Collins's office confirming that the community meeting's still on this afternoon. He saw the evacuation on the news."

"Great," Sylvie said. "The timing couldn't be worse."

"This on the news could scare off our customers," Mary Beth said. "If the losses are too high, I'm afraid the tenants will start wanting rent concessions."

"We won't let our customers be scared off," Sylvie said.

"Shall I try to calm the tenants down?" Mary Beth said.

"Chase and I will handle that. Why don't you remind Betty to set up the chairs and podium before four?"

"Sure. Will do." She saluted Sylvie, her hand hitting the bill of the emergency captain cap she still wore. "I guess these go with the office."

"Keep them for now," Chase said.

"Quite a coincidence, don't you think?" Chase said as soon as she was gone. "The threat coming just a few hours before the forum?"

"What? You think Collins arranged this? A bomb threat is a serious crime. I don't see him taking a chance like that."

"Still, it gives him more ammunition to demand crime prevention funds," Chase said. "And it guarantees media at our meeting."

"Damn, that's right. He'll mention the bomb, so we'll need to counter whatever he says." Sylvie felt sick inside. They were in a downward spiral they couldn't seem to stop. "I hope this won't affect the PriceLess offer."

Sylvie sent out a quick email to all tenants, then she and Chase spent the next three hours going from store to store letting people vent. This was far from the atmosphere Sylvie had expected when she took leadership of the mall and she was grateful to have Chase at her side. In a crisis, a comanager was a gift.

By the time the community meeting was ready to begin, Sylvie's stomach was in knots and she was damp with anxious sweat. She and Chase stood with Detective Lawson beside the first row of folding chairs, welcoming people as they entered. They'd set up at the far end of the mall in an open area.

Collins's assistant, Peter Anderson, bustled around acting important, handing out press packets to the reporters, checking the mic, placing index cards and pencils on the seats for audience members to submit questions for the councilman, who hadn't yet appeared.

The bomb scare had boosted the crowd and the media so that Betty had to bring out two dozen extra chairs.

"When you speak, be sure and point out that Starlight

Desert will be part of the solution," she said to Chase, sliding her clammy palms down her slacks.

"I plan to."

"And you'll call it a prank, right? A stunt?"

"Would you feel better speaking instead of me?" He smiled at her, clearly trying to ease her nerves.

"No. You need to speak for McCann Development. Our tenants need to hear that you're behind them. I'm just... scared."

"I know. You're chewing your lip again and it's killing me." He smiled. "It'll be okay, Sylvie. We'll make it okay."

She smiled back. Today, they truly were Team Starlight Desert, just as Marshall had predicted.

Finally, ten minutes late, Reggie Collins swept onto the speaking platform like a conquering hero. Chase, who would be the emcee, welcomed everyone and introduced the people sitting behind him, including Sylvie and Detective Lawson. He finished with Reggie Collins, who stepped to the podium and raised a hand in welcome, taking over from Chase.

He paused to pose for the photographers with a well-polished grin. Once the cameras stopped flashing, he wasted no time on platitudes.

"The bomb threat this morning was the latest example of the recent lawlessness in this neighborhood. It was only a threat...this time," he said, dramatically sweeping the crowd with his gaze. "Next time, innocent people could be hurt, even killed. That is not acceptable to me and it shouldn't be acceptable to you."

Voices yelled agreement. Collins let the applause build, then finally waved it down. "As your elected representative I have fought long and hard for our share of city services and funds. And I will keep fighting with every ounce of energy, every breath in my lungs…"

Oh, yeah, like he'd fought the developer who wanted to improve the area with new condos. The guy always had an angle, so what was it? What was he really after?

The crowd applauded at the man's staged pauses as he carried on about his ideas for the future. "We must re-envision failing enterprises. For example, imagine a sports complex on this site." He waved out at the mall. "In fact, Mr. Abernathy here—" he motioned toward a man seated in the front row "—represents a group wanting to bring a professional jai alai team to the Valley. Stand up, James."

Abernathy stood, waved to the crowd, then sat back down.

"He just called Starlight Desert a failing enterprise," Sylvie whispered to Chase, who shrugged, a muscle ticking in his jaw. "And how does he know about the jai alai boosters?"

"No doubt he golfs at the same club as Dad."

Abruptly, Collins's assistant bounded to the dais, and motioned Collins away from the podium. While the two held a frantic, whispered conversation, Chase took over the podium and made his remarks. He said all the right things and Sylvie was pleased to see reporters taking notes as he spoke.

"Frankly, as far as the bomb hoax is concerned, my guess is that someone wanted to get out of a day of shopping at the mall. Are you out there?" He pretended to look for the guilty party among the crowd.

People laughed mildly.

Then Collins practically elbowed Chase out of the way to get to the microphone. "I'm sorry for the interruption, folks, but I've been informed that just now a woman might have been mugged in the parking lot outside. *Mugged*."

The audience gasped and murmured.

Chase, Sylvie and Detective Lawson left the podium and ran outside to see what was going on. Lawson got on his phone while Sylvie and Chase scanned the parking lot, which looked quiet. A few shoppers walked to their cars. Two cars pulled into parking spaces. But there were no police or crowd or noise.

"What the hell was he talking about?" Sylvie said, exasperated beyond words.

"No mugging," Detective Lawson announced to them, closing his phone. "A woman had a dead battery. Two officers in a cruiser gave her a jump. That's it."

"We need to announce that," she said, but by the time they got back to the meeting, people were filing out and Collins had gone.

Sylvie jumped onto the stage. The microphone was off, so she had to yell at the departing crowd. "There was no mugging! Police helped a woman with a dead battery. That's all it was."

She chased after a TV cameraman heading for the door. "Did you get that? There was no mugging!"

"I just got footage. Call the assignment desk and let them know." He handed her a business card.

Sylvie and Mary Beth spent the next hour contacting every news outlet to correct the misinformation, but she had no idea if the truth would make it to the anchor desk in time.

Sylvie and Chase urged the tenants not to panic if the news coverage looked bad. There had been a rumor that a bank deposit had been stolen during the bomb evacuation, but it turned out it had fallen behind a desk, so Sylvie explained that and promised that a security guard would accompany any employee who felt nervous out to his or her car. Everyone was jittery.

Who's doing this and why? was the mournful question on everyone's lips. Sylvie smiled and reassured, her mind racing with possible answers the entire time.

Mary Beth enjoyed being in the middle of the crisis, but she would never hurt the mall. Neither would Randolph. Leo had been devastated about the vandalism on his watch. Chase had told him he would hire his nephew Jesse just to make Leo feel like he'd helped in some way.

Could it be a disgruntled tenant? Sylvie couldn't imagine one so desperate for reduced rent or to get out of a lease that he would sabotage the mall like this.

Reggie Collins had certainly gained political mileage from the vandalism and the bomb scare. He'd suggested the mall was failing and could become a jai alai arena and he'd cheerfully passed on the false rumor about a mugging in the parking lot.

But that seemed like political opportunism, not an evil plot to hurt Starlight Desert.

At six, she and Chase sat together in his office to watch the news. Chase squeezed her shoulders. "Try not to worry, Sylvie," he said, but she could tell he was upset, too.

For good reason, as it turned out. The coverage was awful—aerial shots of shoppers crowded behind police barriers and alarmist talk about the "troubled mall" and "declining neighborhood," with shoppers complaining about being stranded with other errands to run.

They showed footage of Collins speaking, while the anchor made it sound that the meeting had been held *because* of the bomb threat, not coincidentally.

At the end of the segment, a reporter thrust a microphone at a woman shopper, asking for a comment. "This has always been a safe neighborhood," she said, shaking her head. "Now, I don't know. Some lady got mugged in the parking lot. Next we'll need bulletproof vests to even walk in the door."

The anchor noted the mugging could not be confirmed.

"Could not be confirmed?" Sylvie blurted. "How about *absolutely did not happen?*" Outrage burned through her. "I'm demanding a retraction."

"That could give the story legs, Sylvie. They'd call Collins for his reaction and he'd fan the flames."

"We have to do *something,*" she said.

"Let it go for now and hope the print stories turn out better."

"This is so frustrating." She dug her fingers into her hair and tugged at the roots, welcoming the discomfort.

"It's been a long day, Sylvie. We need a break. Even your dog is worn-out." He nodded at where Dasher dozed. Taking him for potty breaks and playing tug-of-war with his chew toy had been the only moments of relief she'd had all day.

"*Now* he sleeps?" she said. "He'll keep me up all night." She was bone-tired and her whole body ached.

"How about if I'm the designated walker and we're quiet as mice? Will that help?"

"I guess." She was so weary she couldn't think.

Chase pulled her close. "I know just what will help you relax," he murmured, running his hand down her back, to cup her rear.

Her body responded to his touch, but her mind threw up a wall. How could Chase shift gears like that? He'd set aside the mall trauma for tomorrow and was ready to play tonight.

"I'm too wiped out I'm afraid," she said, gently pulling away from him.

"Oh. Sure." He hesitated. "Then we'll just sleep. Whatever you need, Sylvie." He grinned, clearly assuming he could convince her otherwise once they were in bed.

He no doubt could. Suddenly, she saw how impossible their relationship was. Chase could disengage far quicker than she ever could. When it was time to go, he would leave, content with what they'd shared. Done and done.

For her, it was neither so simple nor so easy. Chase had warned her. She could picture that hazard sticker on his handsome forehead. She knew what she had to do.

"I'm sorry, Chase, but I think I need to be alone tonight. In fact, would you take Dasher with you?"

"Oh. Sure. If that'll help." He was disappointed, she could tell, but he shrugged it off. Easy. Whatever. Which wasn't how Sylvie would have reacted.

They left the mall together, Chase carrying the bag with Dasher's gear, the puppy in one arm. Stepping out the exit, Sylvie nodded at the unfamiliar guard, an extra one, reminding her of the mess things were in.

Chase put the top up on the BMW, left Dasher safely inside, then walked Sylvie to her car. He wrapped his arms around her. "I could just be there for you tonight, you know. Give you a shoulder to cry on, whatever you need."

She shook her head. "Thanks, I'm fine."

He smiled. "No, you're not. You're worried and scared. You don't have to be alone with that. That's all I'm saying."

"I'm afraid I do, Chase." She had to pull back, get some distance from him.

He held her gaze, his eyes full of affection. "You know how much I care about you, don't you?"

Everything inside Sylvie went still. This was big, what Chase was trying to say out here in the mall parking lot in the orange glow of the security light. Was he in love with her?

"I care about you, too, Chase." But it was time to back off. Time to be smart. This would hurt, of course, but sooner was better than later. She stepped away from him. "Listen, I think we should slow down for now. At least until you decide about the mall. We're distracting each other when we need to focus. With Black Friday coming up, the attacks, the way everything's up in the air…"

"Really? Oh. I guess that makes sense." But hurt flickered like a candle flame in Chase's eyes and Sylvie felt an answering pain.

This is for the best, she reminded herself.

Even if Chase *was* in love with her, it was ephemeral, like the gauze curtains she made for her dollhouses, which tore at the slightest tug.

The intensity would pass and then where would they be? Chase would move on and she would be left, heartsick and alone.

"I'm glad you agree." She smiled to hide the trembling of her lips. She wanted to step back into the comfort of his arms, breathe him in, then lie with him in bed, make love, cuddle, his heart beating beneath her ear, his hands on her skin, feeling cared for, cherished and loved.

Instead, she stood there, nodding sensibly, while her gut churned. This meant the end of them. Putting distance between them would snap their connection like an ice floe breaking away in a swift current.

Sylvie had done the right thing, the smart and safe thing, but she felt like crying.

CHASE DROVE OFF THE MALL lot, as torn up inside as Dasher's rawhide twist. Sylvie had just broken up with

him. He hadn't seen that coming at all. He tried to sort
out his thoughts.

But it wasn't his thoughts that were the problem. It was
his feelings. And, man, was he having *feelings*. It was as if
someone had carved open his chest and dumped his heart
into the dirt.

She was right, of course. Things *were* up in the air with
the vandalism, the sale, Black Friday. They were spending
a hell of a lot of time together. Every minute they could.

You're in love with her, idiot.

"Dammit!" He banged the steering wheel with the palm
of his hand. Dasher yipped in alarm. "Sorry, guy."

He'd wanted to be what she needed, to hold her, comfort
her, make love to her or not, it didn't matter to him.

He was in love with Sylvie and she'd shot him down
cold.

What was he going to do about it?

He knew the answer. Not a damn thing. What had she
said they should do if they fell in love?

Ignore it.

That's what he would do. It was the smart thing. He'd
leave and Sylvie would stay. As soon as the mall was taken
care of and Home at Last was in shape, he'd be gone.

It was better this way. He should be glad Sylvie had
been so sensible. They were adults, after all. They could
control themselves.

But, God, he ached for her.

Stick to the mess at hand. And it was big. The mall was
being sabotaged. Someone wanted Starlight Desert to fail
or at least look troubled. Who? The headline-hungry politician? A buyer looking to devalue the property? Mary Beth?
PriceLess? He didn't know and meanwhile, his thoughts
kept racing back to Sylvie.

Get a grip, man. It was simply that he'd never felt like

this about a woman before. He hadn't even gotten used to it, when, bam, she slammed the door in his face. That was a hell of a thing.

He glanced at the dog on the seat beside him. "It's just you and me tonight, buddy." Dasher looked up at him with his big brown eyes. Chase could swear that if the dog could talk he'd be saying, "How on earth did you screw this up?"

CHAPTER FOURTEEN

SYLVIE RETURNED TO HER peaceful home only to find Dasher messes she hadn't noticed that morning. Somehow, he'd managed to chew up a swatch of dollhouse silk, knock over a pot of African violets and leave a wet spot on the Oriental rug.

That dog was pure trouble, no question.

But she missed him anyway. She wished he were here to gnaw on her heels with his pointy teeth and smear her mascara with his pink tongue. She loved the little pest.

Worse than that, she loved Chase. And breaking it off had only made her feel worse. She missed his arms, his smile, his take on things, the way he supported her, believed in her, *got* her. That was completely new for her. To be valued for who she was, to be understood, to be loved.

And she'd sent him away. So she could sleep. Yeah, right.

She tossed and turned all night, drifting to sleep, then jerking awake, in turmoil over Chase, the sabotage, the news coverage, her tenants, Black Friday, everything spinning like objects in a Kansas twister in her brain.

At five, she gave up and was waiting with a mug of chai tea when the carrier tossed the morning paper onto her porch.

Heart banging her ribs, she slipped it from its plastic cover and unfolded it.

The front page was fine, but when she pulled away the first section, there it was. The lead story in B with two photos—the bomb scare and a reprint of the weekly paper's shot of the graffiti.

As she read the article, Sylvie's blood ran colder than the early-morning air through her robe:

In recent weeks, the peace of Scottsdale's Starlight Desert Mall, a 1970s-era mall built by local developer Marshall McCann, has been shattered by multiple instances of vandalism, including insulting graffiti, a bomb scare and rumors of a parking lot mugging.

The attacks, part of rising crime in the older neighborhood, have sparked fear among shoppers, threatening vital revenues on the eve of the biggest shopping season of the year.

Mall officials minimized the incidents, calling them "pranks," though security has been doubled and police patrols increased. Hope may well rest in the possibility of a PriceLess warehouse opening at the site.

The story pushed all the alarm buttons: peace shattered…escalating violence…fearful shoppers…threatened revenues. The community meeting was mentioned and Collins was quoted about re-envisioning failing enterprises. The article did say the mugging was unverified, but, as she'd feared, not until the last paragraph.

Bleary and discouraged, Sylvie headed for the mall, where she spent all morning dealing with concerned employees, tenants, shoppers and citizens. The most troubling call was from the school superintendent, who was worried that his students might not be safe during the Black Friday event.

"I left another message for Roger Munford," Mary Beth told her wearily.

"Still no call?" Sylvie had left two messages with the PriceLess VP, then passed the duty to Mary Beth. The silence suggested the terrible media reports had scared him off.

Things got worse. By noon, four store owners had stopped by to tell her they wouldn't be renewing their leases. They denied it had anything to do with recent events, but Sylvie knew better. Her weathering-the-storm speech hadn't been enough to keep them hanging in. She tried not to feel betrayed—these were business decisions— but she felt like yanking back her stenciled umbrellas all the same. Where was their faith? What had happened to the family feeling she worked so hard to build?

James Abernathy from the jai alai club stopped in to inquire about the possibility of purchasing the mall as an arena, claiming Collins's speech had given him the idea. Sylvie could hardly be polite to the man, who sported a pin that said Jai Alai Is Fun For Everyone! on his sports coat.

Was he a predator circling what he saw as weakened prey? Or had Collins colluded with him in making the offer? His speech sounded rehearsed. Or was she just paranoid?

The worst blow came a little while later when Talley Toombs plopped into her guest chair. "Got a minute?"

"Sure," Sylvie said, scooting close to her desk, bracing her elbows on her blotter, hoping for good news.

"This isn't official, but I had drinks with Carrie Tracer, the Tracers' daughter—she's a friend of mine—and she let it slip that her parents are closing this store."

"They're leaving the mall?"

"It's a shocker, I know. They want to retire soon, so they want to hold on to just the Tucson location, since it's where they live."

No. Tracer's was Starlight Desert's anchor, its biggest draw and its highest revenue generator. This with the other losses put Starlight Desert in real trouble.

Locking in PriceLess warehouse might make up for that, but she couldn't get the guy on the phone. Sylvie's insides seemed to sink to the floor. "If our Christmas sales are spectacular, would they reconsider?"

Talley shrugged. "That depends, I guess. Like I said it's not official or anything."

"What about you? Aren't you upset about losing your job?"

"Oh, you know, when a door closes, a window opens." She seemed way too cheerful for someone about to be jobless.

"And…?"

"And there's a guy." Talley beamed in triumph. "He knows a lot of important people, so…let's just say I'm pretty sure it will work out."

"I hope it does," Sylvie said. "In the meantime, would it help if I talked to the Tracers?"

"God, no. I wasn't supposed to find out in the first place. When I hear anything definite, you'll be the first to know."

After Talley left, Sylvie rested her head in her hands, her usual optimism draining away like water from a cracked cup.

Someone tapped on her door. *What now?*

But it was Chase, Dasher in his arms, and her heart lifted at the sight. It was stupid, they'd broken up, but seeing him made her feel better.

He came to sit in her guest chair. Dasher writhed to get down, then ran to her and jumped against her shin. She picked him up and he licked her wildly.

"Looks like he missed you," Chase said, telling her with his eyes that he'd missed her, too. Sylvie's throat tightened with emotion.

The sound of ripping paper made her look at Dasher, who was tearing at the newspaper on her desk.

"I'd like to shred that dreck, too," she said, prying the paper away from him and smoothing it. "Did you see the story?"

"I did. Not good at all."

"It gets worse. Tracer's might be closing this store. It's a rumor from Talley, but the source is legit."

"That is worse," he said.

"Four smaller tenants say they won't be renewing their leases, either. Also the jai alai guy was nosing around about buying the mall. Could he have been scheming with Collins?"

"I doubt that. Collins was just hyping his so-called vision. At least that's how it seemed to me."

"I don't know, but this is all so crazy. On the other hand, if 'A Starlight Desert Christmas' goes well, I think I can talk most of the tenants into staying. The Tracer's thing might not happen, either. PriceLess would change the whole picture, I know. And if we could just stop the creeps from attacking us again..."

"We'll have weathered the storm and the future will be so bright we'll need shades?" he offered in kindly irony.

"I can hope, can't I?" she said.

"We both can." He squeezed her hand, and for a moment everything seemed possible. But for just a moment.

THAT NIGHT, Sylvie was surprised when her doorbell rang. She wasn't expecting anyone and she was in her robe, planning to turn in soon. Whoever it was stood out of range of the peephole.

"Who is it?" she called through the door.

"It's me. Chase."

Oh, yay. Forget wisdom and good sense, she was thrilled to see him and she threw open the door to tell him so, her heart in her throat.

When she saw him she burst out laughing. He wore his elf costume—a green velvet jacket, red suspenders, green felt knickers, pointed green shoes with jingle bells and a cap set at a rakish angle, the red feather quivering in the air.

"Oh, my God," she gasped. "You are just…so cute."

"I thought it would cheer you up to know our costumes all fit. Now let me in before the neighbors call the cops about a Peeping Elf on the street."

"Oh, sure. Sorry." She moved back and he tromped inside, his bells jingling with each step. "You look great."

He took a slow turn, arms out, to give her the full effect.

Dasher rushed forward, then stopped, ears back, to cower behind Sylvie's legs.

"Great, I'm scaring the dog."

"He's just awestruck."

"I look ridiculous, Sylvie."

"Not at all. I had no idea how sexy green felt could be."

"Please."

"I'm serious. You should wear it for the prep party on Thanksgiving. Think of the morale boost."

"What about my dignity?"

"Overrated," she said, her heart filling up. *I love this man.* She put her arms around him, stood on tiptoe and kissed him. His arms went around her, holding her close.

"What does that mean?" he said when they broke off.

"It means I'm falling in love with you."

"And you can't ignore it? Because I can't, either," he said.

"So what do we do?" she asked, hoping he had an answer that didn't scare her anymore than she already was.

"We go to bed," he growled, reaching for her.

She took a step backward. "Not until we figure this out."

He advanced on her, taking her by the arms, turning her toward the hallway. "Let's just see how it goes."

"You mean, maybe it will burn out?" she asked hopefully as he steered her into her bedroom.

"Entirely possible," he said, guiding her to the bed.

"And no one gets hurt?" Her legs hit the edge of the mattress and she let herself fall onto the bed.

"No one gets hurt," he said, lying over her.

"No one gets hurt," she breathed as his mouth met hers.

Everything in her rose to the contact, as if that kiss held both their souls. This might be foolish, stupid and self-defeating, she knew. She could be pulling a Desiree—throwing her heart like a decorative pillow for Chase to drop. But it felt so right she couldn't give it up. Not yet.

"You're wearing that nice, slippery, easy-to-get-out-of robe again," he murmured, going for the tie.

She looked up at him. "You might want to keep that hat on," she murmured. "I like hearing bells."

Chase laughed and then he kissed her smile until it went away and desire surged through her. She forced herself not to think, to get lost in the moment, to feel how she felt and let that be okay.

They made love with quiet intensity, as if they were crossing an important line. Each brush of a fingertip, each moan, each stroke, tightened muscle and gasp, each answering ache carried them further along, took them deeper into this love they'd created.

I love you, Chase. Stay with me was a whispered song in her head, born of what they'd shared, the feelings growing between them.

Release, when it came it, was mutual and they cried out in unison, their voices blending, almost mournful, and full of relief. Afterward, Chase held her tightly, She rested her cheek against his chest and silence enveloped them.

Helped up by Chase, Dasher nestled above her head on the pillow. Maybe this would run its course, like a fever, and they'd both walk away, content with what they'd shared.

She could hope, couldn't she?

CHASE WOKE EARLY with Sylvie still in his arms. *Maybe this will work out after all.* He'd be around for at least another month. That was plenty of time for them to figure out what to do or maybe even to finish with each other.

Right now, Sylvie felt so good in his arms. When she'd returned to him, it was like a reprieve from a prison sentence.

The dog stirred and nudged his head. Time for a potty break. Careful not to wake Sylvie, he took the dog outside. Then, on his way to the kitchen to fix coffee, he stopped to look in her workroom at all the perfect little houses she'd carefully built. In Sylvie's world, everything was sized to fit and stayed where she put it. That's what she wanted in life—order, control, routines.

That was not Chase's way at all, though this time in Phoenix hadn't been as claustrophobic as usual. Sylvie had helped him get past some negatives. He accepted the General more. He didn't like how his father operated, but at least he understood him. He'd been pleased when Fletcher stood up for himself. Maybe Fletch would do what Chase had harassed him about—grow a pair...and get a life.

Then there was Home at Last. Chase did love the project. He'd liked working with Jake Atwater, too. Intrigued by an urban park Jake was working on, he'd felt the urge to play with designs again. A sideline amusement, no doubt.

Was that what Sylvie was to him?

No. The thought was so abhorrent he actually shook his head. The puppy whined, as if in agreement.

Sylvie had been hot heaven—passionate in bed, smart and savvy at work, and a lovely spot of quiet acceptance in between.

Sylvie felt like home. The way home was supposed to feel. As if he even knew how that worked. He snorted at his own dazed fantasy.

When the coffee finished burbling, he carried a cup with cream, two sugars, the way Sylvie liked it, to bed for her. She opened her eyes and then her arms and he realized they would both be late to work.

AT ELEVEN on Thanksgiving morning, Sylvie headed toward Desert Oasis, her mother's mobile home park tucked into the base of Papago Buttes, with the ready-made Thanksgiving meal she'd picked up from the gourmet grocery store.

Desiree always wanted to cook the holiday meals, but Sylvie knew better. Her mother got sidetracked, letting the sweet potatoes boil over, the turkey shrivel, the pies burn black.

For the past two years, Sylvie had brought the premade meal and her mother warmed up a bakery pie and provided the sparkling apple juice. No alcohol for Sylvie, since the sale prep and mall party would start at three.

The week had flown by for Sylvie, the work taking on a manic pace as they neared Black Friday. There had been no further news stories on the mall's troubles and, thankfully, no more attacks. The PriceLess VP had yet to return her call, but she'd decided to get through the weekend and see where things stood after that. She and Chase spent every spare moment together.

Sylvie knocked on the door.

Her mother flung it open, wearing a kiss-the-cook apron streaked with what looked like frosting. "You have to quit knocking, Sylvie. You're not company. This is your home."

Hardly, but Sylvie did enjoy the cozy space, its walls full of her mother's paintings and weavings, the shelves packed with clay pots, carved figurines and knitted items, along with a happy jumble of half-finished projects.

Desiree air-kissed Sylvie on both cheeks and Sylvie set down her heavy bags, fragrant with the smell of roast turkey, sage dressing and sweet potatoes.

"Pies are boring, so I made a cake." Desiree motioned toward a fondant-covered cake shaped and painted to resemble Starlight Desert.

"Wow," Sylvie said. "That looks amazing."

"The cake overcooked a bit, but I think the decoration came out great. You think I could sell novelty cakes?" She shifted the cake slowly around, studying it.

"That's not part of your business plan." Her mother was talented, but as distractible as a cat. She could run a buzz saw like a champ, made beautiful jewelry, pottery and weavings, but never stuck long with any medium.

"You never know when an idea will score, Sylvie. If you let me sell your stuff online, you could quit the mall and make dollhouses for a living."

"I make dollhouses to relax. I love my job." And she was getting tired of people suggesting she leave it.

"Not lately. I've never seen you so tense."

"It's a tough time right now, that's all." She sighed, taking the containers out of the sack.

"Maybe that's the cosmos telling you to move on."

"No job is fun all the time, Desiree. Could we just enjoy our meal?"

"Of course." Desiree brought the sparkling apple juice from the refrigerator and poured it into two hand-thrown ceramic goblets, then handed one to Sylvie.

Once they were both seated her mother clinked her goblet against Sylvie's. "Cheers! I was hoping we'd be celebrating you being the new general manager. Starr would have wanted that, you know. I'd be happy to give Marshall a piece of my mind."

"There's no need. If everything goes well I'll get the job." As long as the problems worked themselves out and the McCanns didn't get an irresistible sales offer. Sylvie's insides churned at the thought.

"The McCanns take you for granted, that's all I'm saying. You work miracles out there."

"Let's eat before it gets cold." Her mother's extravagant compliments were like so much confetti thrown for effect.

"White or dark meat?" Sylvie asked.

"White, please."

Sylvie put the turkey on their plates, then they served

themselves sweet potatoes, garlic mashed potatoes, asparagus, carrot salad and cranberry sauce.

"Gravy or butter?" Sylvie asked her mother.

"Butter. By the way, I should tell you I'm thinking a mall kiosk isn't the proper sales environment for me anymore."

Sylvie set down the gravy container so quickly liquid splashed onto the table. "You can't leave, Desiree. You owe back rent. Plus, you miss a dozen sales a day when you come late or don't show up at all." Alarm made her voice spike.

"Don't get excited," Desiree said, scooping the spilled gravy with a finger, then licking it off. "I've got a deal cooking on some ceramics. I'll pay the rent, no problem. Don't I always come through?"

"You always try." That was the best Sylvie could manage, considering all the ways her mother had let her down over the years. Talking to Chase about Desiree had stirred up some anger.

"What's that supposed to mean?" her mother asked.

"Nothing." Desiree didn't want the answer to that question any more than Sylvie wanted to give it.

"I'm just giving you notice that when my lease is up you'll have my space to rent. As a courtesy."

"I appreciate that," Sylvie said, praying there would be a mall at all by then. "Are you coming to the mall party with me?"

"I told Margery I'd help her decorate the trailer park. But I have the ornaments for your tree ready." She left the table to bring out a cardboard box. "Take a look."

Sylvie lifted out two. Each glass ornament had a decoupaged photo of one of the stores on it. "These are gorgeous." Her mother had insisted she make them for Sylvie, who was in charge of decorating the mall employee tree. For all her faults, Desiree had a generous heart.

They ate in quiet after that. "Mmm," Desiree said. "This is a fine meal, but you should've let me cook. I have this great recipe for pecan dressing."

"One of these days, when you're not so busy." Which, of course, would never happen.

"So, how's Steve doing?" her mother asked.

"Steve?" Sylvie's potato-filled fork stopped halfway to her mouth. "I assume he's fine. I haven't talked to him in a while."

"So does that mean you broke up with him?"

Sylvie set down her fork altogether. "He moved to Seattle. We stopped dating. It wasn't that big a deal." Nothing compared to how she'd felt during her brief separation from Chase. The intensity of that pain still made her jumpy inside.

"You have to *feel* these things, Sylvie." Her mother looked at her with pity.

"Just because I don't flip out like you do doesn't mean I don't feel anything." Her words held more acid than she'd intended. The stress at the mall was getting to her, she guessed.

"I'm a romantic person. If that's what you mean by flipping out, then I guess that's what I do."

They took a few bites in tense silence.

Finally her mother spoke. "You know, you can talk to me, Sylvie."

"I don't have anything to talk about."

"You never let me help you and that hurts me." Now Desiree was pouting.

God. Enough drama. Even if Sylvie wanted to vent about how scared she was about Chase it would never be to Desiree.

"How could *you* help *me*? You go through one breakup after the next. It's all hearts and flowers and promises until they leave you crying. That's the last thing I want in my life."

Her mother's eyes widened at Sylvie's outburst. "I'm not perfect, okay?"

"Like that last guy. Dover. He was traveling with a band. Why get involved when you knew he'd leave and you'd be hurt?"

"We fell in love, Sylvie. You can't say no to love."

"Sure you can, when you know it will fail." Tears sprang to her eyes for some stupid reason. She blinked them away, not wanting her mother to notice.

"We grew as people, and we shared some lovely moments."

"I don't see the point. I just don't." She drank more sparkling juice to hide from her mother's gaze.

"You would if you'd try. Why are you so afraid to open your heart?"

Sylvie banged down her goblet. "Because I've been hurt enough," she snapped, the words so quick she couldn't stop them. They'd never talked about Desiree leaving her behind. Not once in twenty-plus years.

Her mother's cheeks went blotchy red with shock.

Seconds passed while Sylvie looked down at the bubbles of carbonation bursting on the surface of her drink. "I'm sorry," she mumbled finally.

"I was only nineteen when I had you," her mother said. "I didn't know what I was doing. I tried my best. I didn't have a steady income or normal hours. After the third night in a row of popcorn for supper, with you and your brave smile—*I love popcorn. It's my favorite*—I knew you deserved better. Mom and Dad kept nagging me to give you to them. They thought I was a bad mother. I knew you adored them. You were always begging to spend the night. The school was so much better. It seemed like the best thing for you."

"Why didn't you ask me? I wanted you and our home. I didn't care about the popcorn or the school or having my own room. Did I bug you? Was that why? Did I complain too much? Is that why you never came back?"

Sylvie couldn't believe she was laying into her mother this way, but a dam had broken and the bitter water flowed.

"Of course you didn't bug me or complain. I missed you desperately. I cried myself to sleep for weeks missing you. I thought it was better to stay away so you'd be used to not having me around. And I sent you postcards."

"Postcards?" She snorted. "You thought postcards were enough?" Even as she glared at her mother, the woman's words sank in. Sylvie had always assumed her mother was relieved to be free to flit from place to place with no one to worry about but herself.

"I know you think I'm a flake and a nut and a ridiculous joke of a mother."

"I never said that."

"You didn't have to. It's in the way you look at me and talk to me. It's in the silences between us, the way you bite your tongue and lock your jaw and are always, always polite. It's in the sacks of expensive food you bring because you expect me to screw up again and again." Desiree's voice was shaky, but she was angry, too. For once she wasn't skirting the issue, pretending everything was just fine and cheerful and lovely, a habit Sylvie had herself.

"I know you don't respect me. You may not even love

me." Sylvie opened her mouth to protest, but Desiree held up her hand.

"You have every right not to. But I love you, Sylvie. I always have and I always will." Her eyes, the same clear green as Sylvie's own, crackled with ferocity.

Sylvie had hurt her mother deeply, which surprised her. Desiree had always seemed impervious to criticism, even oblivious to it. What would it be like to have a daughter who rejected you, made you feel guilty every time you saw her?

Sylvie jerked across the table to hug Desiree, the frosting in her mother's hair filling Sylvie's nose with cloying sweetness. "I'm sorry I upset you. We've never talked about this before. I just… I'm sorry." She had to escape this crash of emotions that wouldn't let her breathe. "I should get going to the party."

"Let's have our cake before you go," her mother said shakily, brushing at her cheeks.

The cake crumbled like a giant crouton when Desiree cut into it. "Dammit, I can't even make a cake for you." Desiree's lips trembled and her voice cracked. "I am a screwup."

"No, you're not. I love the cake. The frosting tastes amazing and the decoration is incredible. You could sell it easily. Thank you, Desiree—no, I mean thank you, *Mom*."

Her mother's face lit up like a spotlight. "I'm going to do better, Sylvie. I promise I am."

"Me, too," Sylvie said. She'd been withholding her love out of resentment. That wasn't fair. Their usual hugs were a quick pat-pat and an air-kiss. This time Sylvie held on. They were cheek to cheek and squeezing each other, like a mother and daughter who'd been apart far too long. Which was exactly who they were.

HOURS LATER, at the end of the mall party, Sylvie stood with Chase on the landing, looking down at the mall she loved.

Christmas music played through the sound system, the place smelled of Heaven Scents' holiday candles and each store had placed its special tree out front.

Captain Bean's tree held little wooden toys, Rose's Hobby Hut had craft samples, Lucy's Secrets had Christmas stockings with lacy panties peeking out. The employee tree looked fabulous, loaded down with Desiree's handiwork. Beneath every tree were the gifts for needy families.

Inside the stores, employees were finishing up last-minute details for the next day's onslaught.

"I have to say I'm impressed," Chase said.

"You should be. This is Starlight Desert at its finest," she said. "Everyone working together with all our hearts."

"It's been nice to enjoy this place again."

"I'm glad you feel that way," she said. "Here's to tomorrow," she said, clinking her plastic glass of champagne against his. "I hope it goes well."

"Me, too."

"Don't forget. The *Wake Up, Arizona!* crew needs Santa and his elves in place by 7:00 a.m."

"We'll be there with bells on. Literally." He shook his head.

"I can't wait to see that. Employees are bringing their kids to stand in line for you, since we don't open until nine."

Dasher yipped at their feet and Sylvie bent to pick him up just as Chase's cell phone rang.

He stepped away to answer it, then returned with a serious expression. "Looks like an offer on the mall will come in tomorrow."

"You're kidding." Adrenaline poured through her.

"It's too soon to panic. The offer could be too low. It could fall through. Just focus on making tomorrow go well."

"Oh, I will." But now Sylvie knew that going well wouldn't be enough. With everything at stake, tomorrow had to be perfect.

CHAPTER FIFTEEN

THE NEXT MORNING, right on time, the three McCann men trooped the length of the mall, jingling as they walked, looking like festive prisoners on a Christmas chain gang.

Sylvie covered her mouth so she wouldn't laugh at Fletcher in his green tights and Marshall in his jolly red suit and huge white beard. Chase managed to still look sexy in his getup, but then she'd also seen him strip out of it.

Soon enough, Santa was miked and ready on his gold-and-red velvet throne. Beside him were plaster reindeer and a sleigh, as well as a Christmas tree with dozens of gift-wrapped boxes. While the TV producer talked with Chase and Fletcher, Sylvie approached Marshall. "You doing okay?"

"I feel damn silly like this." He spit out beard fuzz, then shifted his black belt to center the buckle.

"Well, you look perfect to those kids." She pointed to where they eagerly awaited their turn to tell Santa their wishes.

Marshall smiled. "Starr would have loved this."

"She would have."

"I wish my boys had more of her spirit. Neither of them appreciates all the care she put into this place."

"I think Chase is beginning to."

Marshall gave her a thoughtful look. "And that has

everything to do with you, young lady. From what he tells me, you're calling all the plays these days."

"We're working together," she said, pleased that Chase had given her credit with his father.

Marshall sighed. "Truth is, I figured handling the mall would keep Chase occupied long enough to decide to stick around." He shook his head. "Chase goes his own way and always has. I'm getting too old to fight the inevitable."

"I see what you mean." Was that what she was doing by hanging on to Chase, pretending this could last? The idea gave her a chill. Even stubborn Marshall knew that Chase moved on.

Thinking about that made Sylvie's heart hurt worse than it did when she thought about the sales offer on the mall.

Someone gave a five-minute warning and Fletcher and Chase came to stand around Marshall's chair.

After the news segment wrapped, Sylvie thought it couldn't have gone better if she'd scripted it herself. The questions focused on the unique stores, the mall being family-owned and the reporter mentioned the school involvement that day as an example of how Starlight Desert was a good neighbor to the community.

After the broadcast, school buses began dropping off the students who would perform later that morning. If there were two family members spending cash for every kid in a red velvet dress or wearing angel wings or reindeer ears, revenues for the day could top all records.

Sylvie scrambled from place to place, helping out wherever she was needed—directing teachers and students toward the stage, making sure stores had their scavenger hunt items in place, arranging the raffle prizes on the huge cardboard Christmas tree at the employee table. Her handmade fairy-tale cottage rested there proudly, enticing many people to buy tickets.

The walkways were full of people, but traffic flowed smoothly, thanks to the employees assigned usher duties. Jugglers, mimes and a guy in a reindeer costume making balloon animals entertained anyone stuck in a line.

When the first roll of raffle tickets had been used up, Sylvie dashed upstairs for another. She ran into Chase in the hallway. "What are you doing up here?" she asked.

"We haven't yet formed an elf union, but we do get bathroom breaks," he said. "You doing okay?"

"I'm on the fly, but good." She started to take the stairs, but Chase took her arm. "Hang on." He pointed down at the mall. "Take a minute to see what you've accomplished."

All the work and worry had been worth it, she saw. The mall was filled with happy, busy people, all carrying loaded shopping bags. Just below her the chorus from the middle school was belting out "It's Beginning to Look a Lot Like Christmas" for a rapt crowd of proud parents and shoppers.

Farther down, Sunni was setting out the trays of sugar cookies she'd donated for preschoolers to decorate. The line of kids heading for Santa snaked around the workshop, but moved briskly.

In the distance, the playground they'd rented was busy with kids arranging blocks, sliding down the slide or bouncing in the bounce house.

Theo's booth was swamped, his customers sporting his holiday cranberry smoothie in bright pink. Theo had kissed her cheek, thanking her for the most profitable day that year.

"It's going great. Captain Bean had orders to last him until after the holidays. Lucy has to rush-order more silk robes. And Toy Town is wall-to-wall shoppers."

"All the stores are packed," Chase said.

"Talley says Tracer's has never started off a Black

Friday this strong. At this rate I know we'll win over the stores threatening to leave."

"That would be good."

"How's your dad holding up? There'll be more media coverage later."

"He's having the time of his life. Fletcher pretends to be grumpy, but I saw him take a woman's phone number, so somebody must find pointy shoes and jingle bells sexy."

"I certainly do," she said. "On you anyway."

He smiled. "Then it's worth it. These damn tights are hot and itchy as hell. How do girls stand them?"

"I'm more of a bare-legs girl myself."

"That's one of the things I love about you," he said, bumping shoulders with her. She felt good standing beside him.

"I kind of wish Dasher was here," she said. They'd left the puppy with Nadia for the day.

"You going to keep him?" Chase asked.

"Yes, I guess I am." She realized she'd already decided. "He makes life complicated, but like you said, when you love something you find a way."

"Yeah," he said, studying her face. "You do." They both seemed embarrassed by the implications of his words and looked away.

"No matter what happens, Sylvie, you did a phenomenal job here. Always remember that."

"What does that mean? Did you get the offer? Was it good?"

"Not yet, no. Relax."

"I'm trying to. When you see our figures on Monday, you'll be blown away, I know you will." If she could only reconnect with PriceLess, she'd have the best-case scenario for keeping the mall.

Starlight Desert stayed packed all day. The district

superintendent was ecstatic about the money the raffle netted for the schools to spend on field trips, art supplies and band instruments. They would also get a percentage of the day's profits.

At around seven, Sylvie was resting at one of Theo's tables when she spotted tough-guy Rafael from Free Arts loping down the mall holding her whimsical fairy-tale cottage as if it might shatter if he wasn't careful. Evidently he'd won the drawing.

"Hey, Rafael," she called to him. His crew had performed some b-boy routines for the crowd earlier that afternoon.

When he turned, she said, "You won my dollhouse."

"You made this?" When she nodded, he walked closer. "Yeah, it's for my little sister. She'll freak on it, man."

"I'm glad to hear that."

He looked her over for a moment. "So, you're like the boss here, right?"

"One of them, yeah."

"So, yeah, well…" He looked away, then back. He had something to say.

"Have a seat," she said, pushing out a chair for him. "What's up?"

He sat down. "So, like, here it is… The art lady showed us this newspaper story about tags and shit at the mall."

"Yes. We've had some troubles."

"So me and my crew were thinkin' we might know something about that. We saw something wack the other night hangin' in the park. This guy was standing on a Dumpster hefting a box or something onto the mall roof. We figured maybe he worked there, you know?"

"When was that? How long ago?"

Rafael's guess was the same as the golf-cart vandalism night. "That must have been a golf-cart battery he was

throwing up there," she said. "Definitely the bad guy."
Adrenaline spiked in her system. "Do you remember anything else about him?"

"He was far off, but, one thing, his truck ran real rough,
clunky like. We were yellin' like, 'Fix your ride, you
scrub.'"

"The truck was noisy? That's a help. Thank you." She
handed him her business card. "If you or your friends think
of anything more, call me, okay?"

He nodded, tucking the card into his pocket. "When
we're chillin' at the park, we'll keep an eye out. We don't
want this mall trashed out and shit."

"Me neither, Rafael."

"See ya," he said, carefully picking up the dollhouse
and strutting off, not a bit embarrassed to be seen holding
something so girlie. Rafael was a cool head, for sure.

A noisy truck. Why did that seem familiar? Sylvie had
heard a rumbling engine not long ago. When? She ran the
past week through her mind. Then it came to her. The day
of the bomb scare, Leo's nephew Jesse had roared up in
his truck, the engine burbling oddly, then dashed off to
try to help.

They'd hired him after that.

Had *he* messed with the carts to get the job? Had he
called in the bomb threat, too? That seemed extreme, but
he'd likely heard Leo complain about the old carts. He'd
only crippled them, not destroyed them completely. She
would talk to both Leo and Jesse as soon as they showed
up for work.

A half hour later she met Leo in the security office.
When she finished the story, he slammed a fist into his
thigh. "That little bastard. It makes sense now. The day
of the bomb threat, he was at my place too fast. He said

he'd heard it on the news. This isn't a kid who follows the news."

"So you think he would do this?"

"We're going to get him in here and find out, dammit." Leo looked furious. "That kid, he wants it all on a platter. What he wants, when he wants it. My sister spoiled him. I'm just sick that I brought this on us." He shook his head, staring at the floor.

"You didn't know, Leo."

Fifteen minutes later, a red-faced Jesse admitted to the poster-paint graffiti and damaging the security carts, as well as calling in the bomb threat. "I didn't hurt nothin'," he insisted sullenly. "The carts needed fixing. You told me that, Uncle Leo. You said they neglected equipment and stuff."

Leo grimaced, clearly embarrassed to have been complaining about mall management.

"I didn't know they'd get out the SWAT cops and the dogs. The mall needed guarding, you said so, Uncle Leo. You said, 'What would it take to prove it to the bosses?' So I proved it."

He denied vandalizing the inside of the mall. Sylvie hoped Detective Lawson would get the whole truth out of him.

At least the mystery of the attacks had been solved. Sylvie couldn't wait to tell reporters it had been a misguided kid who wanted a guard job, not a crime wave.

High on the news, she left a message for the PriceLess VP explaining what had happened, then went store to store to tell the shop owners. She left a voice mail for Chase, who'd gone to see the real estate guy.

After that she stayed until the mall closed at midnight, reveling in her success. The store owners couldn't have been happier with the day's receipts. Already, two of the stores that had wanted to leave had decided to stay, and, on top of it all, she no longer needed to worry about the vandalism. It seemed the storm truly was passing.

Happily exhausted, Sylvie got home to find a hopelessly huge bouquet of exotic flowers on her doorstep with a card from Chase congratulating her on a job well done. "Get some sleep and I'll see you in the morning."

SO SHE SLEPT. LIKE A LOG. The next morning, Sylvie got out of her car and smiled at the bright facade of the mall, now safe from damage. The winter sun was warm and bright, like her mood.

The morning was crazy busy. Sylvie talked to three reporters and left messages with the rest. Mary Beth nabbed the sales figures from the day before so Sylvie had something to show Chase even before Monday and, best of all, Roger Munford from PriceLess called to let her know they were still interested in a Starlight Desert location.

Randolph came in with a letter of resignation because he'd failed to identify Jesse as the culprit, but Sylvie convinced him the mall wouldn't be the same without him.

As the morning passed, Sylvie kept an eye out for Chase, eager to share her triumph.

It was nearly noon when Cyndi called over the intercom, "I have a Shelley Clark from the *Arizona Daily News* on the phone. She says it's urgent."

Shelley was a business reporter, so Sylvie assumed she was doing a roundup of Black Friday profits from all the malls.

"Put her through," she said, pasting on a smile, knowing it would come across in her voice. "Hey, Shelley, how are you?"

"Fine. I've got a quick question for you."

"I bet I know the answer. Our Black Friday sales were

off the chart. Record-breaking profits. We're thrilled, but not surprised because—"

"Great, but can you confirm that MegaMalls is buying Starlight Desert?"

"Excuse me?" Sylvie's entire body went rigid and she stopped breathing entirely.

"I've been informed that MegaMalls has made an offer and that it's been accepted. Can you verify that for me?"

Sylvie forced herself to speak through numb lips. "Where did you hear this?"

"A reliable source. I simply need confirmation."

"You'll have to speak with Chase McCann, our general manager, who's not here at the moment." The words were dust in her mouth. "Let me have him call you." Her hands shook as she wrote down the reporter's phone number.

Frozen at her desk, Sylvie stared at her door for what felt like hours, but only a few minutes had passed when Chase entered, Dasher on a leash beside him.

"You're selling us to MegaMalls?" she asked him.

His face told her yes. "Where did you hear that?"

"A reporter called."

"It's too soon to talk about it with media."

"How about with your operations manager? Is it too soon to tell me you're selling my life?" Her voice went higher, then cracked. "You promised we'd have the weekend, that you'd decide on Monday."

"I'm sorry, Sylvie, but the deal's too good to pass up."

She just stared at him, feeling hot, then cold, in waves.

"They can close quickly, the price is as high as we could hope for and, frankly, McCann Development needs the cash."

"Why would MegaMalls want us? We're not that kind of mall."

"For the location. The structure's in place. The park acreage will be easy to expand into."

Her mind caught up with the implications of this decision. "They'll put in their chain stores, won't they? We're out. Our stores, our staff, everything gone."

"We'll give the stores at least three months to relocate and staff that long to find new jobs. Some stores might stay."

"No way could they afford that rent."

"MegaMalls may want a transition person and you would be perfect." His words were wooden and his eyes looked sad. He had to know how devastated she was. "Of course, you've got our highest recommendation. Your work speaks for itself."

The horrible truth leached further into her being. "So our record-breaking weekend meant nothing? It was all pointless? What am I going to tell the store owners now?"

"I'll talk to them. This is McCann Development's decision, not yours."

"They'll think I'm a fool you kept in the dark." Her throat squeezed shut. She blinked, her eyes burning. "They'll think I betrayed them." She felt betrayed herself, even though Chase had leveled with her all along.

"They know you. They know you love the mall."

"I can't believe Marshall would agree to this," she said. He was her last hope.

"He's a businessman, Sylvie, and this is a business decision."

"It's all about the bottom line, right? Not sentiment, not family, nothing but money." She spat out the words.

"It's best for McMann Development."

"And for you, right? You get your share of the money? And there's that deal in Oregon, right?"

"That's not why we're selling, but yes." Chase looked puzzled by her bitter tone. "I'll invest in the Portland project and I'll be able to pay back my investors sooner than with Home At Last, so, yeah, the money is nice."

"I thought you loved Home at Last."

"I do, but once all the investors are in place, my job is done. Chet will stay here for the day-to-day and I can—"

"Walk away? Get in, get out, move on?"

"If you want to put it that way, yes." He swallowed, holding her gaze.

"I guess that's the point. We both knew you'd leave. I just didn't think you'd also take away everything I've worked for. The mall. My job. My hopes. All of it." She blinked back tears. "And I've let everyone down on top of it."

"You held the mall together, Sylvie. Everyone knows that. Hell, you even caught the vandal. I know you don't see it now, but this is a chance for you to do something bigger." He spoke gently, kindly, but that made her furious.

"First off, I don't want anything *bigger*. And, by the way, no mall will snap me up to manage it, if that's what you think. The minimum requirement is a college degree or five years of management experience. I'd be lucky to be hired as a marketing assistant."

"So, forget malls then. I know Starlight Desert is special to you, but a mall manager is really just a glorified landlord. Is that what you want? You're smart and good with people and organized and creative and you understand retail cold. You could do so many things beyond this."

Sylvie felt as if she might explode. Garbage was spewing out of the mouth of the man she loved and her heart was breaking and breaking.

"After all this time, after all you've seen here, you don't get it, do you? You don't get me. Or Starlight Desert, for that matter." She glared at him.

"Frankly, in *business* terms, which seem to be the only thing that matters to you, Starlight Desert has just launched its best holiday season ever, the vandalism is over and PriceLess is on board again. If you kept the mall you'd make tons more money than you will selling it. Not very bottom-line of you is it?"

"That's not the direction we're going, Sylvie." Chase's voice was flat. "I'm sorry."

"I know I shouldn't be so angry. I knew this might happen. I just thought you would find a way, that you would see…" She shook her head, fighting despair.

"This doesn't change how I feel about you, Sylvie." He took a step closer to her, arms lifting, as if to hold her.

Nothing would make her feel worse. "Excuse me, but so what? You're leaving for Oregon, right? As soon as you can escape?"

"We have to figure out what to do."

"What to do?" She looked at him from across the cold ocean that separated them. How had she ever thought they could be together? Chase's love was no more permanent than his presence at the mall. "There's nothing *to* do. The mall's over and so are we."

"You're giving up? Just like that?"

"We can't last, Chase, and you know it."

She watched as the truth sank in. His face went slack, his brown eyes murky. "I never wanted to hurt you, Sylvie."

"Too late," she said. "But you did warn me. You told me all about your hazard label, but I walked head-on into the hurt just the same." Chase would never stay here, not for work and certainly not for love. "I'm an idiot."

"No, you're not. You're in love. And so am I."

"It was a fantasy, Chase. Built out of memories and hopes and need. This is reality. It's busted down the door, so let's accept it and move on."

He looked at her for a long moment. "Is that what you really want?"

"It's *exactly* what I want."

"I won't argue with you."

"Good to hear." Sylvie took a deep, shaky breath. She had a job to do for as long as it lasted—to look after the Starlight Desert family. She thrust the message slip she still clutched at him. "The reporter is Shelley Clark. Business section. I doubt she'll delay a scoop this big, so I'll call a tenant meeting for this afternoon so we can tell everyone."

Chase took the slip from her. "I can call the meeting myself. You don't need to be there if you'd rather not."

"Of course I'll be there," she said. "It's my job. I'll do my best for Starlight Desert until my very last day."

"I know you will. But if you change your mind—"

"I won't." Though it would be more painful than she wanted to admit.

"No." He sighed, "I don't suppose you will. You're the most determined person I know. It's been a privilege working with you, Sylvie."

"Just call the reporter," she said, turning away to hide her tears.

At the tenant meeting that afternoon, Chase made the announcement to gasps and *no*s. Sylvie couldn't bear the shocked and pale faces, the long, tense silence followed by an explosion of questions.

Chase answered them calmly, but then he'd had plenty of experience ending things, she thought bitterly.

"I'll do whatever I can to help," Sylvie said, stepping in front of Chase. She had to say something.

"Did you know about this, Sylvie?" Theo demanded.

"No, she did not," Chase answered for her. "The offer came late last night. The reporter got wind of it before we'd even worked out the details or had a chance to talk with Sylvie. As soon as I know more, I'll let you all know."

"Starlight Desert is home for me, too," Sylvie said. "I hope holiday revenues will be enough to cover your moving costs. I just wish…it could be different." And then everything was too much for her. She couldn't bear the weight of this loss in front of people she'd let down.

"Please excuse me." She headed for the door. As she left she caught sight of Chase watching her, his eyes pained and sad. She didn't want his pity, dammit. She didn't want anything from him. Except her heart and she'd have to take that back herself.

CHASE WATCHED SYLVIE walk out of the meeting, his throat tight, his fists tighter. He'd hurt her deeply. He'd had no business getting involved with a woman with as big a heart as hers. It had been as stupid and dangerous as too many peach margaritas that long-ago night.

He'd wanted more somehow, but he'd been a fool to try for it. He was who he was, as Sylvie had pointed out, and people didn't change. Even Fletcher had warned him.

It was just that her rejection had been so swift. *The mall's over and so are we.* Boom. She was right, of course, but it hurt like hell.

He would do what he could to help Sylvie get a new job, make calls, whatever she'd *let* him do, which wouldn't be much, he'd bet. She didn't want to hear it, but she could do far better than be landlord to a bunch of shops.

The sales offer and terms were unbeatable. Even

Marshall hadn't argued against the sale. In fact, he'd been strangely quiet during the discussion.

Selling the mall was the right thing to do, dammit, and Chase wasn't going to let Sylvie make him feel bad about it.

CHAPTER SIXTEEN

THE NEXT TWO DAYS were a wretched blur for Sylvie.

Christmas shopping was brisk, the mall alive with holiday spirit. Heaven Scents' festive aromas filled the air. Santa's workshop was busy with children, the carols playing merrily overhead and the lights and trees made the place seem like the homiest of Christmas scenes.

It was her favorite season in her favorite place, but Sylvie felt empty inside.

Smiling as best she could, she went store to store discussing options and offering advice. The shop owners mumbled that it wasn't her fault, but she felt as though she'd failed them.

Soon, she'd have to figure out her own future, but for now, she intended to do her job as best she could for as long as she could.

She missed Chase, although breaking up had been the right thing to do. Only the comfort of Dasher's easy affection eased her misery. She didn't even mind the middle-of-the-night trips outdoors anymore. Chase had been right about Dasher. She did love him and couldn't imagine her life without him.

Then, midmorning on the third day after the news of the sale, Cyndi alerted Sylvie to a commotion outside.

In the parking lot, Sylvie found a crowd carrying signs, marching and chanting protests. The signs had been stenciled in red paint: "No Mega Monsters in our 'Hood"…

"Negative, MegaMalls"… "MegaMalls Get Out!" The chants conveyed similar sentiments.

While she stood there, a TV truck arrived. She wasn't surprised. The media loved stories like this. People protesting against giant MegaMalls swallowing up the friendly neighborhood mall.

Sylvie could hardly contain her joy. She'd been right. People *did* love Starlight Desert. They *were* loyal. She couldn't wait to rub it in with Chase.

She found him in his office, head in his hands. He looked up at her. "Did you see that mess outside?"

"You mean the loyal customers who don't want us to close? The ones you said only cared about the mall for a smoothie in summer? Yes, I saw them and I'm glad they're there."

"Loyal customers?" He snorted. "Don't be naive. This is a campaign to cause trouble with the sale. There were picketers outside MegaMalls headquarters and the CEO is fit to be tied."

"Really?"

"Oh, yeah. This morning's paper had a letter to the editor signed by 'Take Back Our Neighborhoods' using the same phrases that are on the signs. Also part of the plot."

"You're kidding," she said, sitting down. That did sound fishy. "The business story only came out two days ago. Who's doing this?"

"Someone with the clout and savvy to organize a protest group overnight."

"Like someone political? Like Reggie Collins? He was all hot to re-envision us, remember?"

"He'd have the constituent lists for sure."

"But why would he oppose MegaMalls? You'd think

he'd be trying to take credit for bringing bigger business to the area."

"Fletcher said he blocked permits for a condo project, which makes no sense, either. Who knows what his real agenda is?"

"It would be worth asking some questions."

"Maybe. Meanwhile, MegaMalls is getting cold feet. They hate controversy." Chase looked grim, but he studied her face. "How are you doing?"

"I'm holding up," she said.

"That's good. Is Dasher letting you sleep?"

"Dasher's Dasher. He is who he is."

"I guess we all are, like you said." He looked so sad she felt a twinge in her chest.

His phone rang. "Excuse me," he said.

Leaving Chase to what sounded like a conversation with his real estate broker, Sylvie went back outside to see what she could learn about the protestors. She was sick to death of people using Starlight Desert as a whipping post.

The first thing she noticed was that the signs had been made from Tracer's posters faced inward and stapled together so the blank back side could be stenciled on.

Why would the department store be involved in a protest? Tracer's would be closing whether or not Starlight Desert sold, right? She'd talk to Talley about that.

Also, there were a lot of men among the marchers. Most mall shoppers were women, so that gave weight to Chase's theory that these weren't loyal customers.

She asked a woman holding a big malls out sign how she'd heard about the demonstration. The woman fished out a printed email from her purse with the information from Take Back Our Neighborhoods. The email had been sent out at 8:00 a.m. on the very day of the news story. That was impossibly fast action.

Thanking the woman for the email, Sylvie noticed she wore one of Abernathy's jai alai pins on her windbreaker. So did several of the men walking in the slow circle, waving signs.

Could Abernathy's group have set this up? Or had Collins asked for his help? Were the two men working together?

Her first stop was Tracer's to find out what Talley could tell her about the signs. Talley's assistant promised she would arrive momentarily, so Sylvie waited in the open alcove that held a desk, files and computer. She noticed a box of Godiva chocolates on Talley's desk with a note clipped to it. Twisting her head, she read, "Thanks for… *everything!*" The note was signed *Pete*.

"Sylvie? What's up?" Talley clearly was startled to find Sylvie in her office.

"So is Pete your new guy?" she asked, embarrassed at being caught snooping.

Talley flushed. "No, uh, he's just a friend."

"My male friends don't usually give me Godiva," she teased.

"Anyway, what is it you wanted to ask me?"

That was odd. Talley had been very open about her boyfriend the last time she and Sylvie had talked. Now she was clamming up?

Sylvie decided to be direct. "The protestors outside are carrying signs made from Tracer's posters. Are you or any of your employees involved with the picketing?"

"Heavens, no," she said, but her eyes darted away. "Someone must have grabbed old ad boards from our trash."

"That's possible, I guess."

"Is there anything else?" Talley's smile seemed false and her fingers lay protectively over the note from her "friend" Pete. She was lying. Why? Sylvie thought she knew a way to find out more.

"ARE YOU CRAZY?" Chase couldn't believe what Sylvie had just asked him. "You want us to sneak into shops again?"

"Tonight. Yeah. To look for evidence."

"Really? I don't get why you care. If the MegaMalls sale collapses and we can't find another buyer, you get the mall back, safe and sound."

"Someone's using Starlight Desert and I want to know who and why. It's my job to look out for the mall."

"Your loyalty means a lot, Sylvie, especially under these circumstances. We've been damned lucky to have you—"

"Please, no farewell speeches, okay? Let me tell you what I know and what we need to do…."

She launched into an explanation about jai alai club pins on protestors, too many male demonstrators, the suspiciously early email about the protest and the signs being made from department store posters, ending with how evasive Talley had been about a box of chocolates that might have come from someone at Reggie Collins's office.

"How do you figure that?" Chase said, overwhelmed by the rapid-fire tale, just happy to have Sylvie sitting close by, determination back in her eyes. He'd missed her these past few days. Her spirit, her energy, her heart.

"Because *Pete* could be *Peter*. And Peter Anderson is the guy who set up the community meeting for Collins. He's his assistant. The chocolates could be a thank-you for helping with the protest."

"Pete's a common name."

"True, but Talley loves to talk about her men and she shut me down right off. She's hiding something, I know it."

"Okay…say Talley did help Anderson with the protest by making the signs. Why would she do that?"

"Because they're lovers and he asked her to. Or maybe because he promised her a job. When she told me Tracer's might close, she said her new boyfriend knew important people, suggesting that he'd help her get a new job."

"Okay. And you think Peter Anderson gave Talley pricey chocolates to thank her for picket signs or sex or both?"

Sylvie laughed. "I know it's complicated, but the pieces fit somehow. All we need to do is establish links between these people, figure out their scheme and expose it."

"And you want us to sneak into Tracer's and the jai alai club for…"

"Evidence, yes."

"Why not confront Talley and Abernathy in broad daylight?"

"They'd just lie and hide the proof. This is best. The police couldn't do this without a warrant, but we own the property, so we have the right to enter. Sort of."

"You're serious about this."

"Deadly serious." She managed a brief smile, so familiar and welcome it made Chase's chest burn.

"So what's Abernathy after? If the MegaMalls sale fails, he'll lowball us to build an arena? And why is Collins involved?"

"That's what we have to find out. Are you in?"

"Oh, I wouldn't miss it," he said, knowing he'd do any fool thing Sylvie suggested.

LATE THAT NIGHT, Chase found himself once again unscrewing the vents to the ductwork, Sylvie next to him, swamping him with her cherry-pie smell, burglars for real this time.

"Hurry," she whispered. "The last thing we need is Leo catching us sneaking in."

"After you," Chase said, motioning for Sylvie to crawl into the tunnel. He immediately regretted that because he had to watch her backside sway before his hungry eyes. She hurried past the stores they'd visited together—the candy store, Heaven Scents and the toy store—then banged on the vent into Tracer's. "It's stuck," she said.

He moved closer to help and their bodies brushed. Sylvie trembled at the contact. Their eyes caught and held for a moment. Then, with a sharp palm strike, he forced the vent open.

They stepped down into the stockroom. Security lights lit the area enough that they could find the main switch. Then they searched every shelf and corner.

"Look!" Sylvie said, pointing at a stack of stakes tucked behind a counter, some with blank signs already attached. "Doesn't look like anybody robbed the trash to me. My guess is they had an assembly line here."

Using a small digital camera, Sylvie took photographs of the signs as evidence. They then headed to Talley's office, where Sylvie turned on the computer. While the machine booted up, she flipped through the few upright folders on the mostly bare desk.

"Nothing here that I can see."

"Desk drawers are locked and so is the file cabinet," Chase said after checking both.

"Damn," Sylvie said, staring at the computer screen. "Password protected." She tried a few possible codes, but got nowhere, then sank into the chair. "So all we have so far are the picket signs she lied about. And maybe Pete's chocolates. Let's see what we get from Abernathy."

They made their way down the passageway to the small booster club office. The space looked like a telemarketer boiler room, crowded with desks and phones, each with a call sheet with marked out numbers and comments. The walls held jai alai posters and a white board that seemed to track donor contributions.

Sylvie made a beeline for a big wooden desk at the back of the office. "This has to be Abernathy's."

Unlike Talley's, this desk was messy with paper. Sylvie sat at the chair and began flipping through the sheets. "Just like I figured. He's one of those old-fashioned guys who prints out his email to read on paper. Wow, here's one. It says, 'I'll be there.'" She skimmed the note. "It's about the protest. The header shows a ton of names and the message is a forward from Take Back Our Neighborhoods. So they were part of the march for sure."

Chase wandered through a door to a small room that held office supplies and a small kitchen. He flipped on a light. The room smelled of chemicals. Varnish or paint?

Then he saw it, a can of spray paint next to cardboard alphabet stencils. "Check this out."

Sylvie joined him. "Oh, my God. Abernathy did the lettering for the signs. They were all in red paint."

"So that's a strong link between Abernathy and the protest."

"Also Talley, since she provided the signs."

"We still don't know if Pete is Peter Anderson or if his connection to Talley involves Reggie Collins."

"Wait a second," Sylvie said. She turned and grabbed his arms. "Where else have we seen red spray-paint?"

It came to him instantly. "The graffiti in the mall the night we camped out."

"Exactly. Up until that incident, the paint had been black. Jesse denied breaking into the mall. He didn't have a key, either, as far as I know, but Abernathy sure would have. That attack was different, remember? It was a threat aimed at our tenants…talking about us being a dead mall."

"That's true. We know he was poking around about buying the place. We might be getting somewhere here."

Sylvie took photographs of the stencils, taking one with her as evidence, along with the spray can, wrapping the items in plastic wrap from a box she found on top of the fridge.

After that, she and Chase worked together checking out the papers on Abernathy's desk, fingers flying, eyes skimming page after page.

Fifteen minutes later, Sylvie yelped. "Jackpot! It's an email from Abernathy to the club's officers about forming a Reelect Reggie Collins's political action committee. It says Collins promises to clear red tape out of their way. That could be bribery, right?" She jumped to her feet. "They're paying off Collins to help them get an arena built here. Maybe the condo developer who got stopped wouldn't pay up or something."

"Slow down, Sylvie. They can claim they're just exercising their legal rights to support a candidate who agrees with them. This suggests a bribe, but it's business as usual in politics."

"What about the mall vandalism? That's a felony. I'm sure Detective Lawson could get a warrant to search this office for more evidence."

"If we could prove Collins's office is behind that neighborhood group it would help build our case."

"I bet we have enough to interest Shelley Clark," she said. "As a reporter, she could investigate—maybe confirm the link between Collins and the protest group. I wish we knew for sure that Talley's Pete is Peter Anderson."

"That would take too much time. What if we tell Collins and Abernathy we have evidence that we're taking to the media and the police?"

"You think the threat would be enough to stop them?"

"It might. All I need is an end to the protests and for them to come clean with MegaMalls so the sale will still fly."

"Yeah." Sylvie sighed. "If we win, I lose the mall."

What could he say to that? She was absolutely correct.

She took a deep breath and set her jaw, determination back in place. "It doesn't matter. It's the right thing to do. Tomorrow we'll pin down our strategy for the confrontation."

"You're something else, Sylvie." Chase had broken her heart and killed her dream, but she'd volunteered to crawl through dusty tunnels and paw through emails to do the right thing. God, he would miss her.

A TAP ON SYLVIE'S OFFICE door made her look up.

"Got a minute?" Mary Beth stuck her head in.

"Sure, come on in," Sylvie said. Chase was due soon to talk through their plan.

"First off, I want to thank you for taking me on here like you did, Sylvie. You really saved my ass."

"We're lucky you were available to help us out. How's your mother doing?"

"Much better. She'll be moving in with me next week and she'll be pretty independent, which means I can go back to work full-time. So, here's the deal. I got a job offer."

"You did?"

"Yeah. It's at that new mall on the west side. Roberta,

the GM, is going on maternity leave and she recommended me as her fill-in. It's only for six months, but that might change if Roberta decides she wants more time at home."

"That's great, Mary Beth. I'm happy for you."

"Are you? Really? I feel kind of guilty because I realized you might want the job."

"I don't have your experience."

"Not in years, but after all this and the sale and transition, you'll have quite the résumé."

"You think so?" The idea of hunting for a new job made Sylvie sick at heart.

"Oh, yeah. I'll keep an eye out for any opening that would suit you. I know I let you down by not recommending you to take over for me, though it didn't turn out so great, after all. Looks like I got out in the nick of time. Funny how life works, huh?"

"Yeah. Funny." Sylvie wanted to smack the woman, but Mary Beth was her most recent supervisor, so her recommendation mattered. "Any tips you can give me would be great."

"No problem. You know me, always helping people out. I could have gotten Talley an interview for a store manager job out there, but she says her boyfriend's going to get her something with the city."

"Really?" Sylvie sat forward. "You mean Pete?"

"That's him. I think she said he works for Councilman Collins."

"How did they meet, do you know?"

"I guess he was looking for a tie one day in her store and she helped him. It was love at first sight."

"How romantic," Sylvie said. No doubt, Anderson had figured out how to use Talley to get what his boss wanted from the mall. Talley might have been the one who alerted

Collins's office about the vandalism incident where he'd shown up so fast.

"Anyway, I don't envy you all the hassles ahead," Mary Beth said. "What with stores leaving, owners acting flaky, tempers flaring, all the rigmarole with closing and inspections. What a nightmare."

"I don't imagine it will be fun."

"Oh, no. It will be hell." Mary Beth seemed to catch herself and looked at Sylvie's face. "No one blames you, Sylvie, I hope you know that. For the mall closing, I mean. The timing was just bad, what with me leaving and you taking over right when it happened."

"Funny how that works," she said wryly.

"The stores will find homes. Nothing's certain in this life."

"That's absolutely true." Sylvie had learned that lesson in early childhood and nothing since had proved differently.

"I was wondering whether you and Chase were still okay with each other, considering all that's happened." Nosy Mary Beth was looking for gossip.

"We're fine, Mary Beth. We're professionals and we'll both do our jobs and get through this as best we can." Despite the doubt on Mary Beth's face, Sylvie was determined to do exactly that.

Chase arrived soon after Mary Beth left and Sylvie felt the familiar zing in her heart. When would this stop?

"I have news about Peter Anderson," he said, dropping into a guest chair and sliding it to the side of her desk to be close by, as he used to do.

"Me, too," she said. "He's definitely Talley's Pete. Talley told Mary Beth he promised her a job with the city."

"Perfect," he said. "He's one busy guy. I checked public

records on the neighborhood group and guess who founded it? None other than Mr. Peter Anderson."

"Wow. So we have the connection between Collins and Talley and the protest. Also Abernathy with Collins and the protest. Not to mention Abernathy and the mall graffiti. That's enough to confront them with, don't you think?"

"Maybe we should start with Talley? If she caves, she'll give us more ammunition for the meeting with Collins, Anderson and Abernathy. I'll set that up for tonight."

"Sounds like a plan."

Chase held up a hand for a high-five. "Team Starlight Desert running one last play down the field."

Sylvie's smile almost hurt.

FOUR DAYS LATER, the MegaMalls deal was back on track, thanks to Sylvie and Chase.

"I'm glad we could work this out," Reggie Collins said to the MegaMalls CEO, vigorously shaking his hand. Chase had to fight back a smirk. *Work it out? Really?*

The politician had been terrified he would be arrested.

The culprits had folded like bad poker hands as soon as they heard the evidence. Horrified that she'd been part of a crime, Talley had happily filled them in on all she knew of the master scheme, confirming what they suspected, and promising to talk to any official they needed her to.

Collins, Anderson and Abernathy turned white as ghosts when Chase laid out what he knew of the vandalism, the bogus protest and the bribery. Sylvie played bad cop, threatening to call the Attorney General and the reporter anxious for the scoop as soon as the meeting ended.

In minutes, the men were falling over themselves to, as Collins put it, "correct any misapprehensions we may have inadvertently created about Starlight Desert Mall with MegaMalls executives."

So that was how Chase and Fletcher came to be meeting with the MegaMalls CEO and Reggie Collins, who had assured the CEO that the mall sale had his full support and that Take Back Our Neighborhoods was ready to organize a "Welcome MegaMalls" rally on any date of his choosing.

Once Abernathy had promised to make a sizable donation to Free Arts, Chase agreed not to report the spray-paint incident to the police. He would urge leniency with the AG's office for Collins, though he'd already learned that such a small-potatoes case in a swamped office was unlikely to ever be pursued.

Chase hoped the incident would put enough fear of God in Collins that he'd stay clear of corruption from now on.

He could hope anyway.

As soon as Collins left the room, the MegaMalls CEO turned to Chase and Fletcher. "Well handled, gentlemen. Assuming Mr. Collins does what he's agreed to, we're ready to make a deal with you. My people will get back to you with our revised offer." He shook their hands and left.

"Nice rescue," Fletcher said to Chase. "I'm impressed."

"It was mostly Sylvie. She was with me all the way."

"She's a special lady," Fletcher said. "You sure you don't want to work things out with her?"

"There's no point. I am who I am."

"People change," he said. "Talk to her."

"Since when do you dish out romantic advice?"

"Since I took some of yours. I met someone while I was wearing that stupid elf costume, you know."

"It's a chick magnet, for sure," Chase agreed.

"So I'm going to need the BMW back. She likes convertibles."

Chase smiled at the light in his brother's eyes. "Watch yourself, bro. It's easy to speed in that thing. Bring a warm jacket she can borrow."

The next evening, Chase sat in the living room nursing a whiskey, his laptop open to the CAD program he'd bought. To distract himself from missing Sylvie, he'd begun playing with a few designs.

The meeting to finalize the mall sale was scheduled for next week. The offer was slightly lower, but still attractive, and Portland beckoned. Everything was working out, but he was miserable.

"There you are, son." His father came into the room holding a sack. He always behaved as if whichever son he wanted to talk to had been hiding from him. "I wanted to give you back that Santa suit." He plopped the bag onto the table and sat beside Chase. "What are you up to?"

"Fooling around with some designs. The architect we're using got me interested again."

"Hobbies are good if you don't make too much of them."

"You never believed I'd make it as an architect back then, did you? When it was my major."

"I had no opinion. I never went to college. I wanted you at McCann Development, but as I recall, you complained that the coursework was too demanding."

Chase paused, thinking back. Was that true? He'd felt guilty for wasting so much money and time, but had he complained? It was very possible.

"You were all fired up about finance, I believe. You thought it was more up your alley."

That might have been exactly how it sounded to his

father, Chase realized. Since Chase had taken a longer look at their relationship, he'd begun to see he'd been somewhat unfair. He'd inferred negative opinions from his father out of old resentments and his own doubts. The General in Chase's head had been his harshest critic.

"Kind of like me and fly-fishing," the General continued. "I always had this hope that you two would take over the company so I'd have time to fish. I wanted to hit every trout stream in the Western U.S. before I died."

"I've never seen you with a fishing pole in your hands."

His father frowned. "I fish. I certainly have fished."

"Then go for it. Take off and fish. Fletcher can take over easily. In fact, he *should* take over."

His father frowned. "I don't need any advice on how to run my company. And certainly not from you."

"Because of Vegas? That's getting old, Dad. I made a mistake, but I know what I'm doing and I'll pay back the investors every cent. My word is my bond."

"Of course it is. You're a McCann," he said gruffly.

Chase let his anger go. "All I'm saying, Dad, is that you need to trust Fletcher more. Whether you go fly-fishing or sit around staring at your navel, hand the reins to Fletcher. That's what Mom would want."

His father looked him in the eye. "You're different this trip. You seem more…settled. More like yourself."

"Maybe I am." He wanted to be different—better. He had ever since he'd gotten close to Sylvie. Determination rose in him, hot and strong. He pictured her face, the love he'd seen in her eyes when she'd been in his arms.

His father exhaled heavily. "You know the truth, I have no idea what became of my rods. For all I know, Nadia may have given them to Goodwill. They were pricey, too, let me tell you."

Chase laughed, pleased by his father's admission of weakness. "Hell, we all tell ourselves stories about who we are and what we think we want."

"That may be. I'll leave you with your deep thoughts. Get that costume back to where it belongs. I had a damn good time as Santa, I don't mind saying. That Sylvie." His father shook his head, smiling. "Never underestimate that girl."

"Oh, I won't," Chase said. "I never have."

His father gave him a curious look. "Don't underestimate yourself, either. You're a McCann man. Act like it."

Chase smiled. His dad had turned kindly advice into an insult, but he had a point. Had Chase limited himself?

Had he given up before he'd even tried?

CHAPTER SEVENTEEN

SYLVIE WAS GETTING READY for the mall's Christmas party. She zipped up her dress—black velveteen with a red-and-green plaid skirt—slipped her gold hoops into her ears and looked at herself in the mirror. She looked *limp*. Even her hair seemed heartbroken—her curls were soggy blond sausages.

Dasher lay, chin on paws, at the foot of the bed, watching her. She was bringing him along for moral support and had tied a red ribbon around his collar. He'd been her own special holiday gift from Chase. Chase had given her a lot, despite how badly it had ended.

She gathered up the shopping bags with her gifts—individual acrylic tree ornaments for each tenant. For Marshall and his sons, she had an engrossing board game from Germany that required cooperation to play. For Chase, she'd bought a book on green architecture and inscribed it with a note about how she hoped he would always be true to himself.

After the party, she would focus on her next move, update her résumé and check out the job market. It all made her so weary.

The doorbell rang.

It was her mother dressed in a tie-dye dress in red and green, chandelier earrings in fiery jewel colors. She carried a satchel loaded with tissue-wrapped presents.

Since their talk, Sylvie had begun to see her mother

more clearly for who she was, with all her flaws and gifts. Sylvie's secret grudge had doubled the distance between them and she intended to correct that.

"Hi, Mom." Sylvie leaned forward to hug her mother, Desiree's complicated earrings pressing into Sylvie's cheeks, her scents enveloping her—sandalwood, clay, paint and burned pastry—each revealing one of her mother's passions.

"I love when you call me Mom," Desiree said. "Is that terminally sappy? Listen, I had this new idea—blown-glass water bottles! You refill them, so it's environmentally friendly, and they're beautiful, right? I know it's not my business plan, but it could be, don't you think?"

Her mother was so eager, so wide-eyed. Sylvie could see her as a little girl showing a painting to her sober accountant parents, her fingers and clothes stained and messy. Her restless artist's soul must have befuddled them completely.

Sylvie smiled. "It's worth looking into, Mom."

"But only if I work it out fully—market niche and distribution and all that hoo-hah."

"You're learning."

"I try to be a better person every day, Sylvie."

"Yeah. You do." Chase had asked her if people could change. Her mother was certainly trying to.

"You look pretty damn droopy for someone about to go to a Christmas party. I know this hasn't been easy on you."

"No, it hasn't."

Her mother looked her over. "Let's talk a minute." She led Sylvie by the hand to her sofa and sat beside her. Dasher jumped onto Desiree's lap and curled into a contented ball.

"You know I want the best for you, right? I want you to find love, hon, because that is so—"

"Mom, please—" This was the last thing she wanted to think about before seeing Chase.

"Hold on. It finally dawned on me why you got cranky when I mentioned Steve. You're afraid you're like me, aren't you? That you'll get your heart broken like I do?"

Sylvie didn't know how to respond. "In a way, yes."

Desiree squeezed her hand. "See, that's where you're wrong. You're not me. You're about as not me as you can get." She motioned at how Sylvie was dressed compared to her.

"You're your own person, Sylvie. You won't fall in love the way I do and you won't make my mistakes." Desiree's eyes, the same green as her own, searched Sylvie's face.

"You know how to build a life with someone. You're steady and stable and dependable. Everything in your life proves it. Why would you be different in love?"

Sylvie dropped her head in her hands. "I'm scared. It hurts so much. We're too different. And he's leaving anyway."

"You're talking about Chase, right? When I saw you together on Black Friday I suspected as much."

Sylvie raised her eyes to her mother's.

"Life is risk, babe," her mother said. "What's that bit about the harbor being safe, but that's not what boats are for? Don't make your world into a dollhouse. Sure, you limit your pain that way, but you miss out on so much joy. You deserve joy. Lots of joy."

Sylvie's throat constricted so she could hardly breathe.

"You have to embrace the chaos, open yourself to the world, open your heart to—" Her mother stopped her wild gesturing. "I mean in your sensible, practical way, of course."

Sylvie stifled a sob. She couldn't help it.

"Oh, honey." Desiree pulled Sylvie into her arms. "You know, you've never cried in front of me before."

"Sure I have," Sylvie said, sniffling.

"Not as a grown-up and not when it counted." Desiree leaned away to look at her. "Give yourself a chance with Chase. Don't hold back. You can take it."

"You think so?"

"I know so. You amaze me. I'd give anything for a dose of your good sense."

"You're kidding."

"Of course not. But you could lose the smug eye-roll."

"Deal." She realized for the first time ever, Desiree had helped her. Or maybe it was the first time Sylvie had given her the chance to try.

Sylvie touched up her makeup, they gathered their gift bags, put Dasher on a leash and headed out for the party arm in arm. The whole time, Sylvie's mind raced with the implications of her mother's words.

Could Sylvie be as sensible in love as she was in everything else? Could she be practical *and* romantic?

She glanced at her mother, who was communing with Dasher. *When you love something, you find a way.*

That's what Chase had said about fitting Dasher into her life. Could she find a way with him? He would have to want it, too. And she wasn't sure he did. He might have been secretly relieved it was over. There was only one way to find out.

CHASE WAS SUPPOSED TO BE at the Christmas party, but he didn't feel much like celebrating. Instead, he was in his office looking over the final notes on the contract with MegaMalls. All he had to do was sign these papers and fax them back and the deal was done. Marshall and Fletcher had already signed off.

For some reason, Chase couldn't yet do it. He glanced across the room and spotted Sylvie's red umbrella leaning against the wall. On it she'd stenciled her promise that the mall family would weather all storms.

Sylvie and her mall.

Reaching for the umbrella, he accidentally brushed papers off the desk. Bending to pick them up, he saw they were the printout of Sylvie's PowerPoint presentation, where she'd explained how the mall was unique, the shoppers loyal, the mall employees like a family.

In the past few days he'd seen how right she'd been. The store owners hated moving, even the ones with better locations to go to, and there'd been sincere letters and calls protesting the loss of Starlight Desert to the area.

On top of that, now that they were selling, Chase had become as sentimental about the place as his father.

Dammit. He left the office and walked the length of the mall, remembering what Sylvie had told him about conversion rates and food booths and the shopping tide of early-morning seniors to after-work dash-ins.

Now, the mall was jammed with Christmas shoppers. Revenues were stronger than ever. PriceLess had submitted an even more attractive offer, which they'd had to turn down.

He watched Theo help a woman with her stroller, then give the cranky child inside a free sample juice—something Sylvie had taste-tested no doubt.

There was a silk robe on display in Lucy's Secrets just like Sylvie's. Festive aromas from Heaven Scents, where

Chase had hunted down Sylvie's cherry blossom lotion, filled the air.

He passed the banana tree where Sylvie had tossed her shirt during their campout. He smiled, remembering the crackling-fire screensaver, the hot plate s'mores. They'd forgotten to slide down the tile in the wool socks she'd bought.

He stopped, hit by a memory of his mother and him when he was a child. He'd been about nine and frantic for her to drive him to meet a friend for a movie. She'd been delayed by a store problem until it was too late. He'd been angry. *You care more about this stupid mall than your own family,* he'd said.

She'd kneeled down to talk to him. "You know that you and your brother and father are at the center of me, Chase," she'd said softly, making a circle around her chest. "But out here—" she made a larger circle "—is Starlight Desert."

He'd been instantly ashamed of his tantrum and listened as she spoke more about how the mall was a way for the McCann family to give back to the town, because they'd been so very fortunate.

"Starlight Desert mall is a gift to all the people who shop here and to the people who own the stores and sell the goods they make."

She'd sounded a lot like Sylvie, now that he thought about it. This wasn't the first time he'd noticed their similarities. *There's more to Starlight Desert than its bottom line,* Sylvie had said. His mother would agree.

Strangely enough, he was beginning to himself.

WHEN SYLVIE STEPPED into the McCanns' house, everyone cheered, which made her cheeks heat. The room was bright with decorations and garlands and wreaths, reminding her of that Christmas she'd spent here so long ago. A huge tree with multicolored lights gave off the pine smell of winter.

"Here's to Sylvie!" someone shouted. With a sound like rushing wind, red umbrellas opened up all over the room. Sylvie laughed as everyone slid sunglasses onto their faces.

They were making the best of this sad situation. In fact, everyone seemed unnaturally happy. Were they all drunk?

She looked around the room for Chase, but didn't see him. Shoot. She desperately wanted to talk things over with him. That would have to wait, she guessed.

She did see Marshall and Fletcher. Marshall looked delighted, Fletcher almost stunned. What was up with them?

"Everyone!" Sunni clapped her hands and when all eyes were on her, said, "Sylvie, we want to thank you for teaching us that no matter what happens, if we keep the spirit of Starlight Desert within us, we can weather any storm." She held out a gift box to Sylvie. "This is from all of us to you."

With trembling fingers, Sylvie opened the box to find a ceramic model of Starlight Desert, made by her mother, no doubt, with the words You Made Our Mall Home embedded in the base.

She didn't even try to hide her tears.

She thanked everyone as best she could, then went to get a glass of Christmas punch, trying to settle herself. She would miss these people so much it was almost too hard to bear. Their good cheer in the face of adversity was the best gift she could ever receive.

She looked up to see Marshall motioning her over, grinning like a crazy person. "What's up?" she said.

"Chase had to miss the party, but he wants you to meet him at Starlight Desert. He has a gift, I believe." Marshall's eyes twinkled like the Santa he'd pretended to be.

"He wanted us to tell you he's challenged you to a Nerf duel at dawn, whatever the hell that means," Fletcher said, half smiling. "I'm afraid my brother has fallen down the rabbit hole." He took her hand. "You have my best wishes, Sylvie."

"Thank you," she said, her heart tripping in her chest. What did Chase want to give her?

She had something for him, too—the heart she'd taken back only days before.

SYLVIE ENTERED THE DARKENED mall with Dasher on his leash. Chase had mentioned a Nerf battle, so she headed toward the toy store. As she neared the middle of the mall, though, she picked up the faint sound of guitar music, then heard Chase call her name.

She turned to the central island and he rose from a camp chair in front of a tent. Dasher yelped in excitement and Sylvie's heart silently joined in.

"You got my message," he said, reaching for her hand to help her over the wall. She grabbed Dasher and brought him up, too. The music came from a small boom box. Chase motioned to a clump of votive candles. "My campfire," he said. "I told Leo I'd handle inside security tonight. If he saw these he'd come after us with a fire extinguisher."

She laughed. "What's going on, Chase?"

"Big things, Sylvie. Have a seat."

She sat in the chair beside him, her dress and pumps seeming silly in this setting, but she didn't care one bit.

Chase waved a thick stack of paper at her. "This is the offer from MegaMalls waiting for my signature."

"Yeah?"

"I thought you'd like to watch me finish this thing."

"Why would you think that?" And why was he grinning?

He tore the sheets in half, then half again and again, tossing the scraps like confetti.

"What are you doing? What does this mean?"

"It means you did it, Sylvie. You made me see Starlight Desert as more than a business."

"But you said the offer was too good to pass up. Really? You're serious?" Sylvie thought she might pass out from shock and delight.

"You made me remember what the place meant to my mother. Starlight Desert was her gift to the city and I want to keep giving it."

"But you said McCann Development needed the money."

"We'll survive. Fletcher came unglued, of course, but Dad's decided to semiretire, so Fletcher will have his hands full for a while anyway. Once he read the PriceLess offer, he saw the revenue potential. He'll adjust."

"This is so hard to believe…. We have to tell everyone at the party." She fumbled for her phone.

Chase stopped her hand. "They know. I swore them to secrecy so I could tell you myself."

"No wonder they were so cheerful!" She laughed, then threw her arms around him. "This is wonderful."

"I'm assuming you still want the GM job?"

"Of course. It's been my dream…." She swallowed the knot in her throat.

"Good. There's one more thing to work out. Us."

"Us?" She wanted to sink into his dark eyes, now flaring gold just for her.

He took her hands. "As you so wisely noted, love is nice,

but it's not enough. You need a solid foundation, something Thor might provide."

"But when I said that I meant—"

He raised a hand. "Hold on. Let me finish. So, with that in mind, I ran the numbers on my Thor potential, like I did with the mall. And frankly, I didn't look too good. I mean, I travel a lot, work all the time, don't own a home or a dog."

"That's true," she said, but her heart beat hard with happy anticipation.

He squeezed her hands, his palms warm. "So I threw that out. See, it's kind of like you and the Black Friday promotion. We're going to have to take a chance on projections here."

"Yeah?"

"Yeah. Some good intentions. Some hopes. For the first time in my life I want to stick around. I want to build a life with you, Sylvie. Just you."

"Chase, I—"

"I realized I've been so restless because I wasn't who I wanted to be, doing what I really wanted to do. Let me show you."

He reached for his laptop, clicked the touch pad and revealed an architectural drawing of a house. It was modern, with lots of wood and burnished steel and windows.

"Working with Jake Atwater got me fired up about architecture again, so I started drafting a house I would want to live in. Just to kill the time while I was missing you." He clicked into the details of the sketch.

"One of the rooms I lined with a bunch of shelves and a workbench with skylights for tons of light. I figured I'd use the cork for the countertops in the kitchen like you liked, and some of Captain Bean's wooden shelves and I realized what I was building was a house for *you*."

"Really?"

"Yeah. And I wanted to live there, too. With you."

"How lovely, Chase." Her heart was filling up and spilling over.

"So, I'm going to stick with Home at Last a while, try to expand the project if I can. And I'm going to architecture school. At night, at first. If things go well and the timing's right, Jake Atwater will take me on as an intern."

"That's wonderful, Chase."

"And I want to be with you, Sylvie. Here. So what do you think? Have I got Thor potential?"

"Forget Thor," she said. "Thor's not the whole story. I know that's what I said, but I want passion, too. I want a man who'll sweep me off my feet and adore me and…"

"Watch you sleep and call you ten times a day to ask how your day's going?"

"Yes. Someone who wants my opinion on the Middle East…"

"And whether this tie goes with this shirt, and which diapers stay the driest?"

"Now you've gone too far," she said. "No matter how much you change, Chase, you'll never care about diaper brands."

"Good point."

"And you might as well know I'll never skydive."

"Never say never."

She laughed, then got serious. "I want someone I can count on, who'll be there, thick or thin, who won't lose interest in me when I have pablum in my hair, when I put on ten pounds, or laugh too loud at a client dinner."

"You've got that and more, Sylvie." He squeezed her hand.

"You're taking a chance on me, too, Chase. I've held

back so long, protecting myself, making my world into a dollhouse, I don't know if I can let anyone that close."

"Sure you can. I'll help you. And you'll help me. You with your green eyes that never let me hide."

"Oh, Chase."

He stood, taking her with him, and kissed her, long and slow, his arms warm around her, friend and lover, worth the risk for all the love he offered her.

Dasher barked for attention.

"Find a chew toy, guy," Chase said. "We've got scary stories to tell, Nerf guns to shoot and marshmallows to roast. Where do you want to start, Sylvie?"

"Sleeping bag," she murmured, reaching up to capture his mouth again.

"I'm with you," he murmured back.

"This feels a whole lot like Christmas to me."

"Yeah?"

"Yeah." She had every gift she could want. A new relationship with her mom, Starlight Desert to manage, Dasher to care for and, best of all, Chase and the love he offered her. It *was* a lot like Christmas. And so much more.

* * * * *

Look for the next Dawn Atkins's novel,
HOME TO HARMONY.

HARLEQUIN *Super Romance*

COMING NEXT MONTH

Available December 7, 2010